East of the Shadows

East of the Shadows

by
PAUL HUTCHENS

MOODY PRESS • CHICAGO

Chapter 1

Joseph Fenimore Cardinal was twenty-seven. He was teaching English and biology in Wilkerson College when he met the girl, a senior in his class in Early American Literature, who, he felt sure, was destined—or was it *doomed?*—to become the future Mrs. Cardinal.

Had he known that their romance, so beautiful in its inception and so aesthetic in its development, was to be scarred with imperfections and that there would be disillusioning detours through long and lonely valleys, he might have been more cautious.

But how could he have known that there would develop a love triangle that would be anything but equilateral?

Joe himself was to become the base of the triangle, and his literary-minded fiancée one of the sides. And his equally literary, equally attractive secretary—efficient, alert, constant Janice Granada—involuntarily or otherwise, was fated to play the competing role.

To Joe, until the situation came to startling and very emotional life, Janice had been only a secretary. She had been a friend, of course, but certainly not a candidate for marriage nor a would-be queen to rule his life or his literary career.

And there was yet another dimension, converting the triangle into a ridiculously shaped trapezium. On the horizon, and moving swiftly on cyclonic winds, was the world's way of trying to solve international problems—a philosophy that demanded blind devotion and ruthless sacrifice—the Juggernaut of War.

There was also Joe's friend and counselor, young Dr. Halford Raymond, with whom since their boyhood there had been a companionship like that of David and Jonathan.

Through the years Joe had kept his mind closed against any serious consideration of surrendering what to his friends he sometimes facetiously labelled "a basic human right"—that of remaining a bachelor without feeling a sense of guilt because of it.

There came a day, however, when Hal challenged that right, and at a time when Joe was in no particular mood to defend himself. The cross-examination was on an afternoon at the close of a round of golf two weeks before Joe was to leave for Wilkerson.

"Don't you feel guilty robbing a lonely young woman of her own basic right to marry—a certain young woman I know who seems to have been born just for you? She has an intriguing personality, is literary minded, writes poetry, loves nature, and hates war.

"She would be ideal for you and would complement you in the way your personality requires."

"Did you say complement, spelled with an *e*, or compliment, spelled with an *i*?"

"Seriously, Joe, you need a compl*e*ment, and so does every man."

"Are you accusing me of having some kind of deficiency? If I remember correctly, Webster defines *complement* as 'something required to supply a deficiency.' Right?"

"Right. As a man of medicine, however, I say that every bachelor in the world is suffering from "vitamin-*wife* deficiency." And every young unmarried woman who comes to my office—one in particular— needs a husband."

Joe, who had taken his stance for a final putt at the eighteenth hole, lowered his club, looked out across the fairway, and asked, "You are referring to my secretary?"

"I am trying to open your eyes to see her, Joe. There is a girl who has everything. Now that you've taken the Wilkerson position, one of the wisest things you could do would be to marry her before you go. There's something about being married that gives a man status and prestige."

The ball rolled toward the cup and dropped in. Joe retrieved it, turned, gave Hal a level look, and said, "There is a very important reason why I cannot take your advice. And that is because I think the girl is just right for *you*. Why don't you speak for yourself, John Alden?"

Hal finished the eighteenth with an eagle. They stopped at the soft drink canteen and a little later were at Joe's rooming house.

They shook hands in mock solemnity as Joe said, "Thanks, John, for a good game. And now, you go back to your office, call Janice, take her out to dinner tonight, and speak for yourself."

Alone in his room, Joseph Fenimore Cardinal studied his face in the mirror, grinned, and muttered,

> Mirror, mirror on the wall,
> Who is most eligible of all?

And the mirror answered evasively in the voice of a man, saying, "A thing of beauty is a joy forever."

Hal was right, of course. There was a deficiency—a loneliness which a literary career had not fulfilled. Neither had teaching, which profession he had chosen and in which, to a degree, he had attained success.

He turned now to his desk, unlocked it, took out his journal, and wrote: "A birdie, an eagle, and a broken neck—my par for the day."

He had known there was a weakness in his driver at the point where the shaft joined the head, but he had taped it with a new kind of tape from the pro shop.

"Broke my neck," he wrote, "lost my head—and Hal insists I ought to lose my heart as well. He may be right. He just may be right."

And now, caught up into a familiar spell which came upon him so often—a spell he had known since boyhood—he began to write:

"The conviction still is there, driving me on toward some predetermined destiny. What it is—where it is—I do not know. But the power that pulls and sometimes seems to drag me on has never relented. I cannot resist it even if I would, for it gives me happiness—and misery. It gives me a purpose for living. It seems, in a way, to be a search for myself—to discover what I am and who I am—and why."

The phone rang. It was Janice, her voice lilting, enthusiastic. "I have happened onto something new on *The Hound of Heaven*. The material was so interesting and so thrilling I found myself almost writing the article for you—just as you would do it, of course—sort of like a ghost-writer. And your story on the pheasant hunt is ready. I like it very much—very, *very* much. It's the way I think and feel—"

He had not intended to break in. Certainly he had not intended to do it abruptly and impatiently, but he had always disliked interruptions when he was pursuing a muse. He had been about to write in his journal: "I feel sometimes as if I myself am the Hound of Heaven, in full cry on my own lonely trail. I keep running away from myself,

7

afraid to be caught, afraid the chase will end and there will be nothing left to pursue—and nothing of *me* to do the pursuing."

His mind had raced ahead of him as he wrote, and the thoughts were already jostling for space on the page.

"Janice! Forgive me—but I am onto something I dare not lose. If you don't mind—"

"Oh! I'm sorry. Forgive *me*. I'll call later. Or, if you'll tell me, do you want to pick it up, or should I mail it? I *did* want to talk about what I discovered on the *Hound*. I have a lot of shorthand notes I haven't transcribed yet."

"You can mail it—or— No! I'll pick it up; and if you'd like to be ready, we can take a little spin out to the lake and have dinner at the Beachcomber."

Even as he said it, he had his mind made up. He was going to play John Alden for Dr. Halford Raymond. It would not be easy for Janice to lose her position as his research secretary, but Wilkerson was hundreds of miles from here and— Well, there was no other way. Janice was the just-right complement for Hal—*just* right.

"I'd like that very much," she had said; but there was a quaver in her voice that told him his abrupt interruption had hurt, and the knowledge of it hurt him also.

Until now Janice Granada was the only woman who had seemed the perfect complement he himself required—not for marriage but for mental companionship. With her, roaming the woods, stopping to listen to a wood thrush, watching a sunset's slow demise—these were the refuelings his creative moods required.

Of late, however, he had been aware of an attitude of possessiveness on her part. She was becoming more than a secretary researching his stories, his magazine articles, and his lectures to student groups. So much so that at times it seemed as if he were a puppet, writing and saying the things she suggested and actually wording his descriptions in her language.

When he had hung up, he turned to the coffin his journal had become and glanced listlessly at yesterday's quote from William Blake's "Auguries of Innocence":

> To see a world in a grain of sand
> And a heaven in a wild flower,

Hold infinity in the palm of your hand
And eternity in an hour.

He had been enamored with Francis Thompson's *The Hound of Heaven*. He had phoned Janice to research it and then had quickly dashed off a rough draft for his series of articles on "The Flower Fields of the Poets"—a title borrowed from a Whittier line: "The flower-fields of the soul."

Thompson had once studied medicine but had abandoned it because of his own ill health. He had lived in poverty. He became an opium addict, wrote only three thin volumes of poetry, and died of tuberculosis at forty-eight.

There was an atmosphere in *The Hound of Heaven* not unlike the creative pursuit in his own mind. He loved the imagery, the panting flight of the soul from God, the loving pursuit of God Himself, the singing rhythms, and the colorful phrasings. This was literary beauty of the sort that inspired the reader to soar, the kind his own mother had loved and had sometimes written.

Joe closed his journal and locked it into its desk drawer, hidden from any possible prying by the eyes of a maid or of his landlady, Mrs. Crowley.

A diary, Mother Cardinal had once told him, is for a man's soul to hide in. Never leave its door unlocked.

Words of wisdom had often spilled unawares from Mother's mind; and he had remembered so many of them and built his house upon them: "Never be ashamed to love the beautiful in literature. It is the coin of wisdom, as the French writer Joseph Joubert has expressed it: 'The coin of wisdom is its great thoughts, its eloquent flights, its proverbs and pithy sentences.' Always remember that, Joe. And when you yourself have written something beautiful, it is right to feel a warmth in your heart when you look upon it—as right as it was for God to look upon His own beautiful world after He had created it and say, 'It is *good*.' You must always feel that way about your work, Joe, and never, *never* write anything about which you cannot say, 'It is clean, it is right, it is good.' "

Beautiful Sheilla Cardinal, lonely after Father's death in World War I, had sought and found much release from heartache and loneliness in her teaching and in her own writing. She was, as she expressed it, "Helping God keep on with His continuous work of crea-

9

tion—helping Him prepare young minds for the tomorrows which lie ahead."

Mother had been sunshine and flowers and country lanes to him, and as a faithful mother, she not only counseled but occasionally, when a situation required, disciplined him as well.

"Always be a lover of nature. Be like Longfellow's little Hiawatha, Joe, and love every wild thing of the field and woods. They are all God's creatures. They are all your brothers. Never, never kill except for food or when you might have to, to protect your own life."

At ten he had asked about what had happened in the war. "Did Daddy ever have to kill when he was over there?"

It was a hard question. It was harder still when he asked, "Did Daddy hate anybody when he killed, if he killed?"

She had exacted from him a promise, "Promise me, Joe, that you will always be a man of peace, like the peace the Saviour offers and gives to all who believe in Him."

And he had promised.

That promise had been the drive behind the story of the pheasants, of which Janice had just phoned him.

He was singing in the shower as he prepared for his dinner at the Beachcomber with Janice. This would be their last, perhaps, before he would leave for Wilkerson; and it had to be the occasion of his serious attempt to play John Alden for Hal.

Again facing the mirror and now knotting a favorite tie, the song of the shower was still moving in his mind—a favorite old hymn of the church, which Mother had sung so often in the days immediately after the telegram came telling of Jeffry Cardinal's death:

> A mighty fortress is our God,
> A bulwark never failing.

Mother had found her comfort and strength to keep on living and loving, not only in her work but in her faith in God, the Fortress. She often quoted Luther's hymn and even more often searched the pages of the old brown Bible on her study desk in the den.

Tie knotted, coat inspected for any stray fleck of dust, hair groomed the way he liked it, Joe went out to his car, saying to himself, "All right, John Alden, this is it."

10

Chapter 2

In Longfellow's *Courtship of Miles Standish*, when John Alden had spoken his piece, Priscilla had challenged him, "Why don't you speak for yourself, John?"

Janice might possibly allow history to repeat itself. That was a risk he was prepared to take—and he was steeled against any emotional moment that could tempt him to surrender his "basic right."

As his car moved toward The Towers, where Janice had indicated she would be waiting for him, he reviewed his situation and point of view. It may have been his love for solitude of the kind Thoreau described in his onetime boast, "I have never found the companion so enjoyable as solitude," or it may have been his own inherent need for following a dream. But it had seemed that a wife and home and children could be too interruptive for a man reaching for a literary career. He must march as Thoreau had once counseled: "If one advances confidently in the direction of his dreams, and endeavors to live the life which he has imagined, he will meet with a success unexpected in common hours. . . . As you simplify your life, the laws of the universe will be simpler, solitude will not be solitude, poverty will not be poverty, nor weakness weakness."

It was good advice, he thought; and he had followed it—until now.

Other thoughts crowded in from his childhood.

There was the day of tragedy. After a particularly carefree afternoon in the woods with his favorite neighborhood playmate, now Dr. Halford Raymond, he had come home to find his mother missing. Mother was in the hospital, he was told.

There had been emergency surgery, and from it she had not awakened except to say, "Tell my son I died loving him."

And Joe had become a skeptic, doubting the goodness of a God who allowed such things as wars that kill fathers and sicknesses that kill mothers.

He doubted—yet he believed, for he could *feel* the presence of God all around and everywhere. Sometimes it even seemed God was in his own heart, speaking to him through his conscience.

He had lived his early years in the home of his maternal grand-parents in the lake country of the north. There he had become a little Hiawatha. He had walked and talked with nature and, like Hiawatha, he had learned the language of every beast, called them all little Joseph's brothers, learned their names and all their secrets, and loved them very, very much.

In times of solitude he walked with the sighing pines, ran with the wind in his face, laughed with the hilarious laughter of the loons and mimicked their lonely twilight farewells to the day, and sang with the marsh wrens among the tall sedges of the lakeshore.

In school, his themes dealt with wildlife—beast and bird and flower and tree. Once, when he was fifteen and felt especially sad because of something he had seen that day, he wrote "The Massacre"—the pheasant story which Janice had said she liked very much. He had kept it all these years, and only last week he had discovered it in his file of memories.

Perhaps at the Beachcomber he could talk about it with Janice just before he assumed the role of John Alden.

The story, every sentence polished, every phrase carefully turned, was like a loon calling across the lake, wailing his loneliness. It opened with definitions from the dictionary:

"Bouquet: The flight of a flock of pheasants from the central meeting place of the beaters. It also refers to the meeting place of the beaters themselves.

"Beaters: Those who scour for game. . . ."

The story itself ran:

"The fifteen-year-old boy watched from the crest of the hill over-looking the west forty. He knew the field was alive with pheasants. From every direction the beaters came, moving like the spokes of a wheel toward the hub.

"The boy's heart was pounding with fear—not for himself, but for his brother pheasants.

"The circle was getting smaller and smaller, and from his hiding place on the cliff, he could see the birds getting nervous—more and more as the circle narrowed.

12

"Any second now there would be an explosion of feathers and the bouquet would be born—the only beautiful thing about the whole massacre. There would be a cloud of wings expanding across the sky, a score of shotguns fitted to shoulders—and fire and smoke and thunder would shatter the stillness.

"In such a little while the flight of life in hopeless search of continued life would be transformed into broken pinions and shattered bones, torn and bleeding flesh, and quivering death.

"The boy cringed when he saw the bouquet rise; his spirit reeled within him when the fire and smoke and thunder of guns destroyed the peace of the beautiful little world that belonged to pheasants only. The south forty was their own little nation—and an enemy had come to make war upon them.

"He saw the beautiful birds falling—some dropping without any flapping of wings, others limping on broken pinions to the sedge below. He saw the remains of the bouquet fanning itself against the leaden sky and remembered Bryant's 'To a Waterfowl'—one lone bird winging a solitary way across the crimson sky.

"The hunters had had a successful hunt; they had bagged twenty elusive birds. There would be a banquet tomorrow night in the Range Hall, tales of successful hunts of other days, much laughter and jesting, and for some, a tarrying at the bottle.

"Superior minds had devised a way to take innocent life at a cost of only a little time and gunpowder—minds that could make ammunition which could fly faster than pheasants who could only grow wings.

"The boy dragged home wearily. It was his brothers who had been killed in the war, and it was his other brothers who had killed them. And the boy who had watched from the cliff was angry at the brothers who had superior minds. He sorrowed for them and went home to a supper of pheasant, for one of the human brothers had been thoughtful of his neighbors who were getting old and feeble and could no longer work the way they used to when they were young.

"But the boy could not eat."

*　　*　　*

The story brought his English teacher, Sheldon McMaster, all the way to his grandparents' home to see him. Together they strolled in the woods and along the lakeshore, and when the teacher had gone, Joe was on fire with ambition.

13

"Where did you get the idea for your story?" McMaster asked, and Joe answered: "From my feathered brothers."

In their walk, they came upon a little shack at the base of the cliff. "Here," Joe said proudly, "is my study. This is my Henry David Thoreau cabin."

His desk was made of orange crates, and his chair, a captain's chair salvaged from his childhood home, was the one Mother Cardinal had used when she studied or graded papers or read from the old brown Book.

When McMaster had gone, his words, spoken while his hand was on Joe's shoulder, were like a live coal in his mind: "Someday, Joe, if you keep on working and thinking and keeping clean in your mind and heart, you will help make people understand the ways of God."

* * *

Because of his love for beautiful things and of the ways of nature, Joe found comfort in the beautiful things men had written; and like the squirrels of the forest, he stored them away in his mind—memorizing many choice selections. He came to think of his mind as having an attic where he kept his treasures of thought. The door to his attic he kept always open.

He carried the memory of his little lakeside shack all through the years that followed—the remaining years of high school, teacher's college, and afterward. He continued writing when he could spare the time—and also sometimes at night, when the muse came upon him. But he kept his secret dreams to himself—for there were athletics and class activities and occasional dating with groups. There was so much to learn—until the time when he would build somewhere another and better Thoreau cabin, and there he would write and write and write—and dream and be free from the pressure of society.

Sometimes his own word-paintings filled his eyes with tears and his heart with pride. Comparing his paragraphs and occasional poems with those of history's literary giants, the live coal would burst into flame—and he would feed it with fresh new fuel from the attic of his mind.

The clouded world, made sorrowful because of the loss of his parents, was still beautiful. He had found a new father and mother in the realm of thought.

The years had brought him now to within two weeks of his new

14

position in Wilkerson College. They had also brought him to his role as John Alden.

* * *

Janice was her usual gay and vibrant self—and for an interval as they dined in candlelight at the window overlooking the lake, he toyed with the thought of playing John Alden not for Hal Raymond but for himself. But when he looked down the lanes of the future and tried to visualize her as a wife and mother—his wife, and the mother of his children—he knew she was not for him and he was not for her. There was yet another, somewhere; perhaps she was not unlike his own mother—one who was gifted as she, a lover of literature and nature. But—well—it was simply not Janice Granada. *She* was right for Hal Raymond.

At the right moment—or what he thought was right—he told her so and was startled at her attitude.

"You're kidding," she said. "Hal Raymond? In a roundabout sort of way, he proposed to me himself two years ago, when he was an intern and I was in nurse's training, but we just didn't seem to belong. He's sweet, perfect for almost any other girl, a wonderful doctor with a successful career ahead of him. But I almost hate nursing. I don't like the smell of disinfectants, and I could never stand being jolted awake in the night by the phone ringing, calling him out to some emergency or other."

And then her eyes took on a lonely look. "I'm going to miss my work with you very much, Joe—Mr. Cardinal. It's been very satisfying—and I hope you'll remember me with an occasional manuscript. And any research you need, write or phone me and I'll do it."

He promised, the hour and the crisis passed, and he left her at her apartment.

* * *

And now he was in Wilkerson, ensconced in his position. The months were rolling past, and he was lonely and unhappy. He often remembered Hal's counsel about his need for a complement—and the pages of his diary were filled with yearnings. One entry ran, "I am still on the trail in search of myself and cannot find me. Who am I? Where am I? *Why* am I?"

And in the middle of the year there began to move across the

15

horizon the clouds of war, like the darkness of William Henley's "Thick Is the Darkness."

There had been a discussion of the poem in a recent class. The works of Henley, a British poet of stature, had been compared to those of Browning and Dickens and certain early American poets, including Whittier and Longfellow.

A hand was raised in the back of the classroom.

"Yes, Miss Blanchard?"

Lela Blanchard, daughter of George Wilcox Blanchard, college board member and editor of the nationally circulated weekly, *The Silver Lining,* rose from her seat in the back row. Her voice was quiet, controlled. "I think this poem indicates something serious happening to Henley. When he wrote his famous poem 'Invictus,' he thanked 'whatever gods there be' for his unconquerable soul. He himself was the captain of his fate.

"But in 'Thick Is the Darkness,' he seems to be reaching out for help beyond himself—perhaps to God—when he says:

> Thick is the darkness,
>   Sunward, Oh, sunward!
> Rough is the highway,
>   Onward still onward!
> Dawn harbors surely,
>   East of the shadows.
> Facing us somewhere
>   Spread the sweet meadows.

"He may be trying to say that there is, there *has* to be, a sunrise, and that it is east of the shadows—that God Himself is out there somewhere, and we must keep on looking *for* Him and perhaps *to* Him for the sweet meadows only He can provide—like the Shepherd that makes His sheep lie down in green pastures."

There was silence in the room—not of the thick darkness variety, but of light. And Professor Joseph Cardinal was moved to wonder if Lela Blanchard might possibly be the way out of his own thick darkness.

The shadows of war continued to roll in the east, and Joe, enlisting his mind in the cause of peace, began a series of articles in the Wilkerson College *Breeze* under the heading "Wings of a Dove." His first offering was entitled "The Massacre."

16

Time moved on, entries in his journal began to shine, and he was beginning to sing another of his mother's favorite hymns, "I am looking through the shadows for the beacon lights of home."

His basic right began to lose its chains; he had found the complement of which he and Hal Raymond had talked that day on the golf course.

The class had been studying the poems of Longfellow and for several days had given "Evangeline" particular attention.

"Fair was she to behold, that maiden of seventeen summers."

Literary critics called the meter of "Evangeline" dactylic hexameter, a metrical form that moved like the rhythm of the waves washing the shores of Bluebell Island.

Lela Blanchard, however, was a young woman of twenty-three, more fair, he thought, than Evangeline, and more mature.

He began to be almost painfully aware of her the day in Classroom B when she finished her examination on the history of American literature, rose, and walked down the aisle to lay her test folder on his desk—the last of the class to leave. It was just as he imagined Evangeline might have seemed to Longfellow as he traced her story through its lilting, sorrowful search for love.

When she had gone and he was alone in the room, it was like another line of "Evangeline": "When she had passed, it seemed like the passing of exquisite music."

The textbook had given the historical setting for "Evangeline" as an incident rising out of the French and Indian War. A force of British and Colonial troops had sailed from Boston to Nova Scotia, which was then called Acadia. They had deported the French inhabitants, dispossessing them of their property and settling them among other British colonies in America.

The British had put Evangeline and her lover on different ships, and thus began her lonely search with its aching heart, disillusionments, frustrations, and broken dreams.

Hawthorne had heard the story first, and he had told it to Longfellow; later, when the poem was finished, Whittier read it and said, "Longfellow was just the one to write it. If I had attempted it, I should have spoiled the artistic effect of the poem by my indignation at the treatment of the exiles by the Colonial government."

It was Lela Blanchard's comment on it, clipped to the last page of her examination folder, that awakened Joe's more serious interest in the girl. "How cruel," she wrote, "that they should have been forced to sail in different ships; how thoughtless, how completely harsh to trample upon her heart, and his! And yet, so much of life is like that, as if a stony-hearted fate were determined to thwart us all from finding our personal Holy Grail. We seek, and when we find, we lose again; we are set to sail on different ships. There is too much of shadow, unless one can carry a lantern within to dissolve it."

And there was a final note.

"I like what the English poet Dickens said in his lyric, 'The Children':

> I ask not a life for the dear ones,
> All radiant, as others have done,
> But that they may have just enough shadow
> To temper the glare of the sun."

He was startled at the question, also appended: "Wouldn't that make a good title for a novel—*Just Enough Shadow?*"

That was all, and when he had finished reading the note, it seemed like the ceasing of exquisite music.

There was a local colonial government, and there were two British ships, both captained by small college etiquette, and, Joe Cardinal thought, rightly so. But when the school year is past, and the commencement and her graduation—

Bluebell Island, given its name because from June to September it was carpeted with bluebells and because the island itself was bell-shaped, was the setting for their first serious moments alone.

Chapter 3

Bluebell Lake, one of the many smaller lakes in the area, was part of the Blanchard Estate. First, there had been the wind-in-the-face ride with Lela in George Wilcox Blanchard's white dinghy, driving at top speed to the island itself, armed with camera, binoculars, and an attaché case containing galley proofs of *The Silver Lining*.

When their work was finished and they came back an hour before sunset, their day had changed from carefree make-believe to something which he knew was the kind of love a man should have before proposing marriage.

The conviction had been climaxed as they sat on a little knoll on the island, looking down at the lake and at the waiting dinghy. Their picnic lunch was finished and *The Silver Lining* galleys duly proofed when from the top branches of a maple there came the clear, sharp whistle of a cardinal—"Cheo-cheo-chehoo-cheo!"

Quickly he lifted his binoculars and swept them here and there among the branches. A sweet sharp pain of beauty stabbed at his heart when, from a distance, there came another song—similar, yet with a more plaintive note.

Her hand reached out instinctively as if to silence any word that might frighten or send a startled bird winging away. "It's Evangeline," she whispered. "She's answering."

The touch of her hand on his wrist was only for an instant, but the memory of it stayed. "The female also sings," she said. "I hear him often when I come here, but I've never seen their nest. I only know from what I read that they build it loosely of bark, leaves and grass in a small tree or bush. One day I'll find it, but I won't disturb it. No one has a right to disturb the nest of such beautiful lovers—or any other home of any kind. There he goes now—to meet her out there somewhere.

His binoculars swept the sky and caught a flash of magnificent red

19

slicing across the open space toward a hedge of bushes rimming the hill.

What he said then was unpremeditated; it was surprising even to himself. But when she gasped and then gave a low chuckle, he knew she had understood: "Me, Cardinal; you, Evangeline."

She became suddenly businesslike: "For a long time," she said, "I've been wishing Father would begin a new column that would interweave gems from the literary geniuses of yesterday with a bit of botany—birdlore and animal life. With so much low-level literature flooding the newsstands and the daily papers and the dangerous philosophies that our school kids are reading, such a column would be welcomed. Here's what we have in mind, and please don't let what I'm going to show you spoil a very enjoyable afternoon. I didn't bring you over here just for this. I've had a perfectly beautiful time, one of the finest in my life. But—"

From her attaché case, she handed him a sheet of drawing paper; and on it was a cardinal in full color. There was the striking red crest, the black throat, the black band around the neck and beak, the bill, a light red, the feet, brown, and the eyes—the one visible eye—a tiny pearl of brown.

Below the regal bird there was set in the type of a news caption:

THE CALL OF THE CARDINAL
by Joe Cardinal

An editorial insert announced in smaller type: "With this issue we introduce a new feature which we are sure our readers will like very much. We invite your comments. We know you will enjoy walking with the author down the winding trails of thought, climbing with him the hills which literary giants of old have climbed, and tossing yourself gaily into the little literary whirlwinds he makes for you. Laugh and love and grow and build your nests among the roses in his garden of ideas and high ideals."

It was signed simply, *"Editors."*

Joe Cardinal was pleased, flattered, honored—and also deflated.

He lifted the binoculars again, searched the bushes along the hill's crest, lowered them, and studied the artistically colored cardinal and the brief, poetic, too-complimentary introduction. It had been such a gala afternoon, pretending they were Evangeline and her lover,

Gabriel. How he had enjoyed it. How much he wanted to come here again with her, go anywhere with her, just to be with her.

Daughter of an editor, concerned for the growth and popularity of their paper, she had sacrificed an afternoon—hers and his—and used her most extraordinary feminine wiles to get him to join the staff of *The Silver Lining.*

"Your cardinal," he said simply, "has stopped singing."

Her answer was an announcement: "He has found his mate. They're singing with their hearts now, and we're not supposed to hear that."

"I notice," he said, "that the introduction is signed, *'Editors'*— plural. Does your father know about this?"

Her answer was evasive, he thought: "Father's a devotee of your 'Wings of a Dove' column in the *Breeze.* Only yesterday at the breakfast table he said, 'If I could corral that wild young mind for *The Silver Lining,* we could put a silver lining around the whole world.' "

"You're sure he used the adjective *wild?"*

"He is very careful in his choice of words."

"But *wild* means, *'dissolute, prodigal.' "*

"In the bad sense, yes; but he meant it in the milder sense, which Funk and Wagnalls calls 'frolicsome and gay.' "

"But I'm not frolicsome and I'm seldom gay."

"With words you are. You make them gambol about like lambs, he says; and when you write about peace, it makes all of us want to stroll beside the still waters."

"I'm a little confused. First I'm a wild young bronco, then I'm a frolicking lamb, and now you are asking me to be a redbird. Are you sure your father initiated all these mixed metaphors? An editor of his stature should know better."

"Please! Don't you like my cardinal? I spent three hours doing him yesterday."

Suddenly she was very serious. "You know what the redbird is saying when he cries 'Cheo-cheo-chehoo-cheo?' He is calling 'Peace! Peace! Peace.' And with all the violence in the world—the hating and killing, the thunder of clashing ideologies—a weekly column of peaceful thoughts could help a lot. 'As [a man] thinketh in his heart, so is he.' King Solomon wrote that, remember?"

"But you yourself could write the column. Your colorful introduction couldn't be improved upon."

21

"It took me two hours," she returned. "I suffered through every word of it."

"So does every writer with everything he writes well," he said. "I'd be willing to let you caption it 'The Call of the Cardinal,' if you like. I could give you my name—"

As before, she extended her hand and touched his wrist. "I think I can't stand having you say no. You wouldn't want to shatter a young girl's dream, would you? Make me sail in a different ship? Only the British soldiers could be so cruel!"

She was pouting now in pretty pretense. He liked it, yet he was afraid of it, and he tried to think what her dream might mean to him—the expansion of his literary career? A release from teaching, which he had found too confining? What he said now was a bit mundane, he felt, but he shot the arrow into the air, to let it fall to earth—somewhere: "I make daily trips to the grocery stores and the cafes, and my landlady has a way of requiring monthly rent."

"And then," she disregarded his practical suggestion, "after a few weeks, copies of your columns will be sent to scores of newspapers across the nation and in Canada under the letterhead, Cardinal Features, Incorporated, and before we know it, you'll be calling the nation and much of the world to peace."

"You," he said firmly—and, he felt, defensively, and maybe even evasively—"are the one to write it. You have inherited a talent for expressing yourself literarily. I've seen it in all your compositions and in the little appended notes on your examination papers. And if your heart is set on captioning the column "The Call of the Cardinal," as I offered a moment ago, I'm willing to give you my name—"

"Listen," she interrupted. "There's mother's dinner bell. Hear it?"

Across the lake at the Blanchard place, visible through the shelter of evergreens, like a jewel in a setting of apple blossoms, he saw blue smoke rising from the fireplace chimney.

"We ought to go now, but—" she hesitated, and her tone was as playful as it had been earlier in the afternoon, "I do thank you for offering me your name. I'll have to think about it, but for the present, *you* Gabriel and *me* only Evangeline on board another ship."

And they were off to the dinghy for a fast spin across the waves to the Blanchard dock on the other side.

Their life jackets on and, at her insistence, he in the stern driving the powerful little motor and she in the middle seat facing him, they left Acadia behind enroute for an unknown rendezvous in the future.

At the dock, having secured the dinghy, he said lightly, "It just may be, Evangeline, that we are not the *two* we have pretended to be. I just may be a British officer, and you may fall in love with me and forget entirely your beloved Gabriel. How would that strike you?"

Lela's answer pleased him very much: "When Longfellow shot an arrow into the air, it fell to earth he knew not where—and it was a long, long time before he found it. But when he breathed a song into the air, it was the song of the cardinal, and he found it again in the pages of *The Silver Lining*. Here, be a good little boy and carry this." She handed him her attaché case.

The path to the wisteria-shaded porch was too narrow for side-by-side walking, so he let her precede him and walked behind, with Longfellow's exquisite music accompanying.

"One thing," he reminded her when the path widened at the level place leading to the broad lawn, where outdoor furniture waited always for guest or family, "Evangeline's search was long, weary, and frustrating and was rewarded only when her Gabriel was old and dying in a Philadelphia hospital."

She stopped, picked two purple violets from a cluster near a white iron settee, and handed one to him, saying, "When I was a little girl, Daddy and I used to fight battles with these. We called them Johnny-jump-ups, and we'd lock their chins, saying, 'My Johnny-jump-up can whip your Johnny-jump-up.' Then we'd each give a little jerk, and one or the other would lose its head."

It was a delaying tactic, he thought—hoped, anyway—to postpone their going into the house, where they would no longer be alone.

There was the sound of a car horn at the lane leading in from the highway.

"Daddy!" she exclaimed—and there was a light in her voice as she waved a cheerful greeting and took off on the run for the garage where the car would stop.

He followed her with his eyes, and it was not until father and daughter had come all the way back that he was aware of the violets, their heads still interlocked in preparation for battle. He waited for a chance to give them to her.

23

The moment came when he was alone on the porch, leafing through the galleys from *The Silver Lining*. He was recalling the pleasantries of the afternoon and looking down the lanes of the years ahead when she stopped at his chair. "I forgot," she began, "How did the battle end? Who lost his head?"

"Who lost *her* head, you mean."

"Did we pull, or didn't we?"

He opened his hand, laughed and remarked, "If you don't mind, I'd rather not. How about pressing them between the leaves of a book, just to remember this afternoon?"

Their eyes met, and he saw in hers something he had waited all his life to see in a woman. Quickly, she looked away, went back into the house, and came back out with a book entitled *Complete Works of Longfellow*.

She handed the volume to him and said, "You select the place."

He turned the pages to "Evangeline," where it spoke of the stars as being "the forget-me-nots of the angels . . . In the infinite meadows of heaven." There he placed the interlocked violets, closed the book, handed it back to her, and announced casually, "Not to be opened until Christmas."

She did not reply with words—only with her eyes, and what they said was as a dream of tomorrow. For their love was young and living, fresh as violets under morning dew, and nothing could ever diminish it. No withering sun, no ruthless hand could tear them apart.

Chapter 4

In the Blanchard orchard after dinner, Joe talked with Lela's father: "I've had something happen to me today, Mr. Blanchard. I think it had been happening for some time, but it was climaxed this afternoon. I have fallen in love with your daughter."

George Blanchard was silent, his eyes on the sunset that was fanning out now in a broad span of crimson and gold. "It had to come sometime," he said. "Mother and I have been waiting, wondering a little, thankful that always, when it looked as if serious dating was in progress, she was able to discern. She seems to have an editorial microscope that looks deep into a man's heart; and if there are any plot inconsistencies, the story gets rejected.

"I think I saw one-hundred-percent approval in her eyes when she came running to meet me at the gate.

"If it does turn out to be the will of God for her, you'll find that true love is a growing thing. In times when the fire of romance burns low, always lay the blame on yourself. And, as a wise man once said, 'Every man ought to keep a fairsized cemetery in which to bury the faults of his friends.' Eloise and I have applied that philosophy ever since our wedding day—only I'm afraid her cemetery is a little larger than mine."

Then, as if to change the subject, Blanchard asked, "Did Lela tell you what we have in mind for *The Silver Lining*—and for you, of course?"

"You did know, then?"

"Didn't she show you the lead-in, signed, *'Editors'*?"

"I saw it but I thought it was an editorial 'we.' "

"We," he said, "and in this case, we *three*—Eloise, Lela and I—have studied your column in the *Breeze*. Your call to peace should bear your name, don't you think? I am sure we—and this time it

25

would be a foursome—cannot change the world, but we can help its inhabitants to think peace instead of war, kindness instead of cruelty, generosity instead of greed, love instead of hate."

"If, under the circumstances, I didn't interweave too much *romantic* love."

"The editors," George Blanchard reminded him, "would be alert to deviations—the senior editors, that is."

From across the lake now there came the piercing cry of the loon, a wild, demoniac laugh, a familiar sound to Joe, who had spent his boyhood in the lake country of the north. It was a sound as nostalgic as the call of the cardinal. He spoke now as to a stenographer or a dictating machine: "Beginning paragraph one, of 'The Call of the Cardinal':

"The red-throated loon is a wandering minstrel in the lake country. It wears a triangular brooch of rusty red at its throat, which blends in harmony with the mottled glossy green and white of its upper parts. Its blue-gray forehead offers a gentle hint of its loneliness. Its eerie cry, serrating across the twilight, is charged with melancholy. It is the lonely wail of Evangeline searching the colonies for her Gabriel and never finding him, the bleating of a lamb astray from its mother, the cry of an abandoned soldier on a battlefield after the tornado of war has passed and there is only the pain of his wounds to keep him company—his wounds and his dying."

Interrupting his off-the-cuff musings—coming clear and sharp from the pines near the dock—came now the piercing whistle of the cardinal: *"Cheo-cheo-chehoo-cheo."*

"That," George Blanchard suggested quietly, "could be your answer."

It could be, Joe thought, it just *could* be. The door was too wide open to be ignored. It was almost as if he had heard a call from God.

The voice within came not with sound of wind or storm or fire or earthquake but was gentle and kind, yet with strong authority it commanded him to serve.

It was as if George Wilcox Blanchard, layman of the Wilkerson Memorial Church, had also heard the unspoken words, when he now said quietly, "What I am saying to you, you do not now understand, but you will know after a while."

Joe had heard those words somewhere—or read them. Were they

26

from the Bible—the words of the Saviour, perhaps, to a slow-to-understand disciple?

Lela was standing beside him before he was aware she had come. She spoke playfully, "Now that Mother and I have finished all your kitchen chores, how about all of us taking a little stroll down to the dock? The sun has finished his own chore and the moon is about to take over—in fact, at 9:27, the calendar says; it's a three-quarter moon this week—"

George yawned, "Mother and I have a little matter of business to discuss. You youngsters don't need two old gray-haired people along—"

And from behind him, Eloise sliced in with: *"Did you say two?"*

Joe smiled to himself as he reflected that he understood Lela Blanchard a little better, not only because of his talk with her father but also because of the leak in the dike of her mother's wisdom and humor.

He had not planned to talk seriously of marriage until he could be sure that *Lela* was sure.

If he were not sure, and if she were not, a proposal would be like helping a rosebud unfold before its time had come, and its petals would be bruised or wounded by too much assistance from a too-eager gardener.

This was not their first walk and talk in the twilight. They had strolled before. Twice they had sat on the wooden bench near the boat dock and listened to Nature's sleepy murmurings as she said good-bye to the day—only Nature never really said good-bye, she only changed the tone of her voice.

A proposal of marriage might well be prefaced by something philosophical, Joe thought, so he began by saying, "I was reading Lord Byron's dramatic poem 'Manfred' the other morning, and I ran across a line spoken by the Abbot of St. Maurice. I find some of the choicest lines in all of literature in the things Byron wrote. For instance, when Manfred finished telling the abbot of the torture in his heart because of his sins, the abbot replied: 'The commencement of atonement is the sense of its necessity.' "

He stopped. It was a long way from old England to Bluebell Lake.

Her comment at first was light and equally non-apropos as she

27

mused: "Plato is reported to have said, 'Necessity is the mother of invention.' "

He came back to Byron: "Byron died at thirty-six, a very unhappy bachelor. He did marry once, but it was an ill-fated relationship and lasted only two years. He remained single the rest of his miserable life."

The girl beside him on the bench joined in as if the biography of Byron was the most vital theme of the moment: "Poor Byron. Maybe if he hadn't been left fatherless when he was only three years old and hadn't had a club foot, he might not have become such a victim of self-pity. I feel so sorry for anyone who has a handicap like his. But the poor man was deformed in his attitudes also, and he lived such a profligate life. No wonder when he realized he was facing eternity without God, he wrote:

> My days are in the yellow leaf;
>   The flowers and fruits of love are gone;
> The worm, the canker, and the grief
>   Are mine alone!

Joe's comment was, "It may be that Manfred's despair over his sins was the voice of Byron himself, crying for forgiveness. Who knows?"

"If Manfred had lived today and had talked with our pastor rather than with the abbot, he could have learned that both the beginning and the end of the Atonement were at Calvary. And if Manfred—or Byron—had looked to the cross, or rather, to the Christ of the cross, he would have found immediate forgiveness."

It was a good theological discussion, but there was a time also for love, and human love also was of God. Joe now bridged the gap between the sacred theological and the sacred philosophical by saying, "If I may change to Longfellow and a more apropos incident of literature: You, Priscilla, me, John Alden. I come, O fair maiden, to speak for Miles Standish: 'In the solitude of the forest, sitting at your wheel, carded wool like a snowdrift piled at your knee, beautiful with your beauty and rich with the wealth of your being—' "

It was as if the red-throated loon were giving a farewell call to the day and a lonely greeting to the night as from Bluebell Island there came a long, piercing, melancholy wail. Could it have been the mating call?

28

The answer of the Puritan girl beside him in the solitude of the lakeshore was in a pensive tone: "In the poem, Priscilla fired the shot since heard round the world: 'Why don't you speak for yourself, John?' "

And in that moment before the moon had risen to help romanticize the occasion, John Alden spoke for himself—and Priscilla answered.

There were whispered words, unrehearsed pledges of allegiance, and love expressed with gentleness and courtesy. And, because their love was a sacred thing, there was reverence.

In a lighter moment, she asked coyly, "Why should a wedding ceremony include such an unnecessary pledge as 'Forsaking all others'? There aren't any others, are there?"

"No others."

She sighed. "I am a woman with a cat's curiosity. I'm wondering if there ever *have* been."

"Not a cat," he returned, "but a cute, gentle, green-eyed little kitten."

"You," she accused him poutingly, "are sidetracking the theme of our conversation."

He sighed in pretense of boredom and answered, "Let me count the names: There was one in my teens, an extra-long time ago. She let me help her with algebra problems. And there was another at the University who was my secretary for a while. And before that, Frieda, Iona, Elizabeth, Marilee, Helen of Troy, Harriet Beecher Stowe—but I eluded them all until I met a girl named Lela. She managed to corral the wild young colt."

As if in defence, she said, "But I was only trying to help my father."

"Your father," he returned, "wanted only my wild young mind. You seem to have lassoed all of me."

"I hope so."

From across the lake, as before, came the melancholy wail of the loon.

"It's John Alden," he suggested, "speaking for himself."

"Are you sure? It could be Priscilla answering, couldn't it?"

"And that reminds me—you've listened to my list of has-beens. Now let me hear you count yours."

"I warn you, it will take a long time, but here goes: First, there was Joe, then there was Joe, and after that Joe and Joe and Joe and

Joe. 'I only remember Joey: Joey made me change my name.' " She sang the last line of a new popular song.

A little later, after the lonely loon had called again and again and Priscilla had answered only in whispers, Lela said, "Look! See what has happened during the blackout! What right has a moon to watch the way of a man with a maid?"

"He's only peeking," Joe answered. "Besides, he's only a three-quarter moon, and part of him is hidden behind the trees."

From beside them now came the faint mew of a kitten. Lela shone her flashlight in a little circle until it came to focus upon a small kitten arching its back and stroking itself against the dock post.

"You, too?" she accused him. "You're too young to know about these things. There were three kittens last week, away down the lake where Crystal Creek enters. I managed to catch two of them, but one —this little rascal—wouldn't be corralled. His wild young mind wanted only freedom. Someone must not have wanted them and tried to lose them where they'd most likely be found. I took the two to the animal shelter, and ever since I've wondered about this little fellow. I know it sounds childish—or does it?—but I even prayed for him. Come here, you little darling. You're going to be adopted."

Chapter 5

The curious moon was well on the way to its zenith when Joe's car, with two red tail-lights aflame, moved out of the Blanchard lane into the highway.

Lela, standing at the orchard gate—the kitten in her arms a bit restless at seeming to be ignored, yet purring in appreciation for even a little love—wondered at the ecstacy of her heart and murmured to herself, "When he had gone, it seemed like the ceasing of exquisite music." *Only,* she thought, *he has not gone forever; he will come back, and one day we will go away together and the music will never end.*

To the restless kitten she crooned, "You poor little darling. Happiness, to you, right now, is a pan of warm milk." She carried her newly adopted pet into the house and was busy feeding it when there was a call down the stairs, "There's a snack on the dinette table if you're hungry."

"I'm not hungry. I'm just feeding Little Tiger. I found the other triplet down at the dock."

"Be careful when you introduce him to Big Tom. He hates any cat he thinks might be competition."

Lela remembered another occasion when she had made a home for a foundling kitten. Big Tom had given cautious, green-eyed scrutiny: then, like furry lightning, he had leaped upon the terrified little orphan and would have torn it to pieces except for very forceful intervention.

From the radio, just turned on, there came startling announcements of the tornadoes of war driving madly across Europe: "Germany is on the rampage. Here, to the moment, is the ominous list of the principal events:—The Fuehrer invaded Poland in September of 1939, Norway and Denmark the following April, the Netherlands, Belgium, and Luxemburg in May. May 28 the King of Belgium surrendered 500,000. The Vichy government of occupied France signed an armis-

31

tice with Germany. Hitler invaded Russia on June 22, 1941. The clouds of war move swiftly across the world's whole horizon. What, our statesmen are asking, will America do? What may she be forced to do?"

Fear moved into Lela's heart, for the newscaster was driving on to say: "Thousands of our young men are flocking to the colors, while America prepares for what may be inevitable."

Mother came all the way down the stairs, stopped, and snapped off the radio.

"It's been like that all evening—like it was when the first world war came. You shouldn't be listening to it, Lela. You have too much happiness in your heart tonight. Daddy and I had a special prayer for you a while ago. You're so young and so alive. I hope we can let Europe fight her own wars this time."

Lela was scarcely aware she was quoting a line from a note she had appended to her last examination when she answered: "We seek, and when we find, we lose again; we are set to sail in different ships."

"You really suffered with Evangeline, didn't you?" Mother Eloise commented.

"Mother, I'm scared. It was so wonderful tonight—too wonderful to happen to just me. I can't believe it will last. I keep feeling something terrible is hanging over the whole world—especially over my little world. I don't know whether it's the war and what *could* happen, or what. You ever feel like that, Mother?"

"Often in my girlhood—and my world went all to pieces when your father enlisted. But—there is God, Lela. I prayed for my beloved husband, wrapped him round and round with prayer, and the bullets never touched him. He came back without a single wound."

"You don't think they'd take Joe, do you? He's a teacher and a writer, and—aren't those essential occupations?"

Mother's answer did not offer comfort. It held, however, a spark of hope: "If he were married, it might make a difference, especially if he were a father."

Tiger had finished his saucer of milk and was mewing for love. Lela watched her mother lift the fluffy little orphan, stroke it gently, and heard her croon to it: "You decided to accept our mercy, didn't you? Last week you ran away because you thought our mercy was some kind of judgment, but it wasn't. Now you know. We human

32

beings are often like you, Little Tiger. God is trying to help us, and we're afraid. He waits until we are willing to come to Him—and then He fills our whole life with His peace."

In her room, Lela looked out across the moonlit lake. There was music in the sighing of the pines along the shore, in the washing of the waves against the dock, in everything—in Longfellow's forget-me-nots of the angels. There was a line in the Bible about a time when all the morning stars sang together.

"O world," she spoke, quoting a favorite stanza of Edna St. Vincent Millay,

> I cannot hold thee close enough!
> Thy winds, thy wide, gray skies!
> Thy mists that roll and rise!
> Thy woods . . . that lean, black bluff!
> World, world, I cannot get thee close enough!

But in her moment of fear, when the wild dark future seemed to enter into her and tear her apart with its thunder, she found no courage. There was need for the God of Nature Himself, to clasp her close to *His* heart. "This, O Heavenly Father, I need most of all. And Joe, too, whatever may be his future—may it always be ours—not his and mine, but *ours,* never separated, never estranged, always in love. Let us spend all we have for the loveliness of love."

When, a little later, she gave herself to sleep, she did not realize she had been praying—only that she had held communion with the Father of lights.

And while she slept, Joe Cardinal had begun a new race down a new, wide road—the future like wind in his hair, its prospects like music in his heart. He was in love with a most beautiful young woman, and she with him. He would make for them a home of beauty and love and purposeful living. He would write and write and write—not only the Cardinal column but also a novel that would interweave the beauty and grandeur of being alive.

In his bachelor apartment across the city, Joe put in a long distance call to Janice at Madison.

"Something wonderful must have happened," her lilting voice came singing over the wires. "You sound like a man who has just inherited the stock market or finished a book."

33

"Something better, Janice. I may be able, one of these days, to take you away from your self-employment—at least offer you more than an occasional manuscript. I'll get a letter on its way to you in the morning."

The letter, written soon after he had hung up was addressed:

Miss Janice Granada

Public Stenographer, Research Secretary

The Towers, Room 87

Madison, Wisconsin

"Beginning with the very next edition of *The Silver Lining* I am introducing 'The Call of the Cardinal,' which, according to the editor-in-chief, could quickly become a popular feature running in scores, maybe even hundreds, of newspapers across the nation. He has contacts which will help introduce it on a trial basis to Indiana, Illinois, and Ohio weeklies.

"I'm still working on the novel you know about; and when I come next week to start summer school, I hope to bring the first fifty pages to you for copying.

"I'll have correspondence to the Cardinal directed to me there— and if the mail comes avalanching in, which it just might, because there'll be a little controversy in some of the thoughts, I'll have to have secretarial help. And I know no one I'd rather trust with a job like that than Public Stenographer Janice Granada—unless by this time you have decided to go back to nursing."

Another letter was addressed to Mrs. Charles Crowley and said in part: "If the big front room I had last summer is still available—or can be made so—I'd like to move in early next week. The first semester opens June 15."

Both letters were sent airmail the next morning, and with gold dust in his hair, Joe drove out to the Blanchards to tell the future Mrs. Joe Cardinal what he had done. She would be pleased to learn that he was already preparing for his role of husband and provider.

It was a gay and radiant Lela who met him at the car when it stopped at the garden gate. And, as last night, he was completely under her spell and the equally magic spell of his own happiness.

"I know a place where the sun is like gold," she cried radiantly, "and the cherry blooms burst with snow, and down underneath is the loveliest nook where the four-leaf clovers grow."

"You," he said, "are the fourth leaf."

"Only the fourth? Last night you listed seven—that would make me the eighth, at least."

"Not the least," he said, "but the *last,* and the *most,*" and he caught his bride-to-be in his arms.

They were interrupted, as last night, by the voice of a kitten, begging for attention.

Lela released herself, scooped up the cuddly Little Tiger, and said, "Here, snookums! Meet your adopted father, Mr. Joseph Cardinal. He's the man you were spying on last night down by the lake—remember?"

Snookums' green eyes did not remember, but he was purring his noisy contentment.

"Has he been introduced to Big Tom?" Joe asked, remembering the well-known family conversation piece—the Blanchard's fiercely jealous tomcat, who ruled disdainfully over all other cats in the neighborhood.

"Tom was out on a stormy date last night and ran into a battler who claimed rulership over his own cattery. He's been moaning and licking a nasty wound on his right front leg. It could even have been a wildcat. He's sleeping it off now in his crib behind the grape arbor."

"That," Joe remarked, "ought to teach me something—not to go courting under a three-quarter moon with a very beautiful, adorable, wonderful, lovable, future wife!"

And so began their day.

At the dock, they slipped into their life jackets, stepped into the dinghy, and shoved out from shore.

"You drive," he said, "and let me be the backseat driver—unless you would like to learn that particular skill. All wives are supposed to be backseat drivers, you know."

"I know. My mother is—but she's the silent type, and Daddy reads her thoughts. That could be worse than spoken words, don't you think?"

He watched the lady pilot adjust the speed and mixture control levers until the motor was running smoothly, swing the boat sharply about, paralleling it to the shore, and open the throttle wide.

"We're on our honeymoon!" he called to her. "Evangeline and

Gabriel in the same boat, running away from the British. Do you suppose they'll catch us and take us back?"

He was pleased with her answer: "Mother told me once that there is always a pursuer of some kind trying to capture and separate true lovers. She also said—and she told me just this morning, 'There will be minor separations all along the way—when personalities clash or grate. But always there is the gentle way to understanding. Happy marriages are not made in heaven; they are made by two sensible people, working at it daily.'

" 'It takes a heap o' livin' in a house t' make it home,' Edgar Guest says, and good old Dad paraphrases it a little by saying, 'It takes a heap of *forgiving* in a house to make it home.' "

"I can't imagine anything you'd ever do or say needing to be forgiven," he answered; and above the steady drone of the motor she called back, "Promise me in advance that if I do, I have forgiveness in advance?"

"I promise."

"See that promontory up there? That's where we're going to have our house. Daddy owns the property all along the shore here, and this morning he offered it to us if we like it and want to build here."

She swung the dinghy sharply about, throttled the motor down, and steered toward the shore. "Let's go up and have a look."

When they had climbed to the top, they came out onto a flower-carpeted area more beautiful than anything he had seen in the whole territory. They played house for a while—the kitchen would be here where the view of the lake would be unobstructed, the dining room would be here—and beyond would be a long, wide living room with a fireplace.

"And here, beside the sumac, which we'll have to uproot, and looking out toward your writing tower up there on the very edge of the cliff, will be Joe Junior's room."

Their eyes met, and when he saw she was serious, dreaming of a future which to her was as real, almost, as life itself, he moved into the future with her and whispered against her hair while he felt her tears against his cheek, "Am I dreaming, or are you for real?"

"At times like this, you are willing to forgive me in advance," she said, tossed her head in a mock attempt at gaiety. Then she let him hold her close, while the wind in the pines played silent background

36

to the soft, sweeter music in their hearts. "I don't know who wrote it," he now said to her, holding her at arms length and studying her face, "but whoever composed it was a wise man:

> If I should tread upon a thing you love,
> Or you hurt me with unintended guile,
> Let us forget, for we might be together,
> Only a little while.

And with that the music stopped, and fear moved again into her heart: *We might be together only a little while.*

She tried to switch to a lighter mood by asking, "All morning I've been worrying—wondering if Priscilla helped a little too much last night. Did she, or didn't she?"

"At a time like that, when the moonlight is dim and it's too dark for a man to see what he is getting, he needs a little help. If I had it to do over again, I'd propose to her myself, not get John Alden to do it for me."

"And if you *did* do it over again, I'd tell Priscilla to get lost. I don't exactly appreciate her saying yes for me, being kissed for me, and all in the dark, like that."

"We could do it all over again right up here in broad daylight, without benefit of Longfellow."

They climbed the ragged slope to the promontory and stood looking toward Bluebell Island. "Know what I dreamed last night?" she asked.

"How can a man know what a woman dreams? But whatever it was, it was born of either a wish or a fear. Janice, who's an expert on psychology, says all dreams have one or the other as a nucleus."

"Janice?"

"She's a public stenographer who did research for me when I was in Madison, and I've had her type a lot of manuscripts."

Lela was quiet. He felt her stiffen, as if in some way he had hurt her. His own arm around her tightened, but he felt no response. She spoke then, her eyes searching the lake and the island beyond, "In your list of has-beens last night, I didn't hear the name Janice."

He wondered now if in his gay running of the gamut of names, he had deliberately omitted the name of the girl who had been typing his manuscripts and working long hours in research.

37

He spoke in an indifferent tone and with feigned humor. "That's because she is only a secretary. She's not a has-been but an is-be. She is married to her work and will be helping me with research on 'The Call of the Cardinal' this summer while I'm in Madison grinding out my Masters. She'll also be working on my novel—which, by the way, I've given the title, 'Just Enough Shadow'—that title suggested by the future *Mrs.* Cardinal."

The future Mrs. Cardinal seemed perturbed. He was puzzled at her tone of voice when a moment later she said, "I was going to tell you about a dream I had last night—but—"

She bit her lip, then finished, "But I suppose you and Janice may not be interested."

What had he said! What had he left *un*said! "Look, Lela—Mrs. Joseph Cardinal! Janice Granada means nothing to me—absolutely nothing. You've got to believe that. As I told you, she's strictly business, and I've never dated her seriously. She's just, well, the big-sister type. When you and I take a certain vow next summer, it'll be 'forsaking all others,' including the best secretary I ever had—only she's never been one of the *others.*"

"Did you say *next summer?*" Lela was remembering last night's newscast: "Thousands of our young men are flocking to the colors." Germany, she had heard, was on the rampage; the Fuehrer was invading Poland, Norway and Denmark, and the clouds of war were moving swiftly across the world's whole horizon.

The fear in her heart had been so terribly real. There could be another world war, and Joe would be one of the first to be called.

Her interval with Mother in the kitchen had been only a faint silver lining to the ominous cloud of war: "You don't think they'd take Joe, do you? He's a teacher and a writer—aren't those essential occupations?"

And Mother's answer: "If he were married, it might make a difference, especially if he were a father."

In now's confusing moment, shadowed by jealousy because of Janice and fear because of the world situation, Lela suddenly felt very much alone in the little island world of herself. In a few weeks, or sooner, Joe would be going away to school. There would be hundreds of miles separating them, he would be surrounded by scores of other summer school students, and in an office somewhere he would be working every day—and maybe into the night—with an efficient, businesslike, sisterly, perfect, and probably very pretty, secretary, who would be reading and counseling with him on the possibly intimate scenes of his novel—and she would be here, working in her father's office, helping with the housework under the supervision of her mother!

Joe's answer now to her question was a puzzled "What did I do? What did I say?"

"You said the wedding would be a year from now—and *you* said it! *You* decided it—not *we!*"

Joseph Cardinal, English teacher, writer, columnist, felt a stab of frustration. The thought that came to him was extraneous yet peculiarly apropos: The hero, in "Just Enough Shadow," would have difficulty solving a problem like this one. How would *he* solve it?

Suddenly the answer came, and he said: "Those heartless British! What merciless brutes—separating lovers, sending them away on separate ships! Still more heartless was Gabriel, who stood on the deck of *his* ship, waving to Evangeline and calling, 'See you next June, when we'll be married! In the meantime, don't get too lonesome.' "

There was an interval of tense silence: then Joe added: "I have a very low opinion of Gabriel for being so thoughtless. He has got to learn the secret of sharing—and he will, if Evangeline will forgive him."

And after another interval of *not* sharing, she stooped, picked two purple violets from a cluster growing beside the fallen pine log at their feet, and said soberly, "One of these two is Janice, your secretary, the other your fiancée."

He watched her as with pursed lips she interlocked the chins of the two dainty flowers, gave a quick, sharp pull, and one of the violets lost its beautiful, five-petaled head. Then as if to lighten the atmosphere that had been misty between them, she smiled and said, "There! That settles that!" She handed him the intact violet and gestured with her hands in a little movement that seemed to say, "Think no more of it. The jealously war is over!"

He stooped, retrieved the still-beautiful decapitated head, studied it briefly, and with a gesture of dismissal, said, "Okay, this is it! Here you go—out of my life forever." He tossed it toward the rim of the overhang, where it caught on a mullein stalk, clung a second, and then dropped over the edge.

Hopeful that the jealousy crisis was now in the history section of their lives, he remarked lightly, "You didn't say which violet was which."

"That," she returned, "was for you to decide." She laughed, and it was the beginning again of exquisite music.

"Want to hear my dream now?"

"I do," he answered, and it sounded to him like a bridegroom's answer at a wedding ceremony.

"Remember the picture in our American literature textbook of Hawthorne's outdoor study—a wooden stairway leading up to a platform between the trunks of three or four pine trees, with a railing all around? I dreamed last night that instead of an outdoor study with no roof, where your desk and papers would get rained on in summer and the place would be snowbound in winter, we built a neat little cottage right here. It was a reproduction of Henry Thoreau's cabin on Walden Pond. We named it 'The Cardinal's Nest.' I saw it last night, all finished. Our home was also finished, and I was busy in the kitchen baking things; soon I'd call you to come down for a cup of coffee, which we were going to share on the patio. I could hear your typewriter keys flying—and then I woke up.

"It was one of the nicest dreams I'd ever had. I didn't like it to end so abruptly. I wanted a little time with you, so I tried to go back to sleep and take it up where it was broken off, but I couldn't."

"You know what you need?" he asked. "You need a husband—a better one than I can ever be. Just as soon as we can get this old master's degree and another year of teaching over—we'll have an outdoor wedding right here on this very spot—I mean—Oh, oh— there I go again, announcing both the date and the place!"

"Those heartless British!" she answered.

They discussed their problem seriously. "One chief reason why I thought we might want to wait until next year," he told her, "is that I'd be better able to support a wife in the way to which she is accustomed. With my master's, I can command a much better salary, and—"

She stopped him there. "Are we forgetting that your wife has a bachelor's degree in English from Wilkerson and that I was tutored under the great Joseph Cardinal? I could get a teaching position myself—

"And that," she interrupted herself to say, "might be a good idea. You teach here this fall, and I'll run off and ditto in some other city. Next summer we can pool our resources and have enough money to pay for the wedding and maybe, through a nice mortgage loan, get our home built—"

"Wait! Hold it! It's time you heard the call of the Cardinal. Remember?"

She sighed. "I tried, anyway—but I don't feel all that cheerful, and I am not in a very good humor, not right now, not with things as they are in the world." She bit her lip.

When he realized how serious she was and thought he saw not even a semblance of a silver lining in the dark cloud of her fear, he asked, "The war?"

She nodded, and he let her cry on his shoulder. He listened to the things she told him and gave her the only word of comfort he could think of at the moment, "A college teacher *would* be less likely to be drafted than a free-lance writer."

"But our Uncle Sam won't need as many professors as strong men who can carry a gun. Oh, Joe, what if things do get worse! What if they call you? What if—"

He remembered now a note she had appended to an examination paper, "We seek, and when we find, we lose again; we are set to sail on different ships. There is too much of shadow, unless one can carry a lantern to dissolve it."

He quoted it to her.

"I wrote that?"

"You did, and I loved it. In fact, it was that line that helped me understand you. And from that minute on, I knew I had found the soul-mate I'd been waiting for."

"The cruel British," she said again—and it seemed the expression was going to be an acceptable substitute for certain ugly, unparliamentary imprecations used by others.

"I tell you what let's do," she now proposed. "Let's *not* set a definite date. Let's put our future into the hands of the One who sees all the future, for better or for worse."

He led her down the slope to the dinghy, guided her to the center

41

seat, took his place in the stern, shoved out from shore, pulled the starter cord, and the alert little motor leaped into life.

Playfully she looked toward the overhang, past which they were now speeding, and called, "Good-bye, Nathaniel! Thanks for letting us see your little sanctum!"

He entered into her mood, waved a farewell arm, made a megaphone of his hand, and shouted, "Good-bye, Henry! Until we meet again!"

He gave the motor full throttle and the dinghy shot forward, driving them at top speed into the future.

They were in the same boat, leaving Acadia forever and moving into a commanded future like that of Abraham of old, who "went out, not knowing whither he went." But they were assured that it was toward a land which the Lord their God would show them.

They went back to Cardinal Hill again before he left for Madison. They took with them a tapeline, measured distances, talked, dreamed, planned, hoped, and decided it was going to be too long to wait until next June.

Once, in a moment of hope, when the British were threatening, she said, "It's June now. Isn't one June as good as another?"

Surprisingly, he agreed and answered, "The present June is the best June I have ever known."

From the Blanchard place there was the tolling of the bell. It was yet an hour before noon, so it probably meant Mother wanted them home for some other reason.

That reason, Joe discovered, was a long distance call from Madison. He was to call Operator 7.

"Joe?" It was Janice's lilting voice—enthusiastic, hopeful, almost authoritative. "I've rented suite 1214, on the top floor of The Towers. I've ordered an artist to paint a beautiful cardinal in full color on the glass panel. Your den will be soundproof. I've called Mrs. Crowley, and your room there is vacant and waiting."

Turning from the telephone, Joe saw Lela's eyes studying him, searching, asking questions. He came to where she stood, near the veranda door. "The decapitated violet," he said. "She was reporting to her employer. Everything's all set for the Cardinal, and Mrs. Crowley has my room ready just across the campus from the library."

He was aware of using an apologetic tone—explaining too much—

42

and remembered a line from Shakespeare, "Thy *much* speaking doth betray thee."

But he was thrilled with anticipation. He was seeing on the glass-paneled door of the entrance to suite 1214 a beautiful cardinal in full color—and for a moment it was dueling in his mind with a certain other location—a rustic ten-by-fifteen cabin high on the overhang on Cardinal Hill.

To Lela he now quoted, "They also serve who only stand and wait."

She nodded, and quoted from another source, "Except the Lord build the house, they labor in vain that build it."

"What do you mean?"

She smiled. "I was just wondering about the violet that fell over the cliff—which one it was."

He erased her concern by saying, "I, Joseph Cardinal, do take thee, Lela Blanchard, to be my wedded wife, to have and to hold, as long as we both shall live."

They went out onto the wisteria-shaded porch.

Chapter 6

In Madison a two-room suite in The Towers became headquarters. Here Janice Granada built her throne and thereon sat, ruled "The Call of the Cardinal," and—almost—Joe Cardinal himself. Her philosophy of life, gained through an almost fanatical devotion to the private reading and studying of psychology, was so charged with hate for injustice and a conviction that war was an insult to society and to God, that she saw in Joe's column a voice for her own passion for peace.

Hers was not an "at-any-price" peace but a peace for which a person should be willing to pay any price to win—*except* war. Part of the price which she herself paid was to work late hours on his book manuscript, to fly around the office with the enthusiasm of an executive with a mission, and somehow—he could not understand how—to keep up with part-time stenographic work for others.

She would accept only a token salary, saying, "You pay the office rent, I'll pay the rent on my apartment out of my work as a public stenographer—and we'll make this old world see that peace is God's order for it. Your columns are getting more alive every week, Joe—Mr. Cardinal. I'm proud of you."

One morning, when he was up early to get the office mail, he found the box empty except for a handwritten note: "I was here at six o'clock and got the apples." It was signed, "Little Pig."

He smiled. She was not all serious—she was playacting a childhood story, "The Three Little Pigs."

Arriving at the post office still earlier the next morning, he left a note for her: "I was here at five o'clock and got the turnips." He signed it, "The Big Bad Wolf."

When work was play, it was most enjoyable, and it helped keep the creative fires burning.

In his journal Joe wrote: "An efficient secretary is a good thing. I am leaving most of the office details to her while I bury myself under the words, phrases and pages of 'Just Enough Shadow' and keep the cardinal calling. I *must* keep it calling loud and clear to introduce a cheerful note into the cacophony of wars and rumors of wars."

From Lela, in late August, there came a pathetic little note, "I'm getting pretty desperate out here. I ride around in my lonely little dinghy, wondering where my Gabriel has gone. Have I lost him in the rush of work?

"I'm helping Dr. Wellman in the church office part time—doing research for his new column for *The Silver Lining*. I'm sure you've noticed that Daddy has introduced a new feature, 'Water From the Well.' It's gaining a lot of popularity. Letters and phone calls have come from people of many professions, and what Dr. Wellman writes seems to help everyday people meet their everyday problems.

"Here's a little quote I found for next week's Water column, and I'm getting a lot of comfort out of it myself. It's by somebody named 'Anonymous':

> Build a little fence of trust
>   Just around today;
> Fill the space with loving thoughts,
>   And therein stay;
> Look not through the sheltering bars
>   Upon tomorrow;
> God will help bear whatever comes
>   Of joy or sorrow.

"The only thing is, Joe, my darling, I need *you* to help me, too—very, *very* much. I know God *will* help me bear whatever comes, but when I look through the bars upon tomorrow, I see a lot of things that make me shudder.

"Do you realize it has been a long time since I saw you, Joe—a long, *long* time? I don't like being without you."

His answer to that was: "Even after we are married, you'll be without me so much of the time. I'll be up there in my little house on the overhang, buried in a manuscript, and you'll be down in the kitchen baking cookies and things. I'm beginning to find out that when I'm in a book, it's almost as if I were missing in action.

45

"But one of these fine days I'll be driving into Wilkerson, and we'll have a grand reunion."

He did drive to Wilkerson—and they did have a grand reunion. There were carefree rides on Bluebell Lake and quiet strolls through the woods. They rediscovered mutual values and walked in shared dreams.

Standing on the site of the Cardinal's Nest, they replayed John Alden and Priscilla and dreamed of quiet winter evenings in front of an open fire, when the wind would howl through the leafless maples or sigh in contentment in the silvery tones of the pines.

"You still feel the same way about our not setting a definite wedding date?" he asked, as they stood at the very edge of the cliff, looking down. The mullein stalk, which in June had been only three feet high, was now at least five, and was still dotted with bright yellow flowers.

Her answer was deflecting: "It'll be September or October before it finishes flowering; then, all through the long autumn and winter it will stand like a lone brown sentinel—or, maybe I should say, like a tall tombstone—marking the grave of a decapitated violet."

With an attempt at pleasantry, he asked, "Which violet?"

She spoke calmly: "One day about two weeks ago, Dr. Wellman gave me a verse from the Song of Solomon. It has helped a lot."

"You speak in riddles," he said.

"If you'd care to know what kind of battle I've been fighting out here in little old Wilkerson while you've been away, here is what Solomon says: 'Love is strong as death; jealousy is cruel as the grave: the coals thereof are coals of fire, which hath a most vehement flame.' There are days when I read your column in *The Silver Lining*—the beautiful, tender things you've been writing—and realize that a certain other violet helped you with the research and is with you in all the intimate things you may be writing in 'Just Enough Shadow,' that the vehement flame comes to life, just when I think I've got it smothered out forever. Joe, I'm jealous. I try not to be, but I can't help it."

"Of a mere sister?"

"When you are away so long, anything that separates us is not 'mere.'"

He took from his billfold a color snap of the cardinal on the glass panel of the Madison office. "I had this taken especially for you," he

46

said. "In The Towers, he's only a bird in a gilded cage. His nest, his home and his heart are here—right here—*right this moment*—*and forever*. You've got to believe that!"

"I know it," she said, "but a girl likes to hear it a little more often, and not just by mail."

"Do you know what?" he asked.

"No, what?"

"A certain man I know has been cruel to you. I guess I didn't realize it, but I was *so* absorbed in 'Just Enough Shadow.' I think I can tell you, and you'll understand: Sometimes when I'm alone, and ideas, words and phrases come driving at me, I *have* to get them on paper or they'll be lost forever. It's like a mandate from God. I'm almost *driven* to get the novel done and out into the world before something over in Europe lights the fuse, and America is plunged into the holocaust. Then it'll be *all* shadow and no cardinal at all— maybe not even a *Joe* Cardinal. I'd like to leave behind something tangible to help—"

"Joe!" She closed her fingers over his lips. "*That* kind of talk I won't stand for. Things like that, a person shouldn't even think."

His answer was: "When I was a little tike like Hiawatha, talking with the birds and the animals of the woods, I learned to think about God. He was as real to me then as a baby rabbit trembling in my hand—my faith was, I mean—and I felt I had to protect it in some way—to keep the other animals from killing and eating it.

"God gave me a feeling that little Joe Cardinal was something special to Him—that He had made me because He had something important for me to do for Him.

"I lost that awareness during my teens, and for a long time it was gone—until one day a certain young Evangeline laid a manuscript on my desk with a note attached. I began to know then at least a part of what His will for me was—I had found my mate, and I was beginning to find my life work."

In the silence that followed, while Bluebell Lake rolled quietly below them, it was as if for the first time in his life he had completely opened his heart to another human being.

When the beautiful silence was broken, it was by a spoken word from her, "I am not worthy of your love."

"Wrong, my darling—I am not worthy of *yours*."

47

Her answer pleased him very much; "Sometimes I'd like to write a book about love and what some of the wise old philosophers have had to say about it."

"Any philosopher in particular know any more about it than you and I know right this minute?"

"Victor Hugo, maybe. *The Silver Lining* had a line from him last week—perhaps you saw it. If he is right, then I ought to be one of the happiest women on earth."

"Aren't you?"

"Sometimes. Right this minute I am. Anyway, this is the quote: 'The supreme happiness of life is the conviction that we are loved.' That, Joe, unless I am only dreaming, is what I am."

He answered with a phrase from a popular song, "Beautiful dreamer, wake unto me—"

Their conversation came back to a question he had asked ten minutes before: "You still feel the same way about our not setting a definite wedding date?"

Together they made the decision, and it was: "Whenever *He* sets the date it will be the right time."

* * *

And Joe returned to Madison to be among the missing in action part-time and to keep "The Call of the Cardinal" ringing out across the land.

There were other weekends in Wilkerson—merry and light-hearted, yet confusing and worrisome, for the war across the sea rolled on, and it appeared "The Call of the Cardinal" was only a man-made dam on a minor tributary of a rampaging river that was flooding the whole world.

Then came December 7 and Pearl Harbor, December 8 and the United States' declaration of war against Japan, followed by December 11, when both Germany and Italy declared war on the United States.

World War I, fought so desperately in an all-out effort to end all wars, was so soon followed by this new conflagration. This time America's motive was to help save the world for democracy. As the first world war had been, so also this one was very popular in the United States. Young men flocked to the colors, and thousands almost stormed the induction centers, bringing the total in the armed services into the millions.

48

There were also dissenting views—some of them violent. Suddenly there began to arrive at suite 1214 a new kind of fan letter—letters of fire, of denunciation, of screaming disagreement, of sarcasm, or anarchical emphases.

One letter in particular was very upsetting. It ran in swift, sure strokes: "Thanks for a columnist who dares to be different, who does not follow the capitalistic line.

"Who, actually, cares whether the world is saved for democracy! Who cares, even, whether America is so saved! Keep on writing. Keep on being honest. We are with you."

And another: "I feel like Thoreau, myself. I'd like to find me a little Walden Pond to stroll beside, where I could let my soul go searching for and find 'the leisure to live in all its faculties,' as the Brook Farm people did in our early American history."

And yet another: "The world is beautiful and verdant. It does not need the fertilizer of human blood."

Another, who signed his name simply, "Lazarus," wrote: "Maybe you haven't noticed, or maybe you have, but the beggar has stopped letting the dogs lick his sores. As Daniel Heitmier has expressed it in *Proletarian Unrest,* he no longer lies at the rich man's gate, begging. He is organized now and storming the gates, demanding his share of the wealth. Now, please don't waste a column telling us to get jobs and earn our own living so we can build our own homes and fare sumptuously every day so that we, too, can pass pennies to poor people's palms. We don't want to be rich, for that might make us selfish. You'd better warn Dives we are armed now and that our ammunition is printed pages like yours."

One letter in particular shocked the writer of "The Call of the Cardinal." He could not believe he was getting such reactions. What had he written to arouse such iconoclastic responses? "You strike me as a worthy follower in the tradition of Emerson and Thoreau. I wonder if you would be willing to follow Thoreau all the way to jail for your convictions? Do you realize that he taught civil disobedience and that he went to prison for following Emerson's doctrine? He refused to pay his poll tax because he thought the government itself upheld slavery, and he would not be a conformist. It was when he was in jail that Emerson came to visit him. Surprised, apparently, Emerson asked, 'Why are you here, Henry?'

49

"Do you know what Thoreau answered? He demanded of Emerson: 'Why are you *not* here?'"

"Are you, Mr. Cardinal, willing to go to jail for what your column teaches? Are you trying to stop enlistments? Do you want our boys to refuse to be drafted for conscientious reasons, or would you have them evade the draft because they do not wish to be cowards, as your Emerson taught, 'Conformity is cowardice'? Would you be happy if a Hitler should rise among us and begin a cold-blooded annihilation of one of our minority groups? I wonder to whom you, in your cowardice, are conforming; who or what has changed your beautiful column into a vehicle for anti-American propaganda?"

Joe pressed the intercom lever. "Janice, can you come in a minute?"

Janice, alert, notebook in hand, smiling, azure eyes searching the room before coming to focus on her employer's face, came demurely in. He knew her sweeping glance about the room was to see if anything were out of place—if, while she had been out of the room, anything had been changed, or, perhaps, if the venetian blind needed adjusting to give him just the right amount of light. An executive's eyes must be protected.

Still single, at twenty-seven, she seemed to pacify her mothering instinct by making the office her home away from home.

Competence was her specialty; charm, her key to the hearts of other businessmen in The Towers. Some seemed to envy Joe for having such an alert, efficient, completely dedicated, strictly businesslike secretary-office manager, with personality plus.

Hal Raymond, M.D., whose office was now on the fifth floor, was still without a complement. Only last week he had remarked to Joe, "I suppose you know John Alden spoke for himself several years ago, and Priscilla was not interested. I've been watching for signs to indicate some kind of fever that would need a doctor's attention— but she goes merrily on her way, lost in her work, as if she had a war to fight and no army to back her up. Honestly, Joe, the girl *needs* a doctor—and I need her kind of receptionist."

To which, Joe had answered, "Maybe *she* doesn't need a doctor except to write prescriptions. It's *her* deficiency you ought to be thinking about. Are you sure you can fill Webster's definition of that word? Are you looking for a receptionist or a housekeeper?"

"I'd better be looking for a housekeeper—the wife type. No young doctor is safe not being happily married. All the young marrieds I know in the medical profession have a wife's picture on their office desks—a sort of warning, you know. Even a writer ought to have such a picture."

"I have a wedding coming up in June."

"I know, and I envy you. And if you ever need a specialist in pediatrics, I hope you'll remember me. Seriously, Joe, your girl Friday is an idealist. She's looking for something with real challenge. She's had nurse's training and for awhile was lost in the world of home decorating. Almost, while you were out at Wilkerson, I thought I had a little romance going. I had a dream of how nice she would be to come home to, as the popular song has it."

The self-serve elevator they'd been riding eased to a stop at twelve, and as Cardinal stepped off, he remarked, "She makes an excellent office mother."

Raymond caught the door before it could close and spoke through the crack, "She'd make you a good wife, Joe, if anything ever happens to your Wilkerson romance."

* * *

"You buzzed for me?" Janice now asked.

"I'll be out of town for the weekend, maybe until Monday or Tuesday, so I'd like you to get the apples, peel them and work them into sauce or something. And tell whoever phones or comes in that you don't know where I've gone or when I'll be back."

She flashed him a demurring smile. "You mean that up to this minute I don't know. Is it wisdom for a private secretary not to know where her boss is going for the weekend?"

"It will spare her from any temptation to prevaricate if she doesn't know," he said, and then he saw the hurt in her eyes, as if she were being robbed of something she held peculiarly sacred.

"All right—I'm going out to Wilkerson."

She nodded, and her eyes were questioning. "I hope everything is all right—there hasn't been too much mail with that postmark lately."

"It's been coming to my apartment," he told her.

He handed her the half-dozen critical letters. "Give these the twice-over and let me have your reaction, typed out. You'll know which ones have to have a personal reply and which can stand a form. I'll

51

be back after a trip to the post office. I've a feeling there might be something very urgent."

When he returned, he knew she would have the letters read, identified as to content, and tagged with *F* for "form letter reply" or *P* for "personal." She had been taking care of so many of the personal letters herself that in most cases all he had to do was sign his name. Complimenting her once, he had said, "Your letters sound more like me than mine do—and when you sign my name, it's more like my signature than my own is."

After twenty minutes, he pushed open the door with the cardinal in color on the glass panel, and she was on the phone. He heard her say, "Sorry, but Mr. Cardinal is out just now. May I take a message?"

She waved him a warning hand that said, "You stay outside—you are still out. This is some crank or somebody who shall not get past this desk."

"Yes, I'll tell him. No, he'll be out of town until sometime next week. That's right."

She scribbled a note on a desk pad, "I'll give him your message."

To Joe, when she had hung up, she announced, "Your Lazarus friend, wanting to know if you're going to publish his letter in your column. If you are, he'd like a hundred copies to distribute to all the other Lazaruses in his city."

"And you told him—?"

"That you were not in the office and were going to be out of town for several days. He sounded very disappointed. He wants publicity for his cause."

He was already on the way to his sound-proof den. He handed her a sheaf of letters, all opened and read while he was still in the post office.

"Wait, Joe—Mr. Cardinal. There was one letter only you can answer, and you should have been the only one to read it. It came early this morning. I'm sorry." She handed him an official-looking envelope.

He started, fear wrenching him like a storm on Bluebell Lake tossing the Blanchard dinghy.

His hands were trembling; and when he read, he could not find his voice. This letter needed no decoding and no secretarial identification as to content. It was from the draft board. It read simply: "You have been reclassified as 1-A."

Silence hung heavy in the room, accompanied only by the pounding of his heart—and by the wounded expression in her eyes. It was as if she had received a death notice of a near relative.

He knew that the armed forces were taking men from eighteen up to as old as thirty-nine, but supposed that his occupation would exempt him from the draft. Would he have been exempt if he had continued teaching?

"It looks," he said slowly—and there must have been dejection in his voice, like that of a child running with a scratched knee or bee sting to his mother for sympathy—"It looks as if the Cardinal is going to lose his song."

Below them in the street, another song was being heard. She moved to the window and looked out and down. "Lazarus and his sympathizers," she announced.

He came to look and saw a parade of sign-carrying young men, and with them, a scattering of women and girls. The signs read:

"Make the World Safe for the Conscientious Objector"

"War Is Glorious!"

"The Soil of France Needs New Blood!"

"Heil Hitler!"

"The Cardinal," he said with a gesture of futility, "has been crying 'Peace' when there is no peace. The little dam is breaking."

Beside him now, Janice startled him when she said, "History is repeating itself. There have always been draft riots—even during the Civil War. There was nationwide opposition to Union conscription. There was a bloody three-day riot in New York. A mob overpowered the police and the militia, set fires, and assaulted abolitionists and Negroes. There was over a million dollars damage and more than a thousand casualties."

Joe felt anxiety like a storm cloud, building up and threatening. *I wonder if my column has been helping to start fires like that one down there.*

He recalled a line from a French revolutionist of long ago: "The mob is in the street. I must find out where they are going, for I am their leader!"

53

Janice, at the window, sighed heavily, his change of classification in her hand. He must have given it to her without realizing it, from his habit of handing her the mail to read and answer. There were tears in her eyes and a look of confusion, even of fear, he thought, as if in some way she felt guilty or to blame for the scene below.

"If they take you, Joe—Mr. Cardinal—*no,* I mean *Joe*—if you go to war, you'll take my whole world with you—my job, my security, my happiness, my purpose for living—"

And then, without warning, she was crying on his shoulder.

Chapter 7

What does a man do when he has just discovered that an efficient, ordinarily businesslike secretary has fallen in love with him? More particularly, what does he do when, in an emotional moment, she is telling him so with tears, and on his shoulder—a shoulder on which only one young woman in all the world is ever to have the right to cry?

He could have guessed it. He *should* have, for he had seen unmistakable signs in her eyes—signs he had interpreted as sisterly concern. But she knew about Lela, and that should have been enough. Yet, who could foresee what propinquity might do to a woman who herself was starved for love? He had read of the so-called eternal triangle, but always it had involved other lives, never his own.

He stood sphinx-like and thought ridiculously of a long-ago lesson in entomology—the sphinx-like stance of the green larva of the sphinx moth, which, when startled, raises its head and holds itself rigid until the crisis or the imagined crisis has passed.

I, he thought nonsensically, *am a worm!*

He also thought, The sign on the outside of the door, just below the beautiful cardinal says Walk In.

Anyone could walk in—Dr. Halford Raymond, or even Lela, who might have decided to surprise him.

He remained a sphinx larva; the crisis passed. Janice stepped back and bit her lip. "Forgive me for being a woman," she said.

She dabbed at her tears and said with conviction, "We're going to have to do something about this!" She tossed his draft notice on his desk. "You simply can't go. You know you can't! You're too tenderhearted; you could never kill."

The noise in the street below was more boisterous now. There were shouts and curses, and some were being hurt. Cameras were grinding from atop busses and cars.

The question sprang full-blown into his mind: If the police were conscientious objectors right now, the other conscientious objectors who are breaking windows and upsetting cars could get away with murder, could they not?

"You go to Wilkerson, Joe. Why wait until June for your wedding?"

"What," he asked, "are you saying?"

"I am saying that sometimes there are months after a classification has been changed to 1-A, before a man is ordered to report. Young husbands, especially prospective fathers, are given more consideration than single men.

"And Joe, I don't want you wading around over there in mud and blood. I don't want you buried in an unknown grave." She bit her lip, and he saw her eyes as pools of pain.

He had been right. Janice was in love with him. Yet, she would rather lose him to another woman than to have anything happen to cut short his life.

He spoke calmly, "I think I *am* a conscientious objector."

"I *know* you are, but you can never be exempt for any currently acceptable reasons. You have to have a religious motive."

"Would you say that a love for life and a desire to let others live is a religious motive?"

"It has to have a respect for God's commandments," she returned, "and one of those commandments is 'Thou shalt not kill.'"

"Aggressively? Or in self defense?"

She sighed. "I think I am tired. I'm emotionally exhausted. I've been under strain for a long time, afraid of—of *this*," she indicated the draft notice.

It was the kind of fear born of love, he thought, and he pitied her.

She turned to the window and looked down. "It's over—enough so we can get back to work."

He quoted to her the thought that had come to him a while ago—the ridiculous statement of the French revolutionist, "The mob is in the street, I must find out where they are going, for I am their leader." He turned toward the door of his private office and stopped. "Oh, does anyone around here, or anywhere in the world know where Joe Cardinal is going? And who is *my* leader?"

She answered in another vein, "I dropped your latest column down the mail chute early this morning. The apple was so good, I wanted to get it on its way to all the other hungry little pigs." She smiled, trying, he thought, to dissolve the barrier between them.

"You *what!* I didn't get a chance to look it over for possible typographical errors or misspelled words or—"

"I looked it over—five times. It was all right. I know exactly how you like to say things and what you want to say. You've been trusting me, you know."

"You saved a carbon?"

"I had the girls down on five make three copies. It's under "C" if you need it."

"But," he protested, "I do like to finish a column before you type it finally. I sometimes see something I want to change. The storm some of the latest ones have created has to be considered. Maybe I've been getting too—too something or other for our country's good. Words are like Longfellow's arrows. They not only fall into the heart of an oak but sometimes into the heart of an anarchist. The arrow converts itself into a seed and grows into a thorn tree of dangerous disregard of government—even of rebellion against it!"

She studied her wristwatch. "What time were you leaving for Wilkerson?"

Suddenly there was anarchy in his own heart—a rebellion against Janice herself.

He knew now that he very much needed to get away. There was a wise little lady in Wilkerson who would understand his problem. He felt very much the need of a woman's shoulder upon which to rest his own head, a sympathetic ear into which to pour his troubled thoughts. It had been too long since his last visit.

Unbeknown, his column had been doing startling things to a cross section of young America.

Wise George Wilcox Blanchard would be a good counselor, also.

"There is something special I want to tell you about yourself, Joe, something you may not even know and may not want to believe, but it is the truth. You can be thinking it over while you are in the car."

He could scarcely believe what she now began telling him. He listened, at first fascinated, then puzzled, and finally angered: "The letter about Emerson and Thoreau started me on a tour of your personality, and here, carefully researched, and with dictionary authority

—Funk and Wagnalls in particular—but let me read it to you, and we'll check it for typographical errors."

And this, to his astonishment, was what she read and what he also read from the carbon she handed him:

"I, Joseph Cardinal, am a conscientious objector. I cannot go to war. I simply could not take the life of another human being. My objection is a conscientious one, though not a religious one by definition. I am not an atheist, for an atheist denies the very existence of God; I am not an agnostic, for an agnostic denies that we do or can know whether there is a God; and naturally, I am not an infidel, for that term is used—was used opprobriously by Christians during the Crusades, when they called the Muslims "infidels" and in turn were called "infidels" by the Muslims; I am not a deist, for as Thomas Paine, himself a deist, admitted, a deist admits there is a God but denies that the Christian Scriptures are a revelation from Him; I am not a pantheist, for a pantheist believes that the self-existent and self-developing universe *is* God; nor am I a transcendentalist, for transcendentalism is the doctrine that the principles of reality are to be discovered by introspection. It is a belief in the self-sufficiency of the individual. This cannot be truth, for there is yet Something beyond the self—something that must have created it. I have classified myself as an honest skeptic because I have doubts about the fundamental doctrines of Christianity.

"I am still seeking God. I see Him in everything, yet I do not truly know Him. In spite of all this, I, Joseph Cardinal, feel I am a conscientious objector. My conscience is not God within me, but it seems to be the will of God, somehow getting through to me with a voice I cannot hear but can *feel*—a voice that is identifiable with the will of the Son of God, who claims to be the Christ. His will is making itself real to me in a way I cannot explain—that He would not have me kill another human being which He has created."

The final paragraph finished, Janice looked steadily at him, her eyes asking his approval. "That, Joe, is what you believe. I know. I have studied you and your writings; and since you have no reason that will be accepted by the draft board, you are bound to be on your way to Europe or to some other battle area. It might make a difference if you could really believe in God, Joe."

58

He forced a calm exterior. "Why," he asked, "if I do not believe in God, have I capitalized His name in my self-analysis?"

It was almost unbelievable—what he had been hearing and what she had been thinking and what had been going on entirely without his knowledge. "If you will let me have the carbon of my latest column, I'd like to see what I wrote!"

She handed him a copy from a file marked "The Call of the Cardinal."

"And now, if you will excuse me—" He went into the den, closed the door, and was startled when he realized he had *slammed* the door after him.

Here, in the sound-proof solitude he loved so well, which was like what he someday hoped to have in his visualized Cardinal's Nest above the lake, overlooking Bluebell Island, there was now no pleasure.

His eyes flew down the pages. There was more fire in his mind than there had been for a long time. This was not his writing—not all of it. There were inserts, quotes from writers he knew to be extremists. The column did challenge those extremists' views and answered them, but it did not *fully* answer them. It did, almost, defend them!

This, he decided must *not* be published. He would have to call the syndicate to wait for a substitute column.

When he lifted the receiver, he heard Janice on the phone: "Thank you very much. Just wanted to be sure."

The receiver clicked, and he put the call through. A secretary answered. "Yes, Mr. Cardinal. Thank you very much. We'll wait. We *have* been getting some stormy reactions, so if you can give us a little more Shakespeare and Sandburg, and maybe a little more Tennyson and Wordsworth, it would help. Your readers eat up the 'beside the lake, beneath the trees' sort of things; they're more quieting to the nerves when the world looks so sad."

When he came out into the reception room, Janice had a state road map unfolded and was tracing with red pencil his route to Wilkerson. She looked up calmly, her blue eyes showing evidence of tears. "I've just checked with the Highway Patrol. The bridge at Cloverdale is out, so I've routed you through Cranston; that way, you can see spring the way you like it."

She bit her lip and sighed heavily. "I'm terribly sorry. I guess I've overstepped. But you *had* been letting me make decisions and do the final proofing, and you used to say—remember?—'Your letters sound more like me than mine do.' When I signed your letters, you used to chuckle and say, 'It's more like my signature than my own is.' I knew you hated war and that you had an almost holy reverence for life. I hope you understand I did what I thought was right."

He took the map, studied the carefully traced route, and appreciated her thoughtfulness—unless it were a mother's pointing out to her small son the safest route to his first day at kindergarten!

"Spring might be good for me right now," he said.

She nodded. "The dogwood will be in full dress there. I thought we might want to do a column on the cross sometime. There are so many kinds—the Latin, the Calvary, the Patriarchal, the Maltese. The dogwood flower is an almost perfect Maltese. We could title our column "The Ivory Cross," which is what the dogwood resembles, and move on from there, stopping for a paragraph on Flanders Field and the hundreds of crosses that mark the graves of men who died in wars there. Flanders has had one war after another since the Middle Ages. My father may have been buried there. But the dogwood doesn't know about these things. It unfolds every year; it's the forest's harbinger of spring—like the first robin leads the parade of birds."

He was listening without listening. It was the word "we" that disturbed him. It seemed to have come to this—everything he did was "we" doing it; all his columns were "our" columns, and many of his best ideas were hers.

He broke in to say, "There is a sense in which every man is a part of someone else, or of *many* someones. Is that not true?"

"Is what true?"

"No man is completely himself. He gets lost in a maze of all the personalities he knows, has known, and is learning to know, and he is a part of his past, his present, and even his future."

"If you do decide to take the Cranston route, I'd like you to stop at the cemetery behind the Homefield Community Church and read the epitaph on my brother's headstone. Mother had it chiselled there the week she died. Hers is the tall stone beside it."

"It's not too far from Memorial Day," he suggested. "I could leave a flowering plant there. Or—if you'd like to ride along, maybe stay a few days with friends, I could pick you up on the way back."

"I don't go back every year. When I can't, I've a friend there who puts a plant or bouquet between the stones—Jimmie's and Mother's."

"It'd be good for you," he suggested. "Even painful memories can be helpful if they don't become wallowing places."

She turned to her desk and scribbled a note, which by a sidelong glance he noticed was "Memories, Dangerous Wallowing Places." He knew that soon "we" would be doing a column entitled "Memories, Dangerous Wallowing Places."

"We used to have a hog wallow behind the barn," she said, "but for Mamie and her litter of seven it wasn't dangerous—it was refreshing."

"Because it was natural?"

She nodded, "Sometimes, though, we have to deny the natural if we want to confess the spiritual. I can't go with you, Mr. Cardinal, with so much mail coming in, and most of it demanding a personal reply. And there's always the telephone—long distance, telegrams."

"There's an answering service available," he reminded her.

"Besides," she moved straight on, "Cardinal Features will be phoning to ask about your last column. I appended a note telling them to call. There's an insert I want to put in on page three."

"I just phoned them to cancel it. I'll be sending a new one."

She looked at him, astonished. "You just phoned? You should have let me." She had the tortured look of a beautiful doe, just shot, and dying. Her eyes were pleading, "What have I done to deserve this?"

"In journalism," he said, "when one takes the writings of another and publishes them as his own, under his own name, it is called 'plagiarism.' I've been taking too much credit for what *you've* been writing."

She bit her lip, her eyes welling. "You don't trust me!"

"Should I?"

The silence that followed was heavy with emotion. "We may have done something drastic to my reputation, and we may have hurt our country. I'll have to forgive myself for not realizing it sooner."

"I thought you knew and approved what I was doing. You did

61

trust me last summer, remember? And you commended me for my little inserts and additions."

"But we were writing the usual—nature's wonders and comments on literary masterpieces—not political propaganda."

She bowed her head, "I guess I thought we were partners, challenging the world with new ideas and ideals—sort of like Cardinal and Granada, Incorporated. I hated war so much, because of my father, and I'd been watching the papers and listening to the news. When they widened the draft age, I knew they'd be taking the single men first, and I was afraid I would lose you. I could never stand that. All my life, Joe—Mr. Cardinal—I've been looking for something worthwhile to do, something really challenging. Several years ago, I thought it was nursing, helping relieve pain and rebuild bodies. Then I found you and knew that it was not bodies but minds, the thoughts of people, that needed medication."

She moved to the window again, and while he waited for her to continue, it was as if he were a psychiatrist and she were a patient relating her symptoms.

"You might give me credit for one thing, Mr. Cardinal—Funny!—" she interrupted herself, "that *Mister* between us has the air of a refrigerator. But my motive was high, and my choice of employers was the highest—*the* highest. I want you to know that."

He glanced at his watch. "I should be leaving now." His voice took on the tone of an employer to an employee. "I'd like all mail like yesterday's and all carbons of my latest columns—and the new ones you have sent. I may not have read them all."

"Yes, sir," she said humbly, and he couldn't tell whether she was acting or not. It really didn't seem to matter now.

It was going to be painful to release her abruptly—like trampling on her heart. Of one thing he was now convinced, however. If his future were to be his own, he would have to dissolve the "partnership" of Cardinal and Granada.

He spoke calmly, off-handedly: "I'll very likely be back early next week, and we can take a long look at things. This 1-A classification is going to make a big difference in everything. Maybe while I'm strolling around in God's out-of-doors, He can get His own message through to me."

62

He interrupted himself with a husky laugh. "I forgot, I'm not supposed to believe in God."

He turned toward the sanctum, "I'll keep in touch by telephone, to let you know how to contact me. There just might be something I have to know before Tuesday."

She handed him the road map, searched his files, knew exactly where to locate what he had asked for, and fitted things into his attaché case.

Before leaving, he stopped at her desk and looked down at her— so efficient, so alert to his every desire, so ensconced, also, on her throne—and announced, "I'll stop at Cranston and take a look at Jimmie's epitaph—and I will pick up a plant at the greenhouse."

She was already dialing. "I'd like a Murillo tulip, potted," she told him. "They have them this time of year. Mrs. Oldfield always takes them to the church afterward."

She placed the order matter-of-factly, hung up, and stood.

"Well," he began, like a schoolboy about to tell his teacher goodbye until Monday, "We had a little tussle, didn't we?"

She nodded, "Not so little, but how could it have been avoided?"

"It couldn't have."

"It *shouldn't* have, anyway. I've been too—too—"

In the elevator, he pressed the button for the fifth floor. Dr. Raymond was in and busy, Lucille Branford told him, but she added, "If you have a pain somewhere—just an ordinary little old pain—"

He'd always liked Lucille. So did everyone who came and went in young Dr. Raymond's office. "I have a very sophisticated kind of pain, and I think Dr. Raymond just might help." He showed her his new classification card.

"*No!*" she exclaimed.

"Yes."

She pressed the buzzer two longs and a short, which in Dr. Raymond's office meant "Emergency," and said to Joe, "Go on in!"

The "office call" was brief and to the point—some kind of point, anyway. "You once told me that if ever I wanted a change of secretaries" Joe began, and handed Hal the card from Uncle Sam. "Here's your chance to get one of the finest there ever was or ever will be. She's pretty shaken up, and I think maybe you can help her. Take her out to dinner for me—Sunday, or whenever you can. I'm off to Wilkerson for a feature story."

"Male or female?"

"I'm going fishing," Joe evaded, "Be back Monday or Tuesday, maybe. What I'd like you to do is help prepare Janice for the worst. With a notice like this, and with thousands being called up every month—I might be smart not to wait but enlist."

"But your column!"

"If they send me over to the center of things, I may not come back, and the Cardinal would stop caroling anyway."

"It doesn't make sense," Dr. Halford Raymond said. "It just doesn't make sense! What's the matter with the world, anyway? Did you see that demonstration down there a while ago?"

"I may have helped cause it."

"Your column?"

"Our column," Joe said, but did not explain the "Our."

Hal followed him out into the hall and waited with him until the elevator came. "When you pass through this or that little town, take a look-see for an empty doctor's office. They don't need any more in this town, and I'd like to settle down somewhere to being just an old-fashioned G.P., bringing babies into the world, getting out onto basketball floors and football fields to check over injured players, serving on the school board and the town council—things like that."

The elevator came, and in another half hour Joe was on his way to Wilkerson, his attaché case on the seat beside him, the potted Murillo tulip in the back, a suitcase in the trunk, and in his mind a sense of both relief and frustration. He was thinking:

I am driving toward a destiny. I am neither an atheist nor an agnostic, nor am I a deist or an infidel. I may not even be a skeptic—not a true one, or I would not still be searching.

And why would I feel within me an impulsion toward the goal of God, if there be no God? Why, unless, the urge Godward is itself born of God?

I, and I alone, of all the egos in the world or universe, am a man named Joseph Fenimore Cardinal. I am a self, distinct from all other selves.

In this body or out of it, I will still be a self—in war or peace, in life or death.

I am a man, I am a little boy; I am an oak, I am an acorn; I am a grain of wheat that must fall into the ground and die and rise again in another form.

I am a man of peace, with a civil war raging within me. I am trying to free myself from a slavery.

My name, "Cardinal," means "chief, fundamental, of prime importance."

When I was a boy, I believed in God, and my faith was like a baby rabbit trembling in my hand, helpless and needing protection from those who would destroy it.

"O living God, concerning whom I am a possible skeptic, give me back again the little rabbit. Let me hold it once more in the palm of my hand."

Chapter 8

It was easy to follow the road leading out of Cranston to the Homefield Community Church. He strolled among the stones until he came to Jimmie Granada's marker, and there he read the pathetic epitaph:

> A few can touch the magic string
> And Noisy Fame is bound to win them:—
> Alas for those who never sing,
> But die with all their music in them.

Little Jimmie had died with all his music in him, still unwritten, still unsung, and the world would never know how much it had missed. Only a mother would know—and a sister.

Would the unsung music in a man's soul have a chance to express itself after death? Would the Cardinal's song still be heard—or would there no longer be a need for it?

From his mental attic he now took a book of poems and read:

> Death is only an old door in a garden wall.

He turned to other pages and was comforted with the caressing lines:

> Death may hide but cannot long divide;
> It is as though the rose that climbed my garden wall
> Had blossomed on the other side.

From another book, clothbound and brown, there rose as from a tomb the words once spoken in a Bethany cemetery:

"I am the resurrection, and the life: he that believeth in me, though he were dead, yet shall he live: and whosoever liveth and believeth in me shall never die."

But I, Joe Cardinal, am supposed to be a skeptic; I do not fully believe in the God in whom I believe.

66

He stooped to push aside a tuft of grass at the base of the stone and heard an unfamiliar sound behind him. Turning, he saw first the shining, swing-away footrests of a wheelchair, then the side panels, the chrome-plated wheels and hand-rims and in the seat a smooth-shaven man in his mid-forties.

"Sorry if I startled you, Mr. Cardinal," a pleasant voice said, "but Janice phoned me to be on the watch for you. I saw you drive in and would have been here pronto, but my motorized buggy was in for repair, so I had to use this hand-driven chair. It works all right around the garden and in and out of here and there, but on new gravel and grass it's a little hard to manipulate." He held out a right hand, and when Joe took it, he was aware of fingers missing—two at least.

"Boynton's the name—Charlie Boynton. Janice has me look after the graves—Jimmie's and her mother's. She seldom comes anymore, at least not around Memorial Day. She sometimes defends herself for not coming by saying, 'Every day should be Memorial Day, Mr. Boynton, and we can honor the dead of our wars by being the best citizens we can be all the time.' She still calls me *Mister* Boynton from my having been her teacher when she was a little girl."

Boynton's voice moved along in narrative style: "But she *does* come. I watch her sometimes from the house and see her strolling among the stones, reading the epitaphs and identifications. She always comes, finally, to Jimmie's grave here, stands awhile and leaves a potted plant or quite often a bouquet of wild flowers she's picked in the woods. I get the feeling that, in her mind, the bouquet is a little orphan she has found somewhere, and she hates to leave it. She always stands and looks, and then looks back again and again before finally leaving it.

"After Jimmie died, she was like a little mother hen that had lost her one baby chick. Every stray cat or puppy that came along got adopted and looked after by her."

Charles Boynton rolled his chair to the headstone, stooped, and with a pair of shears snipped off the grass around the potted tulip.

"I've wondered," Joe asked, "what was the cause of Jimmie's death. She never told me—always said it was the war. But the dates—he was only four when he died."

"It *was* the war," Charlie said. "In 1918, when the influenza epidemic struck, there were twenty million deaths around the world, 548,000 of them in the United States and among our armed forces. Jimmie's mother was down with the flu, and so was Janice. Her father was over there helping Pershing, so there was no one to look after them—no one to drive them to the doctor, who was also down with the flu. Little Janice said it was the war that did it. She felt the flu was God's punishment on the world for fighting and killing—and hating. She said, 'Mr. Boynton, God doesn't want anybody to hate anybody.'

"I had a lesson in Christian tolerance one day after school. That little stucco school over there was a one-roomer then, and I was the only teacher of all eight grades. She was in the fourth grade at only nine years of age. She had asked one afternoon if she could stay after school and help empty the wastebaskets and erase the blackboard. Once the board was clean, she began to write. This, Mr. Cardinal, was the astonishing wisdom of her child's mind. It was a quote from a poem the class had had to memorize:

> I saw tomorrow marching by
>   On little children's feet;
> Within their forms and faces read
>   Her prophecy complete.
> I saw tomorrow look at me
>   From little Jimmie's eyes,
> And thought how carefully we'd teach,
>   If we were really wise.

When Boynton stopped, as if overcome by a tearful memory, Joe commented, "If today's youngsters could be taught things like that—and our parents and teachers, too—"

Boynton nodded and went on with his appraisal of little Janice Granada's character. "When she substituted 'little Jimmie's eyes' for the poet's 'little children's eyes,' I knew I had been teaching a child philosopher. I knew it more surely when she turned from the blackboard, eraser in hand, and said, 'Mr. Boynton, little Jimmie didn't get to have any tomorrow because of the war.'

" 'It was the influenza,' I explained.

"She astonished me by asking, 'Do you believe in God, Mr. Boynton?'

"I answered her with, 'Of course, doesn't everybody?'

"And that little dark-haired beauty looked at me with a strange question in her eyes. It was a terrifying look, Mr. Cardinal, and her reply cut me to the heart: 'Sometimes I doubt.'

"She sighed, looked away, sighed again, and qualified her doubt with: 'But only sometimes—when I think about Daddy and little Jimmie. Then I see a flower or hear a wood thrush or a cardinal, and everything's all right again.' "

For what seemed like an extra long interval, nothing was said by either of the men. Then Boynton opened a crack in the silence with, "Sometimes it doesn't take a flower or a bird—only a beautiful silence."

At that moment Joe understood his secretary still better. Not only because of her mother but because, in the formative years, she had been clay in the hand of a skilled potter-teacher who had taught carefully because he was wise.

They moved from Jimmie's grave to the Boynton plot, where among the several stones was one identified with the name "Charles Boynton, Jr."

There was the date of birth and also the date of death.

"Your father?"

"No, his only son."

"I don't understand—the date—"

"There's a story behind it," Charles said. "It happened like this: They were taking men from twenty-one to thirty in those days. Today, it's eighteen to thirty-nine, I understand. Anyway, as soon as school was out that spring, I enlisted. In almost no time I was in basic, and with unbelievable speed I was over there in the thick of things.

"First I was reported missing. Then, after a number of months with no proof I was a prisoner of war, there was an announcement that I was assumed dead.

"My parents had this marker put up for me, even though my body had not been found. They wanted me in the family plot—present in absentia, if there is such a thing. And all this time I was alive but was a victim of amnesia.

"When I came to myself, I looked on my person for identification, and there was none, which is why my identity was not known until I, myself, became myself. Immediately I knew my name and where I had lived.

69

"I had already had surgery." Boynton gestured to his chair and lifted one trouser leg to show an artificial limb. "I lost both legs. They told me I had laid on the battlefield a long time. Flies had laid their eggs and larvae had eaten away the decaying matter; otherwise I'd have died from gangrene. There were a number of other men saved the same way—flies and larvae.

"That led to the medical profession experimenting with live larvae on patients over here and elsewhere. Now, I understand, they have a synthetic chemical that does the same thing—or is supposed to. Medicine has wonder drugs now, of course."

Boynton stopped, sighed, looked toward the sky as if listening, and then continued, "When my family wanted to do away with the marker, I asked them not to. You see, I wanted to make a pulpit of it."

"Pulpit?"

"Not a platform on which to stand, but a doctrine, a foundation. This stone says that I was born and that I died—and I am alive again. It illustrates in a pathetic and very inadequate sort of way the truth of the gospel that Paul preaches in 1 Corinthians, where he says, 'I declare unto you the gospel. . . . Christ died for our sins according to the scriptures, . . . he was buried, and . . . he rose again the third day according to the scriptures.'

"Charles Boynton was not really and actually dead, except as the Bible teaches—that without Christ *all* men are dead, and that *with* Christ, and united to Him, we are made alive.

"Janice told me that she understood the gospel for the first time when I talked to her here one day. She always listens, and she keeps in touch. She sends me clippings and tells me little personal things about her hopes and ambitions. She seems to want to keep on living the days of the little, one-room schoolhouse, when I was her teacher-hero and a sort of father image."

Boynton interrupted himself, looked toward the maples sentineling the church, and said, "There's your bird, Mr. Cardinal—hear him?"

Joe heard—a lilting hilarious "Cheo-cheo-chehoo-cheo!"

Boynton, his sermonette finished, wheeled himself to the base of the marker, snipped off a tuft of grass hiding the letter *C* in the name *Charles*, and Joe heard him say quietly, as in soliloquy, "Now Charles, my boy, don't get to pitying yourself because of your handicap.

70

Always remember that self-pity is a great crippler. Keep your eyes on the Star your wagon is hitched to."

Joe wondered at the man, the self-control, the radiance of his personality, and the simplicity of his faith, and he envied him. Then, when Boynton was sitting upright in his chair again, a shadow crossed the older man's face. He spoke to Joe: "Hitler has ordered the genocide of all Jews as a solution to what he calls 'the Jewish problem.' How can a man be so depraved!"

Cardinal shook his head, and thinking of little Jimmie, he mused, "He should have died with all his discords in him!"

"He will, and soon. A God of justice cannot let a man like that live long. If I were young and well, I might decide to enlist again. But I wouldn't want to go with hate in my heart, not even against Hitler. God doesn't want anybody to hate anybody.

"You going to enlist, Mr. Cardinal? Or maybe you could go as a reporter. You and Janice have a wonderfully readable column. If people don't get new and elevating ideas to expand their minds to new dimensions, they'll stay narrow and self-centered. Holmes expressed it this way: 'Once a man's mind has been expanded by a new idea, it can never return to its former dimension.' "

Later, after getting a picture and permission to write a feature story, "Charles Boynton, Missing But Still in Action," Joe was on the highway again, driving toward Wilkerson.

He was in dogwood country now, and the fragrance was everywhere. The redbud, too, charmed the countryside with its purplish red blossoms, and the woods were carpeted with wild flowers of many varieties and colors.

Life, even in the midst of death, could be a thing of beauty, a mind-expanding adventure.

"Thank you, Oliver Wendell Holmes; thank you very much. I will build for myself a more stately mansion; I will leave my low-vaulted past."

His elation was short-lived. Sorrow came pressing down upon him when he remembered his draft card and thought what an omen it was for sorrow—for Janice, whose throne was so soon to be vacated, and for his beloved Lela; there was, of course, sorrow also for himself. It could mean a termination of the life he had loved—an end to

71

his walks with Nature and to the murmured blessings of companionship with God—the God in whom he was supposed not to believe!

This was spring, and June was just ahead—the time for the singing of birds and of brides and for the mating of mind and heart, making the relationship of husband and wife a holy and rapturous experience.

The delights and ecstacies of romantic love—these were boosters only. Man was more than flesh and blood, and true love was not the food from the table nor soft candlelight and gentleness; rather, it was the touch and cling of the fingers of the mind.

Can You do something about Janice? How does a skeptic address You? God? Father? Heavenly Father? Creator?

He was bewildered by his own inconsistency. A skeptic's prayer was a homemade ladder too short to reach the sky.

He was steering grimly as he swung into the highway which in another hour would bring him to Wilkerson.

Tomorrow entered into him—and in that tomorrow what dreams, what tragedies, what excursions into the valley of the shadow of death! With Pearl Harbor, with nations all over the world declaring war on other nations, with the young men of America thronging to the colors, what right had a columnist and aspiring novelist to sit behind the barricade of his typewriter, breathing the free air of the exempt?

What must be his motive for going, if he was destined to go? To join his fellow countrymen in a war to put a stop to genocide, to stand by a country that is worthy of every drop of a man's blood. He must be able to go without hate. God doesn't want anybody to hate anybody, and, as the adult Janice often had said, "He that hateth his brother is a murderer!"

She had also said, "You're too tender-hearted; you could never kill."

There would be men on both sides who would not want to kill. They would only obey the commands of superior officers, who in turn obeyed those above them.

There had been a story in the morning paper about a policeman who did not believe in killing but who had had to shoot to stop a murderer from stabbing him to death—the same murderer who, in a frenzy, had knifed a half-dozen young women during the past month.

It was a crazy, mixed-up world.

A thought from tomorrow tossed a light into his mind: How can you write from the viewpoint of the young soldier who will be the hero of your novel unless you know by first hand experience what it is like to *be* a soldier?

He would not need to tell the world nor even his close friends—Lela nor Janice nor young Doctor Raymond nor anyone—that he was not as patriotic as he wished he were. It must remain his own secret that his loyalties were divided between serving his country and serving his own ambitions, if he were to finish the book which destiny—perhaps God Himself—wanted the world to read.

"O God, if I am in touch with You at all, let me realize it. There ought to be some way a man can know for sure. Give me a faith like that of Charles Boynton."

Minus his legs, Charles Boynton was still a whole man. He walked straighter and with a more purposeful philosophy than Joe Cardinal did right now.

Yet not with more determination than the new Joe Cardinal. He knew now what he had to do. He had to go over there where Charles and hundreds of thousands of others had gone, and he had to accept the role of being one more policeman to help patrol the thundering world of death and destruction. It was not the servicemen who had to die that should now claim his attention and anxiety—it was the women and children he must help save from a fate worse than death.

In his mind there also ran now the thread of "Just Enough Shadow." He had invented a hero who must live the experiences of enlistment, training, and battlefield terror, but how could he, Joe Cardinal, who hated war as Janice hated it, hate it still more vicariously in the mind of his hero if, as the writer, he himself did not know experientially that of which he wrote?

But how could he tell Lela! And how could he leave her!

Chapter 9

In another half-hour he would reach the Wilkerson highway, a little later turn into the Blanchard lane, and there, waiting at the gate or strolling by the lake with binoculars or book or sitting in the orchard in her favorite writing nook, doing her column, "Musical Musings on the Masters," would be the unbelievably wonderful girl who, in June, was to have been his bride.

No matter what she might be doing, her mind would be searching for the Gabriel she had already found—and was so soon to lose again.

A melancholy thought came now—one he must toss away and refuse to consider, though it might come again and again: When she finds me next time, will I be in a military hospital, old with disillusionment, another Charles Boynton?

More rationally he thought, I am only one man in a world of millions. Why should I expect or hope for special treatment?

He shut off the car motor fifty yards from the house, glided silently along the lilacs, and stopped at the gate, hoping to surprise her.

He heard her voice now, calling to her mother, "No mail—not a thing except a couple of magazines and a few sales announcements! I don't understand it! He always has a letter for me on Fridays!"

Hearing, and suffering a little at her disappointment, knowing her unhappiness was an unneeded proof of her love, Joe thought, "I *do* have a letter for her, but it's one that will break her heart."

That letter lay like an envelope of lead in his jacket pocket. There would be many Fridays in the future when she would receive no mail from him. A series of Fridays that could run on forever.

He rejected the thought.

He would greet her in the new way they had devised the last time he had spent a weekend here. He pursed his lips and let out the familiar whistle, a jumbled musical attempt at a meadowlark's lilting melody. It was supposed to say, "Here, little Lela! Come, kitty-kitty-kitty!"

At the sound of his whistle, Evangeline let out a little cry of delight and ran toward him. He met her half way; and in the moment of meeting and embracing, he felt as he always did when he was with her. It was the almost unbelievable happiness that lovers know, only it always seemed to him that no other lovers could possibly experience the ecstacy they had found in each other.

Mother Eloise came out now and ordered them, "You two youngsters skedaddle out of here so I can get my work done! Go down to the dock or somewhere. I'll ring when I need you."

There were so many things to talk about: the strange slant his column had been taking, and why; the iconoclastic "fan" letters he had been getting; his visit with Charles Boynton in the Cranston cemetery; the particular problem he had with Public Stenographer Janice Granada; the interval in his office when he had been a worm; the letter in his pocket—heavy and hot and tormenting.

"Know what I want us to do?" she said, as they followed the little brown path through the orchard and down the gentle slope to where the dinghy danced on the afternoon wavelets washing the shore.

"Do we have to *do* anything? Can't we just do nothing except make up for the long and cruel time I've been away?"

"I want to go down where the moon comes over the treetops of Bluebell Island and let John propose to Priscilla again, just like he did that other night."

"By the way, I never did ask how our little tiger kitten got along in his new home. Is he still around, or has Big Tom scared all of his nine lives out of him?"

"*She* is fine, very fine," Lela answered. "She's been a jolly little companion on my walks by the lake, and she's helped me with 'Musical Musings.' Only she's not little anymore. She grew up so fast, like kittens do, and now we have a new problem."

"Problem?"

"What do we do with five new kittens?"

"Unbelievable," he answered. "And what does Big Tom think about that?"

"Tom?" She sighed with the word. "Tom never got over his battle wound. We had to choose, Dr. Sloan told us, between having him a

75

cripple for life or putting him to sleep. It was pathetic. I drove him to the animal hospital myself, and he climbed up on the back of the car seat, leaned against my shoulder, and purred all the way to town. Every time I think of it—I just *can't* think of it. I don't dare. He trusted me, Joe, and when I left him for his long sleep, his big green eyes stared at me as much as to say, 'I love you!' and he hobbled across the floor to brush his sides against my ankle."

Joe's arm around her tightened, and he let her sob a moment on his shoulder.

It was not a time for words, and neither of them spoke until she sighed and said, "Yesterday, when I was browsing in the library, I found something I had planned to save for our honeymoon. It was by an unknown author, and it seemed to have been written just for us. I have it here somewhere."

She searched a sweater pocket, and while they sat beside the lake beneath the trees, while the wavelets, like Wordsworth's golden daffodils, fluttered and danced in the breeze, she unfolded a slip of paper and read to him:

> Oh, let me lay my head tonight upon your breast,
> And close my eyes against the light. I fain would rest;
> I'm weary, and the world looks sad: this worldly strife
> Turns me to you; and oh, I'm so glad to be your wife.

And in that moment, Joe knew he could not now tell her of the change in his draft status. He felt a desperate need for the counsel of someone with a mature understanding of what seemed to be one of life's greatest problems—that of heartaches and how to heal them.

* * *

George Wilcox Blanchard understood, and his counsel was that of a man schooled in the wisdom of much reading and of having lived through the devastations of war.

"Lela will stand the test," he said when they were together in the dinghy, its motor silent, anchored in the shadow of Bluebell Island. "I've studied her all the way from childhood, and while she may seem to fall to pieces in a crisis, she herself always knows where the pieces are and puts them back together. I'm not bragging about her parents when I say Lela will rise to any occasion. She's made of the kind of material that survives tornadoes and is like John Bowring's cross in the hymn, 'In the cross of Christ I glory, Towering o'er the wrecks of time.' John saw that cross still standing after a terrible devastation had left everything else in shambles. Lela has the story in her 'Musical Musings' this week."

They talked also of "The Call of the Cardinal," and George listened to the story behind the altered slant, and of the letters that had come.

"What does Lela say?" Joe asked, while he baited his hook, and cast out near the end of the dock. "She didn't mention it when we talked a while ago."

"Lela doesn't know," George said. "We haven't run anything new for the past four weeks; instead, we introduced an editorial note saying that by request we were doing a rerun of your favorite columns. She hasn't asked any questions. I was waiting to talk with you when you came. There *was* something pretty seriously wrong with the slant, Joe, as you've already told me. I confess I feel a lot better about the column—and about my future son-in-law."

"You say 'By request'?"

"Eloise and I requested it."

"Thank you *very* much. But I think maybe Lela ought to know."

"She *can* know now. That would have been an occasion to which she would have had a hard time rising."

They talked of wedding plans.

"My advice is to go ahead as if you expected to be deferred. Perhaps if you had taught this year, it might have made a difference, but I think Uncle Sam may not consider a magazine column quite as important as teaching, especially a column that has been doing what yours has been doing. I wouldn't want to be unpatriotic enough to think the draft board had been reading your columns and were influenced by them."

A thought came now, and Joe decided to lay it out for George Blanchard to examine. It was, "And my secretary, who hates war intensely, may inadvertently have sent her employer off to war."

"Could be, it just could be."

"Back to June 6th—you and Mother both think we should go ahead?"

George's fishing line went taut, and there was an interruption for a few minutes until a sizable crappie lay among its fellows in the net. Farther out there was a stirring of the waters to indicate that a school

77

of them was in the vicinity, ready to strike any bait that might look enticing.

From across the water now there was the ringing of the dinner bell, and the fishermen said good-bye to hungry fish at a time when under other circumstances a mere dinner bell could be ignored for at least another half-hour.

George drove the thundery little motor, swinging first up the lake, where, with a gesture of the arm and with a raised voice, he said, "It's going to feel good having you kids living up there. Mother and I can look up the hill and see what's going on. And you can look down and watch your parents-in-law growing old and keep right on with your writing."

"*If* I come back, *if* I am sent over, and *if* I am intact."

George jammed the speed control lever wide open, and the dinghy shot forward at top speed toward the Blanchard dock, where, Joe noticed, a young girl was standing waiting. When they were near enough, he saw also, on the wide lawn near the wisteria, a picnic table spread, a fire in the barbecue pit, and smoke rising.

Nostalgia caught at his heart. He did not deserve all the good things that were happening to him—or were they the sentenced prisoner's last meal before the long walk to the gallows?

* * *

Across the water, the war raged on, new nations declared war overnight, the whole world became an inferno—and the honeymooners took up residence in the Blanchard guesthouse on Bluebell Lake. The office in Madison was closed, and Janice Granada's shrine was reduced to ashes. There was a new address to which "fan" mail was to be sent: The Silver Lining, Box 765, Wilkerson, Wisconsin.

The big bad wolf was the same, but there was a new little pig who vied with her husband for an occasional early morning visit to the post office.

The make-believe lost a bit of its glamour when Joe told his slightly jealous wife that the game of the little pig and the big bad wolf had had its inception in the Madison office.

In a moment of simulated courage, on a day when she came back with the mail and tapped on the door of Joe's hideaway-den twenty yards from the guesthouse itself, Lela said, "*You* little pig, *me* big bad wolf, and I am going to come down your chimney and eat you up!"

He let her in, and she ate him up. Then her face took on a serious expression. "Can we have it understood that there will never again be a certain other little pig? It's been like a shadow between us ever since I learned about it—about *her*, I mean. I think I've had just about enough shadow." She was fighting tears. "I don't want to be this way, Joe, but after all, I am a woman, and you have quoted her quite a lot lately—or haven't you noticed?"

He shuffled through the mail and noticed that the return address of one was: Janice Granada, The Towers, Madison, Wisconsin. It had not been opened.

In a gesture to let in enough sunshine to dissolve any remaining clouds, Joe handed the letter to Lela, saying, "*You* secretary, *me* mere husband."

Her hands were trembling as she used the letter opener, then she handed it to him with the remark, "It *could* be personal," to which he replied, "Anything personal that comes in our mail, has to be personal to both of us. You believe that?"

The letter from Janice was in her own handwriting. It said in flowing style, "I was up at seven o'clock this morning and got the apples for Dr. Halford Raymond. Did I ever thank you for asking him, once upon a time, to take me out to dinner? I find he is a man of habit. He does over and over again what he has decided he likes to do. I do miss the good old days, but the new ones are a challenge. I owe more to you than you will ever know. Someday I want to meet your sweet little wife—I'm sure she must be that."

The letter, on Janice's personal stationery, was signed, "Little Pig."

He handed it to Lela, studied her face as she read, and saw her eyes narrow and her lips purse. When she finished, she moved to the window and looked out toward Bluebell Island, where, this azure morning, if one were so attuned, he could hear music in every dancing wave and words of love in every whisper of the pines.

He tried to read her thoughts, wondering if she were remembering a night when a three-quarter moon had stolen a look through the feathered tops of the trees and a small tiger kitten had mewed its way into their hearts. This brief letter from Janice, telling of her friendship with Dr. Raymond, ought to dissolve her every shadow of jealousy.

Apparently it did not. She turned to him with: "This big-bad-wolf-little-pig thing—am I right—began *after* the three-quarter moon?"

His answer, he felt as soon as he had given it, was a little too defensive—in its tone, anyway: "It was just a smattering of pleasant inter-office communication. Nothing more."

She shot an arrow from Poe's quiver: "Quoth the raven, 'Nevermore!' " And she dropped the letter into the wastebasket.

He retrieved it, moved with it to the fireplace, struck a match from the mantel, held the flame to a corner of the letter, tossed it into the firebox, and turned back to say, "There! The decapitated violet has been tossed over the cliff, the little pig has been eaten up, the big bad wolf has gone up the chimney in flames." He swept her into his arms and would have kissed away any remaining doubts, but she seemed not ready for the shadows to be gone.

"Okay," he said as he released her. "Tell me what else I should do—a wife does have to trust her husband, doesn't she?"

Her answer was disconcerting, but it did let in a little more light, "She can trust him, but can she trust all of his friends? I don't know—but I seem to feel something."

He shuffled the stack of letters to see if there might be anything else of a personal nature. Janice would have had them all cataloged in her mind before opening them. That was the way the original little pig had worked.

One letter had a return address indicating it was from the draft board—and his sun went down on a horizon of blood. Quickly he slipped it into a desk drawer. It could be a deferment, or it could be a notice to report for immediate induction. He could, with time and love, resolve the small war that had broken out between them, but the greater war that slaughtered peoples—women and children as well as armed men—was suddenly about to crash in upon him—upon *them*.

Chapter 10

They were strolling on Cardinal Hill, having their last walk and talk before he was to be inducted into the army. Suddenly her arm through his tightened. "Can we rest a minute? I'm afraid I'm getting tired."

His heart smote him. "Of course. I'm sorry, I guess I'm a little slow realizing. It's new to me—being a prospective father."

"You're always thoughtful, Joe dear."

"Always? How about the times when I'm buried in the shadows of 'Just Enough Shadow'? I'm going to miss my hero and heroine. They've become almost a part of me these months."

"Aren't you forgetting? You *are* your hero. Every important thing that happens to you over there you'll interweave as an incident into the life of Vern Gregg. Only I hope he never forgets while he's in Paris, if he happens to go there, that his Judy Frost is back home waiting."

He seated her on the flat top of an oak stump—one that had had to be cut down because it was growing in the place where Junior's sandbox would be built. Work had been started only a week ago— trees and underbrush had been cleared away and the foundation had been poured—and then had come the draft board's final notice. The deferment which had come the morning the big bad wolf had gone up the chimney in flames had kindled hope that the young teacher-writer-columnist might be in an essential occupation and, especially since he was now a prospective father, that he might never be inducted.

"The Call of the Cardinal" had lost its political slant. It had become, as originally planned, a lively little rill of wisdom and a voice for peace in a time of international unrest. Many a disheartened reader had written to say thank you for medication to quiet a fevered mind.

"Think you can climb up with me to the Cardinal's Nest?" He now asked.

She sighed, "If I can lean on a strong man's strong arm."

"I can carry you if you like," he said.

"Maybe not—maybe not both of us. You're forgetting—"

"I'll never forget." Then he added, and regretted the melancholy of it as soon as the words were out: "While I'm over there taking lives, you'll be back here giving the world a brand new one."

The place where his den was to be built was an area about one hundred feet in diameter. There would be room enough not only for his hideaway but also for a picnic table and lawn chairs for guests. He seated her on a fallen ponderosa log.

"I found something in the Psalms this morning," she told him. "I thought maybe we could have a secret verse while you're over there getting ready to come back and I'm over here waiting. The days may get dark enough to seem like nothing but shadow, and we can remember."

He drew her to him gently. These months of living together had been almost impossible to believe—the blending of personalities and the sacredness of love in bloom. There had only been an occasional interval when, quite unintentionally, they had hurt each other's hearts, turning them to ashes. But then repentance and honesty had rekindled the fire, burning up the old wolf and all his kind.

She searched a jacket pocket, drew out a small New Testament with Psalms, and turned its silver-edged pages to the bookmark.

Strange, he thought. Where is the skeptic Janice told me about? When he was with Lela, it was easy to believe. It was only when he walked alone with his musings that he doubted—not the existence of God but His availability. Could He—*did He*—disclose Himself only when a man reach up with the arms of faith?

And what was faith? Was it a thing apart from God, or was faith true only when it was anchored in something solid? And what, in a world of hate and greed and foggy creed, was solid enough to make a dependable anchor?

"Read to me," he said. "I like to hear you. I *feel* something when you read from the Book—that Book."

While she read and talked about the things she had once heard in a sermon by Dr. Wellman, he studied the sky. He let his eyes stray

82

from tree to tree and focus for a moment on the jagged spire of the stump of the ponderosa. This tree had once ruled the area, and they were now seated on its prostrate trunk.

In California it was the redwood that ruled over all the other trees of the forest, but in this part of the country, the ponderosa pine reigned. Only one had had its throne upon this hill—but it had not been able to stand against the madness of a tornado that once had swept through the area.

The laws of Nature never change, he thought, but then he began to doubt. How could God, if all things were controlled by laws, interfere to bring about an answer to a man's prayer without upsetting the course of nature? These immutable laws that reigned in the universe—could even God dare to break them?

The marker fell from the little brown book. Lela retrieved it and tucked it into a place in Romans.

"Thank you," he said. "Thank you very much."

"For what? What did I do?"

"A law of nature made the bookmark fall. When you picked it up, you did not violate that law, you only introduced another law. Your strength was greater than the pull of gravity."

"Speaking of law," she said, "I like what it says in Romans, the eighth chapter and—let me see—here it is, verse two: 'For the law of the Spirit of life in Christ Jesus has made me free from the law of sin and death.' Oh dear! There goes my marker again."

The wind caught the little slip of paper and whisked it toward the mullein stalk of long ago.

He caught it before it could fall over the edge and handed it back to her.

"Want to see what I found in Elizabeth the other day? I jotted it down just for myself, but it might be good for us—all three of us."

From the marker she read to him a thing of beauty from Elizabeth Barrett Browning:

> In the pleasant orchard closes,
> "God bless all our gains," say we;
> But "God bless all our losses"
> Better suits with our degree.

Was it philosophically elevating to thank God for our gains and not for our losses also? Did the Creator have some way of gathering together all the pros and cons of life and weaving them into a pattern of symmetry? Was there a higher law in operation in the area of the soul to unfold the will of God in such a manner?

"All the pros and all the cons," he said. And she answered, "All our gains and all our losses. Right now, Joseph Cardinal, you are my gain, and I promise you I will never, never, never—even in the smallest way—be one of your losses."

He sighed, helped her to her feet and steered her carefully down the slope to the place where the architect's identification read:

Future Home of the Joe Cardinals

The beauty of the area was disfigured now with downed shrubbery and with huge gashes made in the soil by bulldozers and other tools of the contractor's trade.

His mind flew back to the Towers and to a note he had found in the mailbox one morning. Janice had introduced a new game. Her note was a quote from Keith Preston:

> The great god Ra, whose shrine once covered acres,
> Is filler now for crossword-puzzle makers.

Joe quoted it to Lela, who answered with pretended gaiety: "Hurrah for Ra! I ran across him one day last summer. I was browsing around in the *Britannica* looking for ideas for Musings, and I got a very pleasant surprise. I'd seen the word in quite a few crossword puzzles but hadn't bothered to look it up. He was quite a figure in his day, and his shrine really did cover acres."

He was learning that when she wanted to tell him some new thing, it was good to let her talk. This was *her* life. So soon they would be separated, and he would miss the gay, necessary nonsenses of her chatter, the playful things she said to relieve tension in serious situations:

"In Egyptian mythology, Ra was the god of the sun. He created himself by union with his shadow. How about that! A god, spelled with a small *g*, who had no previous existence, creating himself by union with his own shadow—which he couldn't possibly have had! And millions of people believed it! How credulous can you get!"

His eyes were still focused on the words, "Future Home of the Joe

84

Cardinals," and the area itself seemed to him like the remains of a battlefield. "The great god Joe," he said aloud, "whose shrine once covered acres."

"Don't. Don't say such things! Before you know it, the war will be over, you'll be back, and we'll finish our house. You'll be up there in your den every morning, and I'll be down here being a good little housekeeper."

He shook his head. A wave of melancholia swept over him. "I will not have made enough of an impression on the world, good or bad, to be filler for a crossword puzzle."

"How can you say such things! Junior and I won't stand for it—will we, Junior?"

This brought him back to a more current reality. He stooped, picked up a piece of flint shaped like an arrowhead and, brushing off the dust, remarked, "I wonder if this little artifact went through somebody's heart long ago."

"Joe!"

"All right, all right! I *won't* say such things. But maybe it is psychologically better to get them out of the mind than to keep them rotting in the attic."

There was silence between them until she broke it with: "Some arrows are *good* arrows. I remember one that was shot into the air and was found long long afterward in the heart of an oak—and a cardinal's song was found again in the heart of a friend."

Before leaving the hill for the spin back to the Blanchard dock, she told him how she had used her information—not in "Musical Musings" but in her Sunday school class, named facetiously "The College Brain Trust." "Some of those kids are really searching for God, only they don't know it. If Augustine was right in saying that no person will ever find peace until he finds it in God Himself, then all their searching for pleasure, every restless activity, and every yearning for identity, could be interpreted as searching for purpose in life which can be found *only* in God.

"Anyway, I suggested to them that most of our little gods, while at times seeming so large they cover all our own little acre, eventually diminish to fillers for crossword puzzles. Only the true God, who is self-existent, who gave His name to Moses long ago as the 'I Am,' or the 'I am He who is forever,' can truly satisfy the heart. And Joe, all of a sudden, while I was talking and telling them about the great I Am, something wonderful happened. It was like coming out of a narrow place into a room as large as all the universe. Even though I had known so much about God, I discovered Him in a new and mind-expanding faith. My own heart had found satisfaction *in Him!*"

Her voice choked. She turned to him and was lost for a moment in his arms. "Joe, darling, this has got to be our anchor for the next few months."

He felt her trembling in his arms and felt also her tears against his cheek—and was glad to be the husband of such a wonderful woman. "I am not worthy to belong to you," he said.

She sighed with contentment and released herself, and they strolled toward the place where Little Joe's playpen would someday be. They stood looking down the long slope and across the wide pasture to the orchard and the Blanchard place nesting like a jewel in its setting of green. He watched her and wondered how he would ever be able to stand the terrible separation.

"Lela," he said, "I don't see any reason why you and Dad can't keep on with the column. You know what I believe and what the world needs, and you and he and mother can keep it going until I get back. In the meantime, I will give *full* time to the hero of 'Just Enough Shadow.' I think I've worked out a compromise motive for my going. It will not be just to help save the world for democracy and to reduce the great god Hitler to a filler for crossword puzzles, but I will, in a vicarious sort of way, *be* my hero. Through him and his experiences, I can help show the world the futility of war. When I come back, *if* I come back, and am intact enough to run a typewriter, I can finish the book. One has to live a death in order to write about it—"

She closed his lips with her fingers. "John Alden! When you use that big little word 'if,' you are not speaking for Miles Standish nor for me—nor even for the Joe Cardinal I married."

In the dinghy, they set out across the water, circled Bluebell Island, and were racing at top speed when they came back and drove past Cardinal Acres, a trail of turbulent water in their wake.

"Goodbye for now, Mr. Hawthorne!" Lela called, and waved a mock farewell. "We'll be seeing you!"

"Goodbye again, Henry!"

At the Blanchard pier, he looped the anchor rope around a dock post, walked with her up to the level area near the barbecue pit. He had not removed his life preserver. She called it to his attention but did not seem surprised when he answered, "I won't be gone long. Just long enough to think a thought or two."

She stopped him with her eyes, then said, "I understand. I'd feel the same way. But you keep this little old vest *on*. Here, let me tighten the strings."

She watched him as he strode down the slope, then ran after him and was there to help him with completely unnecessary suggestions: "As I said, keep your vest on, don't drive too fast, be sure to head into the wind if you run into heavy water—"

"And if," he cut in to add, "your boat capsizes for any reason, and you get thrown out, don't panic. Stay with the boat, keep your head above water, and hold on. Eventually, the waves will wash you to shore. Right?" It was a routine any boy scout would know.

"And here," she suggested, "just in case you'd like to take a peek at our secret verse. It's Psalm 23, verse 4." She pressed her New Testament into his hand and clung to him with her eyes, which, he noticed, were brimming and more expressive because of what she was saying through tears: "I don't like to have you away even for a few minutes, Joe. How can I lose you for months!"

A hundred yards out, he waved, caught her wave in return, and set his face toward Bluebell Island. He was Gabriel in a boat without his Evangeline, about to begin their long separation.

Driving past the Bluebell dock, he searched the bushes along the shore where another cardinal couple had begun their honeymoon, and laughed without mirth. Then he voiced a prayer that came uninhibited from his subconscious, "Let me be like Michelangelo—as humble and dependent."

There was a phrase in a poem by the great painter which, translated by Wordsworth, expressed the loneliness of his spirit at this moment:

> My unassisted heart is barren clay.
> Unless Thou show us then Thine own true way,
> No man can find it. Thou must lead.

No man's heart could, of itself, be anything but barren. The seed of God's truth was the breath of God in a believer's mind. And it would take time, even for a seed from God to quicken and reproduce.

One did not plant a seed and then demand of it, "Grow *now!* Grow *fast!* Let the world know that you have life!" Nor did one dare to scold the soil of the soul for not accomplishing immediate germination.

On the far side of the island he stopped the motor and let the dinghy drift until he had read their secret verse. Then he tucked the book into a shirt pocket, started the motor, and steered straight for Cardinal Acres. There was a farewell to be made.

He docked at the new pier, built especially for them, climbed the winding path leading up to his mesa-like throne, crowned with spruce, pine, and silver maples, carpeted with wild violets, trout lilies, and bloodroot. This was to have been—and someday would become—the location for his study, overlooking the whole area around it. It would be his throne.

Here, "in quietness and in confidence," as written by Isaiah of old, the world shut out and himself shut in with his thoughts and emotions, inspiration and perspiration teamed with a mutual yoke, he would send his light to all men everywhere. "The Call of the Cardinal" would be heard round the world, and always there would be just enough shadow to make the sunlight pleasurable—not a glare nor a creator of deserts.

Seated on the bole of the fallen ponderosa, he noticed in the sand at his feet a half-dozen inch-deep conical ant-lion pits, food traps constructed by the larvae of the nocturnal damselfly-like adults that are sometimes known as doodlebugs. For a brief interval he reflected upon the strange habits of this unique insect: The adults drop their eggs upon the surface of the soil; the plump, hairy-bodied larvae, immediately upon hatching, dig their conical pits, burying themselves, except for their heads, at the bottom of the cones, and wait. When an ant or other insect tumbles into one of the pits, the voracious little ant lion seizes its prey, paralyzes it with a poisonous secretion, sucks its body of all juices, and then, by an upward jerk of its long jaws, tosses the skin up and out, and awaits the next victim.

I will *have* to come back. For no man could be robbed of his future—not if the Creator had planned for him some particular future.

Standing in a little garden of flowering bloodroot, he began to write his farewell column, carried along by the winds of the words of One who once said, "Consider the lilies of the field, how they grow."

"It was Elizabeth Barrett Browning who once wrote," he began, " 'God bless all our losses,' thus voicing the heart's desire of us all. Even nature suffers loss and is blessed by those losses. Its losses are the seeds of gain. The plowshares also that open the soil: the gains spring to life from the wounds. 'First the blade, then the ear, after that the full corn in the ear.'

"How brief, the fragrant life of the bloodroot's flowers. When those flowers have dropped their last delicate petals and their perfumed life is done, the mother plant gives her whole attention to another pre-destined task. She pours her energy into leaf-making. The small leaves, stunted in the first weeks of their life because the plant's energies are taken up with flower- and seed-making, begin now to really live. They grow rapidly, and take on a brilliant green sheen not possible while they were denying themselves for the sake of the flowers.

"The bloodroot gets its name from the bloodlike juice in its reddish root; the juice itself is sometimes used to make certain types of cough syrup.

"*Sanguinaria canadensis*—what mysteries unfold in its brief span of life. The orange-red juice of this beautiful little member of the poppy family was used by the Indians to dye their robes and blankets. The whole plant gave up its life to this higher purpose."

Because it was to be his last column, Joe penned yet another paragraph:

"I, too, must give up a life I have loved—to serve my country. Will I leave my blood to fertilize the soil of a battlefield, or will I carry it back in my veins to the America I love?

"Do these words, themselves dripping blood, seem maudlin? Perhaps they are. Is not every man entitled to a little self-pity now and then? Yet excessive self-pity can be a great crippler, deforming the soul, dwarfing and robbing it of its beauty, and robbing the world also of its God-given potential.

"Guest columnist during my absence will be Mrs. Joe Cardinal. Be kind to her, keep your hearts at rest no matter what happens to you or yours, remembering the promise made by the Prince of Peace long ago: 'Come unto me, all ye that labour and are heavy laden, and I will give you rest.' "

The column completed, Joe gave it a final proofing. In Cranston,

Charles Boynton would read and understand. Lela would read and break into tears. In Madison, Janice would open her mail box one morning, turn the pages of *The Silver Lining* or some other paper which featured "The Call of the Cardinal," and absent-mindedly look again in the box to see if the big bad wolf had left anything personal.

Back at her typewriter, in her own office, Public Stenographer Janice Granada, would sigh for the territory she once ruled and, being a believer in God, would pray for her former employer's return. She would hope he could come back whole, not as Charles Boynton had returned, and she would fervently desire that he might not be left to rest under a cross in Normandy or elsewhere—after he had first waded through mud and blood.

Joe tucked his notebook into a pocket, stood looking out across the water to Bluebell Island, then gave momentary attention to Lela's little Book, remembered the tears in her eyes when she had pressed it into his hand, and read again the note she had penned on the slip of paper used for a bookmark: "God bless all our losses."

He saw now, on the other side, a poem by Whittier. It was one he seemed never to have noticed in all his reading:

> We search the world for truth. We cull
> The good, the true, the beautiful,
> From graven stone and written scroll,
> And all old flower-fields of the soul;
> And, weary seekers of the best,
> We come back laden from our quest,
> To find that all the sages said,
> Is in the Book our mothers read.

His thoughts took flight now to another Book, lying on his mother's desk. He saw his beautiful, brown-haired mother reach for it, open it, turn its pages and, her voice gentle and reverent, read to her son such favorite passages as, "Get wisdom, get understanding," and "Let not your heart be troubled, neither let it be afraid."

"In the Book our mothers read!" Joe Junior would be exposed to all the sages said, from early childhood to adolescence and beyond. But Joe determined, Don't let him become a skeptic; don't let his much reading, his searching for truth in the words of men, rob him of the truth in the Book.

And there was the burning bush story—the command to Moses:

"Put off thy shoes from off thy feet, for the ground whereon thou standest is holy ground." This hill could become holy ground—every bush and flower, every whisking chipmunk and bartering trade rat, by the alchemy of God, could become a living flame, aglow with the presence of God—and a man's every written word, phrase, sentence, paragraph, and column could burn with celestial fire.

This place of stones and grass and bush and tree and bleeding flowers—this, Joe, is *your* holy ground. To this place you will return —to this throne. From it the voice of the Cardinal will be heard once again, and in the metamorphosis of your music there will continue to be the beautiful modifications of Peace.

Someday the world would know peace, but the price of it would be the rulership of the Prince of peace.

Joe moved to the edge of the garden of bloodroot, and because he remembered a woman whose husband had died in battle, and had knelt before an open Bible and prayed for strength to carry on, so now he knelt and prayed aloud, "O living God, make Yourself *living* to me— and I will follow wherever You lead."

When he was aroused by the ringing of the dinner bell, it was as if he had been on a long journey.

At the foot of the hill he worked his way to the new dock, stepped into the dinghy, shoved out from shore, seated himself in the stern, started the motor, opened the throttle wide, and steered for Bluebell Island. He wanted one final wind-in-the-face ride to the place which so reminded him of the island of his own self, where conscious and subconscious communed and where new thoughts, words and phrases were born for interweaving into his column. It was here that he had first heard the very special call of the cardinal and had fallen in love with the daughter of the owner of the island.

"Little old dinghy," he addressed his flying steed, "don't carry her Gabriel too far! Bring him back safe and well and strong. And keep Evangeline free from stress and too much shadow."

Circling the island and heading into the wind and the higher waves that rolled nearly always on the side opposite the lee, he looked again toward the site of their future home. He was startled by what he saw: As if carved in his absence, shaped by the slant of the sun on the rocks and on the overhanging branches of the junipers, there was the face of a man.

91

It could not be. Yet, bewilderingly, there it was—forehead, nose, lips, jutting chin, even a giant left eye. The whole profile was unmistakable.

It was a replica of what, in his mind, as a boy, he had imagined Hawthorne's Great Stone Face had looked like.

He laughed to himself. I am seeing things! The overhang which we have called Hawthorne's Haunt has created for me a Great Stone Face of my own.

But even as he looked, steering straight toward it, it faded, as had the lonely bird of William Cullen Bryant's "To a Waterfowl":

> Thou art gone, the abyss of heaven
> Hath swallowed up thy sight.

He swung the dinghy about, set out for the island again, circled it, came back, and searched the profile of the overhang. But he saw only its former rugged features; the Great Stone Face had disappeared.

He kept on driving hard toward the overhang, and when he was within hailing distance, he raised his voice to call as once a retreating general had called, "I shall return!"

When the dinner bell rang again, as if impatient at being apparently ignored, he mused, I am not looking for a Great Stone Face but for the great and holy face of the Creator of the universe, as the Book claims Him to be, revealed in the face of Jesus Christ. Will I find Him, perhaps, where Charles Boynton found Him—on a European battlefield? If so, may it be so!

Lela met him at the Blanchard dock, and they walked hand in hand toward the barbecue pit and the wisteria-shaded porch. "You noticed I rang the bell twice?" she asked, and the tone of her voice seemed to say, "Should a man's lonely wife be required to wait so long for him to come?"

"I came as soon as I could. But I had to have a last fling at the lake. Then, when I rounded the island, and looked toward the overhang, I thought I saw—you'd never believe what I thought I saw."

Lightly, she answered, "I'd believe you *thought* you saw something, even if I thought you *didn't*."

He reached up and tucked a pendent branch of wisteria under a stronger, higher, primary branch. "I thought I saw Hawthorne's

Great Stone Face. When it faded out, I went back to see if I could see it again. But it was gone, like Bryant's waterfowl."

Her hand on his arm tightened, "I'm glad," she said. "I saw it once myself, when the sun was right and the clouds were cooperating. But only once.

"One thing about Hawthorne," she went on, "I've been studying him lately, and am very unhappy with the way he pours his hatred for evildoers into the Puritan mold. In *Scarlet Letter,* for instance, while he does make it clear that there is a moral law that actually forces evildoers to pay the full price for their sins, he portrays the church leaders as merciless, cruel, vindictive hypocrites. I'm afraid our younger readers will develop a dangerous prejudice against the church. I can't believe the Puritans were that bad."

He was willing to talk of Hawthorne, though the undercurrent of his thought was not of a genius of literature of the early American days but of a little corner of history being born at this moment. He listened almost absently as she said, "Dr. Wellman has the best understanding of how sins are to be forever expiated—not by the sinner himself suffering for them in a sort of purgatory of the heart but, as he expressed it one Sunday morning, 'through the Saviour Himself who has *already* purged our sins. The true purgatory is Calvary,' he said."

It was a good thought, and he would try to remember it and use it in some way in his novel. "If Hawthorne had known that, a lot of his writings might never have been."

"I still feel sorry for Hester Prynne, and I despise the hypocritical self-appointed religious judges. It's not fair for an author to depict Christian people in such hideous caricature."

"You are my Hester Prynne," he said. "You *have* no sins. You are my perfect wife, and I love you to the nth degree." He swept her into his arms and said, "I love you, love you, love you, now and forever, and I promise you I shall return."

93

Chapter 11

It was nearly midnight, and Joe had slept fitfully. The strangeness of his surroundings, together with the many and varied disturbing noises, had kept him intermittently awake.

Ever since the forty-two prospective privates had clambered, shuffled, and scrambled their way aboard, undressed, and jacknifed themselves into their berths, there had been such a bedlam of banter, groans and guffaws, mixed with wisecracks, that at times the men had seemed to drown out the roar of the train itself.

The nine-car Pullman was carrying nearly four hundred American men to an unnamed reception center.

Lurch, sway, swing, roll—grind. The brakes were on again; Joe could tell by the feeling of his head being pressed hard against the partition at the head of his berth. It was not exactly an artistic piece of furniture—not at all resembling the velvet cathedral headboard Lela had selected for the master bedroom of the new home on Cardinal Hill. That was to have been padded, deeply hand-tufted, and of king-sized width.

The grinding came to a crescendo now, and the train lurched to a hurried and violent stop.

He searched for an adjective to describe the emotion that for the moment was on the throne of his mind. When he was able to start working again on his novel, he would need the exact word to describe the way Vern Gregg would feel in a similar situation: sullen, sulky, ill-tempered, morose, depressed, melancholy—perhaps disconsolate. An old hymn had invited the disconsolate, "Come to the mercy seat, fervently kneel."

Don't worry, Vern, he thought, I'll get you through your trouble some way. A book has to end happily, or it has not ended at all—and even happiness is supposed to be only the *beginning* of an ever-after.

Soon I'll have you over where the thunder of flaming death is tearing the world apart, leading, driving, dragging and blasting blindfolded men, women and children into cemeteries of terror—and then after a terrible while, I'll bring you home again. I have predestined you for a happy ending.

The Psalmist had been sure that goodness and mercy would follow him all the days of his life and that he would dwell in the house of the Lord forever . . .

One other thing Lela had told him about Dr. Wellman's sermon that morning. The pastor had quoted a London minister as having said, "The Christian lives in the house of the Lord *now,* and will continue to do so; then, at death, he will go upstairs to live in the upper story of the house of the Lord forever."

There was a beautiful outdoor upstairs overlooking Bluebell Island which, someday, would have a rustic stone stairway carpeted on either side with wild flowers.

Feeling a need for the anchor of faith he and Lela had talked about, Joe fumbled in his pocket for the little New Testament with Psalms and reached up to snap on the lamp above his head. He gasped and drew back his hand with an exclamation as the lamp went out with a blinding flash.

Burned out! he muttered. That's the way you yourself *could* go out, Vern. Just like that!

"Joe Cardinal!" he heard Lela say. *"Don't say that. You're not speaking for Miles Standish, nor for John Alden, nor for yourself!"*

There would be another bulb at the other end of the berth. Joe sat up—something one could do better in an upper berth than in a lower. He fumbled in the darkness for the switch and turned it on, but there was no response. That lamp had either already burned out or was missing.

It was missing. The government, in requisitioning enough cars to move Uncle Sam's soldiers, could not be expected to guarantee perfect accommodations.

He could not see well enough to read, so he fumbled at the button and buttonhole of the curtains that hedged him in on the right. Pushing his tousled brown head through, he found himself looking straight into the serious blue eyes of a red-haired, square-jawed fellow directly across the aisle. Their faces were not more than three feet apart.

The redhead grinned good-naturedly, and said, "Looks like we both thought of doing the same thing at the same time."

"You happen to have a flashlight? One of my bulbs just died, and the other is missing in action. I don't like to bother the porter."

"Flashlight?" Joe thought he saw a pleased expression in the blue eyes. "Sure thing. Something I got at our induction center the other day."

The red-head disappeared behind the curtains, and Joe recalled a moment at the county fair last month when a game operator had pushed a wire-masked Japanese face out from behind a canvas curtain —and men paid fifteen cents for three baseballs to throw at the Japanese head. He had turned away, sickened at the very idea.

The red head came out again, and a large brown hand gave Joe a tiny, bullet-shaped combination key ring and flashlight. "I have several," he said. "I've been giving them away. You're Joe Cardinal, aren't you?"

"How'd you guess?"

"I didn't, exactly. I'm Ned Boynton, Charlie Boynton's nephew. Your former secretary gave me your picture before I left and told me to watch out for you. She thought you might get lonesome. I've liked your columns a lot, Joe—most of them, that is. Your last one —the one about the bloodroot—came just before I left. It made it easier for me."

Joe pressed the plunger on the base of the bullet-shaped flashlight, which shot a tiny but effective beam toward the ceiling. "Thanks," he said. "I'll get it back to you after a while."

"Keep it," Ned returned. "That's what it's for—to introduce whoever uses it to the Bible verse on the outside."

Alone again in his berth, Joe toyed with the miniature flashlight. Janice, he thought, is still fighting to keep or regain her throne; the little pig is still having its influence on the big bad wolf.

The train was moving again, picking up speed, doing sixty, maybe seventy.

He was glad he had been assigned an upper berth, for he had wanted to be alone, to think, and maybe even to scribble a few notes for his column to send back to Lela. For a minute he was gliding along in the dinghy, slicing a trail through the waters of Bluebell Lake, feeling the wind in his face and the splash of spray deflecting from the prow—peering through the mist for the Great Stone Face.

This time next year or sooner—much sooner, probably—he would be jouncing along in a jeep, or sitting at the steering apparatus of a tank, driving over shell holes or through swamps and across the broken and bleeding bodies of men he would have helped to kill.

He wished he could raise a blind in the Pullman and look out on the flying fields under the moon—under a three-quarter moon. Bluebell Lake would be beautiful tonight.

Had he heard a kitten mewing?

His mind examined critically his first experiences at the induction center. There had been things he did not like but which he had accepted because it was routine and necessary as far as the army was concerned: the neck-to-hip X-ray, the stethoscope pressed to his heart and lungs, a special test of his blood.

He had been sworn in, along with five hundred other inductees, all at once, with right arm upraised: "I, Joe Cardinal, do solemnly swear that I will bear true faith and allegiance to the United States of America, that I will serve them honestly and faithfully against all their enemies whomsoever; and that I will obey the orders of the President of the United States and the orders of the officers appointed over me according to the Rules and Articles of War."

And now, induction was forever past, and reception was just ahead —at seven in the morning. Joe focused the powerful little beam of light upon Psalm 23:4, and gave his thoughts to Wilkerson and his farewell to the one who, he felt, was the nearest to perfection a woman could ever be.

"Through the valley of the shadow of death"—all the way through.

The tie that bound a man to his home was the tie of thought, of visualization, the power of the mind to leap with lightning speed from here to there and walk within his moods as a man walks among the trees or climbs the hills—or drives a dinghy across a lake.

He was getting sleepy now. Better hand back the flashlight—he didn't like to have a bullet-shaped article in his possession—not yet.

He worked his face through the curtains again, only to meet a similar action by Ned Boynton across the aisle, who grinned as before and said, "Great minds still running in the same channel?"

"Or groveling in the same trench—or don't they use trenches any more?"

"You do what you have to do to live. I was just hoping that when we're shipped out tomorrow or the next day, we'll be sent to the same center. Janice would like that. There's a good girl, Joe—Mr. Cardinal. Once I thought maybe she'd be nice to come home to, but she didn't like the idea of being a minister's wife."

"You a chaplain?"

"No—missionary—almost, that is; but the draft caught up with me. It's not going to be easy, going out to kill some of the very people you've been praying for."

"Don't they have permanent deferments for ministerial students, missionaries, and ministers?"

"Not always—my orders came through before my mind was fully made up. It was too late after that."

"It's a crazy, mixed-up world. While men and women are being oppressed and ground under the heels of tyrants in one part of the world, others are going out to preach the gospel of the Prince of Peace."

"Where I was going," Ned said, "tyrants do worse than that. They kill and *eat* the prisoners of their wars. They've been doing it for centuries. I was going out to try to stop a little of it by giving them the gospel—the one power that can change men's hearts."

The train was standing now, its engine panting at a water tank. Up and down the aisle, heads were out of bunks, curtains were moving and bulging, and voices were mumbling, complaining and laughing.

"Hey you birds up there!" a voice barked from the other end of the car. "Screeching brakes, train whistles and starts and stops I can stand, but endless chatter—no! Maybe the early bird gets the worm, but I know two birds that are going to get a *boot,* if they don't close their yappers."

It was good-natured banter, and Joe knew that under other circumstances, he would have enjoyed, even entered into it, heartily. He contented himself now by tossing down, "What about the early *worm?* Aren't you worried about what will happen to *you?*"

These were only the little shadows which his hero, Vern Gregg, would walk beside. And Judy Frost, lonely and filled with heartache because he had gone to walk through the valley of the shadow of death, would walk through a deep, dark valley of her own.

The train was going again, and he knew he must get to sleep. Tomorrow would come too soon. He arranged his pillows by shoving a fist into one of them to push it out of his way and fluffing up the other, adjusted the nozzle of the air conditioner at his left so it would blow toward the foot of the berth, and drifted off to sleep.

Riding the dinghy, swinging and swaying, riding a jeep, riding a tank, wading through forest and swamp and mud and blood, bloodroot in bloom, red dye and cough syrup, climbing Cardinal Hill, climbing and climbing, never getting over the garden wall so he could blossom on the other side. He was going to blossom in only one color.

He was all the way to the crest now, and there was a wide field below—a battlefield strewn with tanks and dozers—and children's playpens.

* * *

He had needed his sleep, for the next day at the reception center was tiring and hard to take in spite of its being interesting. Vern Gregg did not enjoy it.

From the depot, the whole nine carloads of them went in buses to the reception center and waited in a tree-shaded park until their names were called. For awhile he and Ned Boynton did not see each other. Blood-typing was first, then a series of motion pictures on social disease—enough to scare any adventurer in that realm into using his common sense—and then came a lecture by a chaplain who, Joe and Vern felt, was trying hard to make their task more understandable and purposeful. Nothing poetic, Joe thought, nothing to make a man feel he could walk through a woods and see the footprints of God— for they were not going to take a leisurely walk, as Thoreau walked, nor as Emerson hoped, to live within all the faculties of the soul.

After dinner there was an IQ questionnaire and a talk about bonds and insurance.

He would have to make a will, he decided, and he would make Lela his beneficiary. There was no use tossing aside a reality—he might *not* come back. He had become a worm crawling through a field of conical pits dug by ant lions. So easily, he could fall into one of them.

They handed him a form to fill out. He controlled his reluctance and filled in all the blanks with the data required, and when he spelled out the name Mrs. Joseph F. Cardinal, he thought of Joe Junior and was thankful that they would be provided for.

When his policy was finally written up and Lela made beneficiary, he heard Ned beside him say, "I'm making the mission board my beneficiary, so that if I *don't* come back, they can use my insurance money to carry on—and my life will have been given for the cannibals anyway. By the way, did you ever stop to think that every soldier who fights over there—every one of *us,* I mean—is actually fighting *for* his enemy as well as against him?"

A burly soldier overheard that and said, "Not this bird. I'm fighting for *my* country and nobody else's."

They were alone, these three, at an outdoor writing desk—a park picnic table under an elm. Ned's answer sounded mature and carefully thought out: "We're fighting the armed forces of the enemy for the sake of the women and children and unborn generations of those enemy countries, to free the people from their own tyrants and from their godless rulers so that the next generation will have a chance to live in peace. And on top of that, we're fighting, if you care to look at it from another angle, so the gospel can be preached in all the world, as the Lord commanded, to reopen doors which have been slammed shut to missionaries and, it would seem, in the face of God Himself.

"And there's one other angle. In the Bible God has promised to bless all those who bless the children of Abraham and to put a curse upon all who curse them. Do you suppose maybe He could be using the Allies to carry out his judgment against Hitler and his cohorts? In that sense, He might use war as a vehicle of holy vengeance upon the enemies of the chosen people. I do remember that it was through Israel that the Saviour came."

The soldier beside them yawned, stretched, unfolded his legs, stood and said, "You're in the army now; you've got to be hard-boiled."

The next day, after being measured for army clothes, Joe was in the line of march to that certain spot in the room, marked by footprints on the floor where he was to stand for a few seconds and have both arms jabbed at once with immunizing needles. Just ahead of him also stripped to the waist was Charles Boynton's nephew. Ahead of *him,* a husky fellow said over his shoulder, "Listen, Parson. How do you reconcile your new job with the one you're giving up. Instead of being eaten by cannibals, you're going out to help the British Lion and the Russian Bear eat up the Nazis?"

Ned's answer was interrupted when the man at the head of the long line of stripped-to-the-waist soldiers couldn't 'take' the double-barrelled inoculation and fell like a bomb to the floor, to be picked up bodily by assistants, carried away and given first aid for fainting. The next man, a stripling, took it standing and didn't even wince.

It was not until afterward, when they were again in their barracks, packing their civilian clothes to ship home, that Ned finished what he had started to say in the lineup.

"It's this way," he began, carefully folding and tucking in his dress shirt. "God sometimes has to allow war in order to save the world from worse catastrophes. Our country makes some terrible mistakes, but we have to look at it like one of Lincoln's most vigorous supporters, Carl Schurz, who once said, 'Our country, right or wrong. When right, to be kept right; when wrong, to be put right.'

"Without the Revolutionary War, there might never have been any *'our* country,' and there wouldn't have been any *United* States if we had let our nation tear itself to pieces back in the days of the Civil War."

Joe finished tucking the last item into his suitcase—a new tie, a birthday gift from Lela. It was good that Janice had put Ned on his trail. She would not agree with Ned's every point of view, but she was trying to help.

They walked together to the post office and sent their suitcases home. In a day or two a package would arrive at the Blanchard mailbox. But there would be a letter following—or maybe preceding—and Lela would know it was only routine army business.

Chapter 12

The pain in his shoulder was throbbing now. No longer did it feel the way it had the instant the bullet had plowed its way through—fast, sharp, vivid. Now it was a pulsating, pounding thing, like the beating of a heart. Like the beating of *my* heart. My heart is still beating, and I am alive.

Joe's hand fumbled inside his jacket. He drew it out again. It was wet, sticky and red. A sickening sensation enveloped him. How long would it take to die? How long would it be until every drop of his blood had filtered into the thirsty brown soil of the Normandy orchard in which he was lying? Strange, he thought, that he should have fallen in battle here—in an orchard.

The sky, visible through the shattered branches of the apple tree above, was blue. There were millions of apple trees in Normandy, he had heard, and the sky above them was as blue as the sky that domed the Blanchard place at Wilkerson.

Lela's mother had wrapped George Wilcox Blanchard round and round with prayer, and he had been spared. He had come home without even one small wound.

A melancholy mood moved in to darken the shade of the apple tree. Someday, at the picnic table in the shade of the old Jonathan tree, Joe Junior would pray, "God is great and God is good—" And at night he would kneel at his mother's knee and say, "Now I lay me down to sleep. . . . If I should die before I wake—"

The throbbing was not nearly so pronounced now. He could be getting weaker; perhaps he was bleeding internally, also.

"Mommy! Where's Daddy? I'd like to have a Daddy, too, like the other kids."

Wish somebody'd come; wish the first-aid men would hurry. He had been told there would be aid men swarming all over the battlefield, giving first aid and marking the spot by sticking the bayonet into the ground, leaving the gunstock upright as a marker for the litter men. The bayonet was bloody.

First time I ever had to use it. But it was either me or him. And the German soldier had been just a kid—a teenage boy who hadn't wanted to die. But I had to kill him. O living God—the Great I Am, I didn't want to do it! He looked like he was hardly old enough to shave!

And the boy's heartrending cry when the bayonet tore its way through!

Looking down into the horror-filled face, Joe had said, "I didn't want to do it!—I didn't hate you!"

And the sobbed-out answer of the boy: *"Ein' feste Burg ist unser Gott!"*—the opening line and the title of Martin Luther's best-known hymn, translated literally by Wordsworth: "A Strong Tower is Our God."

Somewhere in the German lad's boyhood, someone had taken him to church, and there he had learned to sing a hymn of worship and faith.

"A Mighty Fortress Is Our God." It was not *his* God or *my* God but *our* God.

And again Joe could not understand the ways of war. He had come to help police a situation and had found that a vicious, Jew-hating Nazi was only a terrified youngster whose major enemy was the great god Hitler.

Joe's eyes focused feebly on the apple tree in whose shade he was lying. There was an ugly wound below the tree's lowest branch. He had helped repair damaged trees back in the Blanchard orchard. "Make the wound smooth by saw or chisel and mallet; do not loosen the bark around the edge of the wound; cover the edges with shellac to prevent injury to the cambium layer; use lampblack, white lead or linseed oil." He recalled the time Lela had steered the lawn mower too close, making a jagged-edged wound on the old Jonathan. After first aid the wound had begun to heal, and the tree had kept on bearing fruit. Apples and trees and people and war and teenage boys were crying *"Ein' feste Burg ist unser Gott!"*

Wish the aid men would hurry; the litter bearers might never find him.

A fly lit on his cheek. He twitched a face muscle, and the fly lifted.

103

He heard the buzzing of its wings and felt it light again; his left hand brushed at it feebly.

Two flies—more than two, a half dozen, maybe. Flies and Charles Boynton.

Somebody had died by crucifixion once. Pastor Wellman had said in a sermon that in Calvaria there were huge Oriental flies that swarmed all over the crosses.

He drifted into unconsciousness.

* * *

The sun was in his eyes now. He tried to move a little, just a little. He was extremely uncomfortable, yet there was not as much pain as before: the throbbing in the shoulder was scarcely noticeable. That could mean there was not enough blood left in his body; that might be why his heartbeat was irregular. In a little while it could stop. It had been like Longfellow's muffled drum long enough, beating his funeral march to the grave.

He could not move his shoulder—nor his right leg. He didn't seem to care to move them, anyway. All he wanted was to lie still. Even his desire for the aid men was feeble.

"The wounded soldier has ninety-seven chances out of a hundred to recover," he had been told. Red cross machinery was prepared to pick up the wounded and take the worst cases by plane and the others by LST back to American hospitals in England. Sulfa drugs, penicillin, plasma—everything was in favor of ninety-seven percent of the wounded not dying.

But there was that other three percent. Three percent and flies.

He watched an ant crawl across his pale left hand and onto his sleeve. The sun was in the west now; it had been in the east a little while ago when he had been shot. Maybe I've been asleep all this time. I could be dreaming.

He sighed and then sighed again. He'd been doing that a long time now, he realized. Lela had done that once. Seated at the breakfast table in the guest cottage, she had sighed and turned pale. Alarmed, he had carried her to the bed where she'd kept on sighing, unable even to sit up. Her heart had been erratic also, as if it were skipping beats or more likely beating twice in quick succession then resting an instant before deciding it was supposed to keep on beating.

The doctor had given her a transfusion. She'd been as pale as death itself, and he'd stood helplessly beside the bed and watched and suffered until the red showed again in her cheeks and lips, and the eyelids were red inside again rather than the pale pink they'd been when the doctor first examined her.

She had needed blood.

I need it, too, more than the Normandy soil.

He was sighing harder now. Might just never see Lela again standing at the wisteria-shaded porch, laughing with him over some little nonsensical remark one of them had made. No warm kiss, no clinging arms, no lingering over breakfast, chatting of things, planning and hoping. Their boy would go through high school and college and be somebody. In history, he would read of a far-off war, where his father had given his life. War and rumors of war. Pearl Harbor. London bombed. Normandy. They used to sing, "When the lights are on again all over the world."

That Nazi was just a kid, just a kid. "You're government agents, men! You may have to kill a few, but you'll save thousands. This is war! Nations are responsible to God to put down international gangsterism!"

He couldn't lift his arm now to shoo away the flies. There were dozens of them now, but there was no sunlight in his face. It must be hours later.

Faintly now, he heard a voice.

"Poor fellow! How'd you get clear out here? Wonder I ever found you. What'd you do—crawl?"

He remembered now. He'd tried to crawl to a shady place, and that was all he remembered until only a moment ago.

The helmeted aid man was on his knees, doing something—pouring sulfa powder into his shoulder wound and mixing something, too. It looked like water and some yellowish-brown liquid—blood plasma and distilled water, perhaps.

Now there was a tube being inserted in a vein in his arm, at the crook of the elbow, the way the doctor had done it to Lela that day.

The shoulder was throbbing again and beginning to hurt. Joe heard himself groan. He opened his eyes. The face of the helmeted aid man was close to his own. He was listening to his heart beat.

"Feel better now, Pal?"

Joe's answer was a mumbled, "Feel worse, couldn't feel *anything* before. There's a letter in my pocket. If anything happens, answer it for me. Tell her I died loving her; tell her you found me under an apple tree and that I was trying to climb up the hill to Hawthorne's hideout."

"You're bound to get well, Pal," the aid-man said. "The bleeding has stopped and you've got enough plasma to make it until we can get you to an aid station where they'll give you some real blood."

Joe heard himself groan again.

"Too much pain? Sure you have. Here."

Joe felt the needle go into his left arm and felt almost instant relief. He felt cheerful and sleepy. Morphine, perhaps.

"Thanks, Pal," he mumbled.

"And now a little note to the litter men so they'll know what I've done to you—and so the medicos at the station will know."

Joe was already sleepy and relaxed. He could feel the throbbing in his shoulder, but there was no pain. The waves were washing now, lapping at the dockpost.

He brushed at a fly, lifted his hand to brush at it again, and let it fall to his chest. His fingers closed on a bit of cardboard. He forced open his eyes. The cardboard information tag tied to one of his jacket buttons was a bright red, like the juice of the bloodroot that grew on Hawthorne's Haunt.

Red meant *urgent*. Urgent, pounding, sleepy, red, blood shed for the remission of sins. "Just as I am, without one plea."

Chapter 13

Joe was at the beach evacuation post when he regained consciousness. He was feeling cheerful—too cheerful for one whose heart was beating so rapidly. He was thankful for medical science and the fact that there was relief from even the most excruciating pain.

A helmeted aid man passed by, looking at identification tags on a dozen or more wounded men on stretchers on the beach. He stopped beside Joe.

"Oh, there you are. I was looking for you. I won't have to write that letter you mentioned. Here—"

"Letter?"

"You know—you asked me to write to your wife if anything happened. Well, you're going to be OK."

*　*　*

"You're going to be OK!"

Joe, in an American hospital now, somewhere in England, recalled those words spoken on the Normandy beach. If only they were true. It might have been—it could have been, if the weather had been right. Strange, weather could do to a man what mortar and shrapnel had failed to do.

But he wasn't all right, and he never would be. Oh, he would get well and be better off than the thousands who had been killed, never getting beyond the sand of the invasion beach. For so many a wooden cross would mark the spot; for others it was both arms or both legs or a lung or a face. For still others, the body would be intact but the mind would have disintegrated, and they would be like vegetables. A psychic casualty was worse than a physical one. Yes, his lot was better than some who even now lay in the same ward with him.

His lot was better than that of the lad who slept beside him last night, who this morning had been wheeled away to emergency and had not come back.

Tomorrow it would be his turn. He would come back from surgery minus his right leg. There'd been a double fracture back in Normandy; the bone had shattered. Sulfa drugs and careful dressing had first made it look as if the leg could be saved. But the weather had been against him—the weather and the channel that made the evacuation beach a prison where he should have stayed, perhaps, until the wild wind had stopped blowing. But there had been too many wounded coming down for evacuation—too many who couldn't stay for treatment in France but who had to get to England and hospitalization.

He recalled it now. Wind shrieking, waves pounding and breaking against the shore—the same shore whose horror he remembered so well—the wild, terror-filled climb up and up and up, over fallen buddies, over slippery rocks, through bullets and bombs and cries of death before, behind, above. And now he was going home. He had accomplished his purpose. He had killed a German boy, who had died sobbing out his faith in a Mighty Fortress.

How wildly the boat had reared and plunged; it seemed they would never get beyond the surf to the LST two miles out. It had been a mistake, he knew, that they'd decided he should go along. Only the slightly wounded should have been evacuated in such a wind. But it was too late now.

Too late he had realized what might happen as a mighty lurch of the boat tossed him against a buddy who lay beside him on his own canvas stretcher. In his leg he felt another fierce stab of pain.

In calmer weather, they could have ridden smoothly out to the LST in a duck and clambered up the LST's ramp with the ease of a bundle of fodder riding the conveyer into the threshing machine.

It seemed only yesterday, but he knew it was at least a week ago, that he had gone through the nightmare of the evacuation. Without medication, it seemed even worse than the agony on the beach—except there had been no flies, only salt water spray—and the groans and curses of men in pain.

He was aware now of a nurse at his side, saying, "And how is Wisconsin this morning?" She was blue-eyed like Lela and had a dimple in her left cheek when she smiled, which she was doing right now. Lela's smile would dissolve when she learned he was going to be a cripple. He could face most anything except having her know. It was

108

not that she couldn't rise to the occasion, but there would be confusion in her heart until she was strong enough to begin the business of piecing her world together again.

He struggled up the steep slope to the acres of the great god Ra, and then came back to the hospital to answer the polite question of the nurse, "How's Wisconsin this morning?"

He grinned. You were supposed to do that. All GI Joes grinned when a pretty nurse in white came into their ward. "Can't wait until tomorrow," he said. "I'd rather have a surgeon's knife any day than a jagged-edged Nazi bullet."

Just talking, trying to keep his chin up. He couldn't let a smiling nurse think he was down in the dumps.

A buddy in the cot on the other side was grinning, too. He'd come back two days ago and was doing well, minus a leg. He broke in with, "They used a *saw* on me. I heard them filing it for you just as I was leaving. It was dull when they got through with me."

The nurse was alert to the situation. "You had too much iron in your blood, maybe."

He came back with, "One of my legs was too long. That's why I couldn't run fast enough to get out of the way of that shrapnel—not that I was running away, of course."

It was good-natured banter. It went on all the time in the ward— safety valves for surplus steam that could explode a mind. Joe had tried to enter into it, making himself do it while on his couch he lay in anything but in pensive mood. He was doing it, he felt, so as not to spread his own gloom to the fellows who couldn't stand any more than they had already endured.

First, there'd be the operation; then, the long period of struggle, maybe between life and death again; then, more transfusions, more morphine, and more and more. Some of the fellows were already beginning to feel pain where there wasn't any, in order to get the "hypo." It felt so good to drift away into a world of lethargy, where one could live in all the *emotional* faculties of the mind without having to think or worry or plan or be disillusioned. The psychic thrill sometimes persisted for several hours after the shot. The only problem was that a person could become an addict, and then there would be the tortue of withdrawal symptoms that are more excruciating than physical pain.

The nurse slipped a thermometer under his tongue and took his pulse. He knew how fast his heart was beating—117 the last time he had checked it. He knew also that he had a fever. There was— or had been—infection.

The thermometer had been under his tongue five minutes now, while the nurse had gone down the length of the ward, leaving similar "temp sticks" under a dozen other tongues. He wondered how high his temperature was. Had a right to know. A man's temperature reading was no military secret.

He read the thermometer, tucked it under his tongue again, and closed his eyes. The reading was an even 101. Not bad—but trouble. Fever always meant trouble—it also meant his body was still fighting and his blood was still busy carrying away poisons.

"I saw you peep," the nurse said when she stopped again at his cot. "Think that's fair?" Her tone was only playfully stern.

"It's my fever, isn't it? And England's a free country, or is it?"

"Surely—and you're *my* patient."

He had not intended at all to say what he now heard himself saying, but he wanted to seem lighthearted and playful, so it came out: "I am the big bad wolf, and I am going to come down your chimney and eat you up."

"Sorry," she said, "but I'm promised to another bigger, badder wolf over in the other ward."

She was cleansing a place on his arm with alcohol, getting his hypo ready. He watched her skilled movements—how careful she was that there should be no air bubble in the syringe.

With a quick, smooth jab the needle was in. He watched the transparent liquid until the plunger was pressed all the way down. She sealed the prick with sterilized cotton.

A man could believe in God more easily when he saw one He had created giving herself to help others. That was God's chief concern, it seemed. He *so* loved the world that He *gave*. That was part of the last sermon he had heard by Dr. Wellman.

Already his mind was beginning to drift—in the dinghy, riding the waves—and he was remembering to keep his life jacket on, tied so carefully and so surely.

The nurse—or was it Lela?—busied herself at the tray. There were others waiting down the ward.

110

*   *   *

Lela's letters had been giving him strength, lifting his spirits and making him want to get his surgery over as soon as possible and get the healing business into the history section of his mind. Her last letter had ended, "And now, goodbye, darling, I'm praying for you night and day—and waiting, while I'm also waiting for Junior. I've never felt better in my life, and I'm not worrying even a teeny weeny bit, although naturally I'm sobered at the thought, because it's our first. How wonderful to bring a new life into the world, to project our personalities in this way for the potential blessing of the human race!

"I'll miss you, I know, and I'll need you; but Junior and I will wait patiently for your return. Yesterday, I took him up to Cardinal Hill, climbed up to your 'den,' and told him all about you. I guess I stayed away too long, because all of a sudden Daddy came driving around the bend in the dinghy to see if everything was all right. No, I didn't take the boat, I don't go out alone anymore, but I drove your car, coming in by the new lane we'll be using when we move in. Dad and Mother think we'd like a road leading all the way up to a parking area, rather than having to park down below and climb up every time, and I know you'll agree. The contractor is working on a carport now. We're leaving the Cardinal's Nest for your final approval of the plans. I'm making them leave it wild all around, the way nature now has it."

Joe was reading the letter again when Dr. Burnell came through, stopping at every cot in the ward. "Hi, Soldier. How's the foot? Hello, Montana! You're going home next week, according to schedule, I see. For goodness sake, Terry, of *all* the places to get shot! We've got a new ear ordered, and as soon as we can find a tailor—or a seamstress, whichever you prefer—on it goes, and you'll be even more handsome.

"Hi there, Joe. I've been listening for the call of the cardinal, but you never complain." He studied Joe's chart. "Surgery in the morning, eh? You're in good shape. Blood count OK? Morale good?"

"Not too sure about the morale," Joe said.

"Listen, Doc, I—isn't there any way to save the leg? I'll need it when I get home. We'll be living up on a hill, and I'll have to do a lot of climbing."

"We're saving the upper third, as it is. What do you want, the whole leg?"

111

Joe grinned. Doc surely knew how to make the fellows like him. Pleasingly grumpy—purposely so—when every fellow in the ward knew he was 100 percent for him. Being boisterously grouchy was his way of saying "Fellows, I'd take your place right now, if I could!"

"I do want the whole leg," Joe answered.

"We had to choose between saving it and saving you, and we chose you. But we'll order you a new one that'll stand shrapnel, mortar, bayonets, and everything. Fact is, if you'd been wearing it when you struck out across Normandy, you wouldn't have felt anything except that little scratch on your shoulder. You should have had it before you started."

"Seriously," Joe said, "I—"

"People get well faster when they're not too serious."

Joe felt the gray-blue eyes searching his. They were kindly—inviting him to talk. "It's this way, Doc. I have this letter—"

Burnell noticed it lying on the bed. "From home?"

"The little wife."

"Everything all right?"

"She doesn't know about your having to use the saw on me—and how's a fellow going to tell her? I think she's been praying I'd come home safe and sound—like her mother prayed for her father—and he *did* come back from World War I without a scratch."

For the first time Doctor Burnell frowned. "I'm not much of a Christian, Joe. Part of the time I've been anything else *but,* I suppose. But my old dad used to teach us boys a lot of things about the Bible—and he told us we ought to be careful not to ask God for just anything. He put it this way: 'When you pray, you ask for things in the name of the Saviour, and when a person uses *His* name on a check, he'd better be careful how he fills it in. We can't use His name as a sort of magic wand to get only nice comfortable things.'

"I'm guessing your little lady will be able to take whatever she has to take a lot better than if she weren't a Christian. Just as soon as we get you all sewed up and you feel up to it, you get a letter off to her and tell her the truth."

The doctor had his stethoscope to Joe's chest and heart, listening. When he spoke again it was in his usual gruff manner. "The old pump's working like a million dollars. We'll make you a beautiful new leg nobody'il ever see except your family, and you'll be a good hus-

112

band and father and look back on the war as a little interlude—nothing more."

Joe's answer was with a forced gaiety, " 'Quoth the raven, nevermore.' "

"If your shoulder could take it, I'd slap you good and hard on it—just consider it done." And gruff old Dr. Burnell was off down the ward to fire up the morale of as many others as he could.

* * *

"Darling Joe:

"Well, our baby is one month old today, and I'm feeling fine. I'm able to walk around the place. I went all the way down to the dock yesterday, and do you know what? One of our little tiger lady's quintuplets ran along beside me, as well as on ahead, and it was almost as if she was going back to see the place where her mother was the night we adopted her. She's a little darling—the only one with a white streak down her nose.

"When the telegram telling you'd been wounded in action came, it was terribly hard to take—a blow to my faith at first. Then I was reminded—I think by the Holy Spirit—that we do have a God who takes all the pros and cons, as you once said to me, and weaves them into a pattern more beautiful than pros alone could make.

"I think I'm beginning to realize that there is suffering of one sort or another for everybody in this life, and it's how we take it, and by whose strength, that decides whether we can ride the hardest waves. Bringing Junior into the world helped me to see that, I think.

"Now that it's over and I'm well again, it's safe to tell you that Junior was very stubborn about being born, and for a while it looked as if I might not make it. Anyway, that's the way it seemed at the time. I had a wonderful doctor, who recently set up his practice in Wilkerson. But it was one of those nights when a doctor just has too much to do. There was a head-on crash out at Crebs Corners, and the ambulance brought in five teenagers who were a sorry mess of broken bones and cuts—and two of the kids were dead at the scene.

"I heard the sirens going, and radios were on in the houses across the street—and the war news came in through the window.

"Did I tell you about taking a special prenatal course on what to expect, and how to take care of a newborn tiny tot? There are odds and ends of little emergencies that might arise during the first months

113

and years. I feel quite competent—and you can trust me to look after the greatest little guy in the world.

"Oh well, it's over now, and even though the doctor couldn't spend a lot of time with a very slow, young mother-to-be, his nurse was there every spare minute.

"But that's all history. I've been looking through a catalogue of artificial limbs, and in it there are pictures of men and women, some of them famous, who have lived normal lives—at least normal for them—in spite of having only one leg. Joe, darling, my love for you mounts higher and higher, and when I see you again, I know I'll be so happy I can't contain myself. I'll love you more because you've been hurt.

"Oh, Joe, *I love you so!* And I'll be waiting for you just as you are, for no matter what they do to you, you're always my Joe. Must close now. Junior is calling in his own lusty manner. I'm writing this from the green lawn chair by the barbecue pit. Oh, oh, there's a four-leaf clover!

"Always, with all my love,

Lela"

Chapter 14

Very soon now, he would be going home. This morning, as he sat in the little chapel in the hospital listening to Chaplain Conrad's final words of counsel to wounded servicemen, he felt a surge of thankfulness.

The world, with all its terrors and disillusionments, was still a thing of beauty. There was a peace a man could have within his own heart. There were still available the phrase gems of men whose minds walked with trees, sang with birds, and gathered fragrances from all the flower fields of literature. Joseph Cardinal was strolling the little brown paths of Bluebell Island, listening to the call of the cardinal in his own mind.

He had been so proud of the way he could walk; his limp was scarcely noticeable even to himself. Vern Gregg was going back to his Judy Frost, and they would be married and live happily ever after; there had been just enough shadow to make them appreciate the sunshine that God gave to all whose eyes He Himself had opened.

"Be prepared," Conrad was saying. "Brace yourselves for the shock you will get when you discover *how* shocked your friends and relatives —your relatives especially—will be when they see you.

"You will be irritated, and if you show it and make too much of it, it'll be like World War III in your mind. It may seem a little like you've been to hell and back—and it's up to you whether you make a hades out of the world you're going to have to live in."

Sitting with the others in the hospital chapel, Joe's leg was without pain, yet he was aware of every missing toe and even of the ankle and heel.

He felt the chaplain's eyes were focused on him, as if to remind him, "You need what I'm saying, Joe, you'll *really* need it when you get back to your Lela and your Little Joe and to the stares of the home-town folks."

115

He snapped his mind to attention and listened:

"Instead of handing out a list of rules for *you* to be governed by when you arrive at home base, we've devised a set of six rules for the friends and relatives of wounded servicemen. We have ordered it printed in all American newspapers and periodicals. These rules may help make your homecoming a little less rugged. You are not going to be able to hide in a fox hole, but you'll be in full view, and the thought-bullets of both friend and foe will strike hard. You can dodge some of them—but you'll have to be hardened to the rest.

"Here, men, are the rules we hope all your friends and relatives will read:

1. Remember, they are not cripples—they are *men,* human beings.
2. Ignore missing arms, legs, etc. Display no pity or grief.
3. When your man gets home, he will probably enter into a period of lethargy and apathy. He may appear depressed and lazy. This will be a perfectly normal phenomenon. Do not goad him.
4. Don't stare.
5. Never help him unless he indicates he needs it.
6. Remember, the family can irritate more than anyone else."

Family? Joe thought. *How can my wife ever irritate me? How can my son?*

On the battlefield and in the hospital, Lela had been an angel. Her perfection was without even one hint of flaw.

All through the months of recovery and the making of adjustments to his handicap—the weeks of recurring pain, the interludes of self-pity, the emotional upsets, the times when powerful medications had had to be used to calm jittery nerves—Lela's face was before him, the perfect woman, the paragon of faith. There was no perfection like Lela's perfection.

During the days of healing—the waiting weeks and months, the healing for his mind also—he had had long and lonely walks in the valley of the shadow, but there was light ahead, and home. There would be walks and talks in the orchard, togetherness as they climbed the hill to Hawthorne's Haunt, carefree rides across the lake, strolls along the shores of Bluebell Island hand in hand, arm in arm, heart interlocked with heart. There would be times when they would sit across the table from each other in a little café; her eyes would smile contentment, and joy like the New Testament's joy unspeakable would move into his mind.

There would be no more war and frictions at all. Being married to an angel, he would have no need for Chaplain Conrad's rules.

There were also times of deep depression, when his creative mind was like a desert with no oases anywhere. In those times he walked among the books in Conrad's library searching for ideas for his novel, so long interrupted in its creation. He sometimes found strength in the lyrics of Wordsworth, Tennyson, Byron, Longfellow and Holmes. There was a touch of sadness in all their beauty—and there was beauty in their sadness.

In those intervals he moved to the typewriter and tried to capture the colorful thoughts winging in his mind like a thousand migrating monarch butterflies.

On another day he strolled the poetic flower fields with Irish poet Thomas Moore and sang with him a well-known hymn, "Come Ye Disconsolate." In the last line of the first stanza he found release from the chains that bound his mind: "Earth has no sorrow that heaven cannot heal."

It was the final stanza that winged his thoughts back to the States and to Janice Granada's analysis: "You are not an atheist, nor an agnostic, nor a deist, but a *skeptic.*"

> Go, ask the infidel what boon he brings us,
>   What charm for aching hearts can he reveal.
> Sweet as that heavenly promise, Hope, sings us—
>   Earth has no sorrow that God cannot heal.

This same Thomas Moore had written the lyrics for the well-known and much-loved secular number, "The Last Rose of Summer."

And in that poem, also, Joe found new music for his column and for Lela's "Musical Musings on the Masters."

On a particularly depressing day he was searching for yet deeper truth—for solidity beyond the truth of beauty, for truth itself. And he found, like a jewel in a setting of sorrow, from the pen of the beloved disciple, John, these words in John 20:30-31:

"And many other signs truly did Jesus in the presence of his disciples, which are not written in this book: but these are written, that

117

ye might believe that Jesus is the Christ, the Son of God; and that believing ye might have life through his name."

And as he read, it seemed to Joe he had never known it before. He had heard it without hearing it, seen it without seeing it, read it but never really read it, believed it without truly believing it.

In the solemnity of the moment, Joe bowed his head and prayed: "Thank You, O Living Christ. I believe!"

There were tears in his voice as he exclaimed, "I am no longer a skeptic! My war with God is over. I am a believer in Him. I have experienced Him. He has revealed Himself to me through His Son!"

There moved into his consciousness a beautiful exhilaration, a sadness that was gladness, as if a thousand years of blizzard had suddenly dissolved into sunshine.

Knowing the mind of man and the psychology of its workings, he knew this beautiful emotion could not be sustained. It was the moment of the lamp's first lighting. There would be intervals of discouragement, but none that heaven could not heal. There would even be times of miserable *un*awareness. But, he thought, I am a child of God through believing in His name, and I have life eternal now.

He moved to the window, looked out and across the haze of London, and saw faintly, caught in a slant of dusky sunlight, the silhouette of a cross. And he was pleased to hear himself humming a familiar melody:

> In the cross of Christ I glory
> Towering o'er the wrecks of time.

Towering over the war, along with the devastations, the bleeding and dying, the bombs and bullets, the thunder of death, and the crosses that marked unasked-for graves!

There was the sound behind him of someone entering the room.

Turning, he greeted Chaplain Conrad.

"I hoped you would be here," the chaplain said, "there's a new man down in ward 7. He was transferred from the Liverpool hospital. When he learned you were here, he gave me a note to you.

Joe read the slip of paper and said, "Thank you, Chaplain. I'll get to him right away. I was just looking out across the fog or smoke or smog or smaze—whatever it is—and, have you noticed it? The cross? The mists seem to curl around it like Byron's 'mists that round the mountain curled.'

"Did you ever read the little ditty about the great god Ra, whose shrine once covered acres, but Ra himself is now only filler for cross-word puzzle makers?

"I was just thinking about how many of us have had our little shrines blasted out of existence, and only the cross remains."

"That," Conrad answered, "is what has happened to the young fellow in bed 19. I think maybe you can help him."

And Joe, still walking in the aura of his new experience, hurried down the hall, and in a little while was stopping at the designated bed.

"Ned Boynton!" he exclaimed, looking down at the ringleted red hair of the nephew of Charles Boynton—the hair disheveled now and in need of a barber.

Ned reached out a pale hand, clasped Joe's and clung to it. The voice, once heard from the upper berth of the old Pullman car so long ago, was only a rasping, guttural whisper as Ned pointed to his throat: "Bullet!"

Their visit was the fellowship of men who had fought, who had died a little, and for whom World War II was forever history—except that part of it which would hide in the caverns of the subconscious and make itself known to the conscious mind again and again and again.

"They tell me I can learn to talk without vocal cords," Ned wrote in a little notebook. "But it won't be the same. Maybe I'll have to learn to be a writer—if you'll teach me. When Janice found out about it, she wrote a wonderful letter. I think she sees in me another little chick who needs to be adopted; and when I get back, she'll start mothering me in the same way, I'm sure. Wonderful girl—Janice. She'd have made a good missionary. She'd make a good anything— nurse, secretary, missionary, anything to anyone who needed love— and who doesn't?"

Joe read, nodded, and handed back the notebook. There was pain in his heart for this once-strong, vibrant person, who had dedicated himself to go into the world and preach the gospel—even to cannibals.

To Ned, Joe now said, "It's a deal. I'll teach you to write, and you teach me to preach."

To the doctor, just coming into the ward, Joe said as he left, "My friend, Ned Boynton—how's he doing?"

"He had a problem for a while—psychological—but now seems to have an anchor of some kind. He's going to be all right. You notice

119

his clear blue eyes? He talks with them. Some of the fellows are snapping out of their lethargy when they see how the cross he talks about towers over the wrecks they themselves have become. He's been here only a few days, and already he's chaplain to at least six fellows. They send him notes, and he writes back."

"Make *me* number seven," Joe said and walked as if under orders down the long hall. In a few days he would be on the way home.

Lela, with her childlike faith and unbelievable loveliness and understanding, would be so glad of the new thing that had moved into his mind and heart—the realization of the presence of God, which, he was convinced, was the true destiny meant for every man.

Chapter 15

Though it was exhilarating to be going home, it was hard to be leaving England. And it was harder still to leave behind so many whose stay in the hospital was to be long.

He felt something akin to guilt, realizing that he could go back to the States when many were still in the battle theaters. Many would yet suffer wounds severe enough for them to be released; the wounds of others would channel them into eternity. But each must live his own life and walk through his own valley of the shadow.

There was the private farewell to Ned Boynton, who, even yet, dreamed of the time when he could be God's missionary.

"I've learned one thing," Ned wrote, as Joe was making his final stop at bed 19 in ward 7. "When the Lord said, 'The field is the world,' He did not mean just one little corner of it. The field is the *whole* world, and if He has a plan for me in the States, and I can find out what it is, I will be a missionary there."

"Thank you," Joe said in reply, and was surprised to hear from the pillow a guttural whisper, "I have something for you. It's my first try at writing. It's poetry—I think."

Ned reached a pale hand under a pillow and brought out a sheet of paper. He handed it to Joe, and with eyes that looked from deep caverns of heart hunger, he said, "I hope you can use it some way in your column—or maybe in your novel."

That poem Joe carried with him when his ship set out across the Atlantic, and it was still in his possession when he left Chicago for the last two hundred miles to Wilkerson. Lela would love it, and so would Dad and Mother Blanchard, Janice, Charles Boynton, and the readers of "The Call of the Cardinal."

Lela ran into his arms the minute he stepped down from the train, forgetting, apparently, the fact that he might be knocked off balance. But only for a moment. After the embrace, which was so eager, so filled with happiness for her, she released herself and stepped back to look at him. Her eyes leaped to his right shoe. It was the same kind of shoe as the left. "Oh, darling! We're together again!"

There were others there to meet the train—and there were hand-shakes, backslappings, and covert glances toward the place where his right leg had been, and where now, camouflaged with sock, shoe, and pantleg, a new light-metal jointed leg was adjusting itself to service.

Some of the handshakes were a little too enthusiastic, and they made his shoulder hurt—the shoulder where a bullet had shattered the scapula. Both the shoulder and the leg had been aching today, maybe a little more because of the damp weather.

There was rain in the air.

In the car, Lela, at the wheel, said, "I'm sorry. I didn't ask if you'd like to drive. I guess I must have thought—"

He knew she had read the six rules and was trying hard to remember them. She would expect him to be a little on edge.

"There's only one thing I want to do right now," he said, "and that's thank my wonderful wife for keeping her letters coming, for praying, and for bringing our baby into the world safe and sound."

He studied her profile. Her hair looked freshly washed, every strand in place like a young girl prepared for a date. He saw the firm set of her chin; her eyes were straight ahead on the graveled road.

Her answer was in the spirit of their former make-believe: "If you mean the old wolf wants to come down my chimney and eat me up, I'll take you straight to my little brick house."

They were nearing the Y in the road now, where a left turn would take them to the Blanchard place and a right would lead them to the new dock and the path that led up to Cardinal Hill. The little brick house in her mind was probably down near the old beech tree on which they had carved their initials.

He became aware of the rain only when the windshield wipers began their nervous plick-plocking, beating a very determined rhythm, not unlike the breathy raspings of the katydids on hot summer nights: "Katydid, Katydid, Katy-she-did."

"Maybe," she said gently—and it was the same gentle tone she had often used when she was changing his mind about something. "Maybe we should hurry on home now. Aren't you eager to see our Joe! What a wonderful baby God gave us! He's just perfect in every way! His nose is yours, his eyes are blue, his hands are strong, his shoulders are broad, his smile with the dimple in the right cheek is like yours. Joe, darling, nobody's baby was ever so perfect, and I'm not just bragging about myself when I say it but about both his parents."

He'd waited so long, anticipating the moment when he could take her in his arms and whisper his love, feel the warmth of her kiss, and know once more the way a husband felt when his wife's head was resting on his shoulder.

And now rule number six dropped its bomb: "Remember, the family can irritate more than anyone else." He felt the flame of anger burning in his mind. It was a terrible feeling to have at a time like this. He hated it, remembered his artificial limb and the pain in his shoulder—and he heard Charles Boynton saying, "Self-pity is a great crippler."

When he was silent and the car swept on toward the Blanchard estate, she spoke gently, as if she were sorry about rule six, even more sorry than he: "I'm hungry too. Starving, in fact. But we've got all the rest of our lives to have roast pig for dinner. It *could* rain hard any minute, and it's time for Junior's feeding."

And in that moment, Joe Cardinal, Sr., realized he now had a rival in the family—a perfect baby with whom he must share his time and attention.

"Fine," he answered her, and felt the sharp jab of his words in his own heart. "And while you and my rival are together, I'll be walking out beside the lake, beneath the trees."

She pressed the brake pedal, the car slowed, and she reached across with her right hand and pressed his knee in a gesture of understanding.

He asked now, "Did *The Silver Lining* publish the six rules for relatives?" His voice was raised, to drown out the rasping katydids, and her answer was also necessarily loud: "I memorized them. And if I ever break even one of them, I want you to tell me. Promise?"

"I promise," he answered, and swallowed. She didn't even know she had hurt him by squelching a dream of many months.

He did not dare let her know she had hurt him, for *that* would hurt *her*.

"One of these days soon we'll drive baby Joe to Cardinal Hill, climb to your hideaway, where I've spent a lot of time lately myself, planning, hoping, dreaming, and loving a lot, and we'll read Browning to him. I want him to be like his father: poetic, kind, gentle, a bit of a dreamer, and a person who could never knowingly hurt another.

"In fact, just the other day, I was reading to him while he nursed. We were in the orchard at the time, and I was especially lonesome for you, so I read something by Wordsworth I'd never seen before. It was:

> The best portion of a good man's life—
> His harmless, aimless, unremembered acts
> Of kindness and of love.

"I said to Junior, 'Wordsworth was writing about your father.' Dad came along while I was reading—and crying. Yes, I was crying, and with every tear I was loving somebody named Joe Cardinal, Sr."

Beside her, Joe now thought, *First the knife, then the anesthetic. But she doesn't know—and I shall not tell her.*

"Dad stood looking down at me; then, as he does when he sees Mother or me crying, he said, 'Women cry when they are sad, when they are happy, when they are lonely, and when they love somebody so much it hurts. Women are wonderful.' Then he lowered his bee veil and went on to the apiary.

"As soon as I knew he was gone, I turned to my favorite passage in Browning, and read the lines you were always quoting to me: 'How do I love thee? Let me count the ways.' Just for my own comfort, I started to count, and I discovered I needed an adding machine."

Her voice choked, and he thought, *Women cry when they love somebody so much it hurts. Maybe I'm too sensitive. I might just need to heal an ugly little wound in my own character.*

The light shower was over and the sun was breaking through when they turned into the Blanchard lane, and the car nosed slowly up the lilac-bordered drive.

Lela's father and mother were on the porch swing at the time. They came hurrying out. In Mother's arms, cradled in a receiving blanket, was baby Joe.

"Here!" Lela cried excitedly. "Let Joe have him. Let him hold him!"

Joe looked for the nose that was Joe Cardinal's nose, the strong hands, the broad shoulders, the blue eyes, and the smile. The nose was buried in a fighter's fist, the eyes were closed, and the perfect baby had no welcome for his father at all. What did a little tike like him care about a father anyway?

In Joe's arms, the baby with the closed blue eyes, the strong hands, the broad shoulders, and missing smile was a dead weight. Joe felt what he had hoped was a new father's pride and was surprised and disappointed that it was not a stronger emotion.

He carried his sleeping son toward the house, walking as much like a soldier in a parade as he could. The others, walking behind him, could notice his limp and maybe even the shoulder which, in spite of all he could do, drooped a little. The missing scapula would have left an identation except for the padding in his coat.

Lela would have to find out about the shoulder, which he hadn't had the heart to tell her about in his letters. He would prepare her ahead of time so she wouldn't have to fight too hard not to notice.

Chapter 16

Because the rain would have made the grass on Cardinal Hill too wet for enjoyment and because, to her, at the moment, Joe Junior was the most important thing in the world—they postponed until tomorrow their visit to their new homesite.

During the night rule 6 came mercilessly alive.

If only the perfect baby had been more cooperative! He kept waking and crying, sleeping for brief intervals, and whimpering for some uncomfortable reason. And there was the problem of his feeding.

"You sleep, dear," Lela told her husband. "This is a mother's responsibility. Besides, I can get to him quicker—I mean—"

She *was* trying hard not to offend, he thought. He'd had to show her the new artificial limb, the one that could have taken a bullet and there would have been no pain. He had told her about grumpy old Dr. Burnell and his contagious humor. "See? The wound has healed perfectly. I use this powdery solution on the stump to keep it lubricated and to keep it from hurting when I walk. That's a lot of weight to put on it—my 157 pounds!"

When she first saw the wandering, many-stitched scar on his shoulder, she gasped. Then she scolded him gently. "You should have told me. You don't ever need to be afraid of my reactions. But I love you for not wanting to hurt me."

"Let *me* count the ways," he said. "You're always counting yours, and it's not fair for me not to get a chance." He knew he was talking lightly, but he was thinking about wounds and about the One who was wounded for our transgressions. In a few minutes now he could begin to tell her of his "great awareness."

"There's something I want to do," she told him—and before he could say, "What?" Joe Junior interrupted with the little whimper that

126

warned of something wrong in his crib—or maybe nothing wrong— maybe only a baby's way of demanding attention.

"Remember what I used to tell you Mother always did when I fell or hurt myself or got a drawer slammed on my finger? She'd give me a kiss where the pain was, and it always made it feel better." She kissed the scar.

Joe Junior was making himself heard now with dynamic wailings. In the shadows of the night light, Joe Senior watched his wife move hurriedly to the bassinet, heard her gentle cooings, saw her doing little things only a mother knew how to do, and thought, *She has two babies to look after now.*

It seemed to be a night for crying. From the orchard there was the uninterrupted buzzing of the cicadas—harvest flies, the ranchers called them—their lonely, persistent whirring rising and falling but always on the same pitch.

Once Joe Senior wakened with a cry of his own, and Lela came quickly to his rescue.

He heard her calling as from a distance, "Joe! Joe, darling! You're having a nightmare!" She shook him as she used to, and his waking was abrupt and confusing—and filled with pain. She had done the inadvertent thing, not remembering his shoulder.

"Sorry," he apologized and then made himself say, facetiously, "I ought to think of others when I'm asleep like that. Why bother my wife with what goes on in the attic?"

In the past, they had always told each other what their dreams had been, but this time he could not. This was one memory he hoped he might never have to share with her. "Did I say anything? Was I calling for help, or anything?"

"I don't think so, but you were saying something about a teenage kid. It'll be a long time before our Junior will be a teenager, so you just go right back to sleep and give him a dozen more years. Then we can start worrying about his adolescent problems."

He sighed, "Thanks for waking me."

She had to go again to Junior's crib, and while she was gone he prayed: "This is going to be a hard thing, Father, remembering the boy and the bayonet. Help me nòt to think morbidly. Don't let it become a wallowing place."

He could, by the power of will, refuse to make a slough of despair out of the Normandy orchard. That is, he could during his waking hours. But what could a man do while he slept, when his subconscious mind, which, psychologists claimed, never tires and never sleeps, tore itself loose from all inhibitions and sometimes indulged itself in orgies of terror?

Right now Joe wished something rational could be done about war. If the individuals or groups of individuals who initiated it had to do all the fighting and dying—and living lives that were only half lives— if they could spend just one day in the body of a man who must live in a dilapidated house of blood and bones and mind—or of *no* mind, with the psyche twisted and deformed—or if for only a brief time they could know the tortured confusion of being a vegetable—

Lela was still doing things at Junior's crib when the "great awareness" came again.

Perhaps it was the night light near Junior's crib and Lela's quiet movements that made him remember Leigh Hunt's "Abou Ben Adhem," or else it was the slant of moonlight on the framed painting of an angel on the wall.

The drama of the brief poem moved swiftly through his mind— Abou Ben Adhem's awakening and his vision of the angel writing in a book of gold the names of those who loved the Lord.

> "And is mine one?" said Abou. "Nay, not so,"
> Replied the angel. Abou spoke more low,
> But cheerily still; and said, "I pray thee, then,
> Write me as one who loves his fellow-men."
>
> The angel wrote, and vanished. The next night
> It came again, with a great awakening light,
> And showed the names whom love of God had blessed—
> And lo!. Ben Adhem's name led all the rest!

Memorized in the little grade school of long ago, this poem had remained a growing thing in Joe's subconscious. Tonight it brought its own light, and he was identifying himself with Ben Adhem and feeling the love of God, greater than the light of sun or moon, shining within him and all around him.

He was responding to that love. In his thoughts he was standing in Chaplain Conrad's library and seeing a gray cross caught in the swirl of a London fog. He remembered reading Adelaide Proctor's

"The Triumph of Time" and thinking how the flowers that grow on pine-starred hills or bloom in Flanders fields would always fade. Man's bright hopes, watered with tears, would suffer the desert winds of swiftly passing time, and wither.

But the love of God could never change, nor could it ever die. "Hush, for the ages call," Proctor wrote. "The love of God lives through eternity, and conquers all!"

In the aura of that morning in London he had gone down to ward 7, bed 19, to visit—and to be startled by what he saw: a strong, brilliant young man diminished to a skeleton, with no voice with which to preach the gospel of the incarnate I Am, the One who had lived and died, and who had been buried and raised so that those who believe in Him might have life in His name. Ned Boynton, who lived as if the power of the resurrection were within him, was going to adjust to a handicap and learn to *write* the gospel.

With the coming of the "great awareness" tonight, less dramatic than when it had first moved into his consciousness, came also a still small voice. It was not audible but was a quiet yearning to use an already developed talent to tell the world of the love of God, that lives through all eternity. Men must be taught not to fight and devour one another.

When Lela was beside him again, he said, "Tomorrow, I want to tell you something wonderful."

"The same old story, or something new?"

"It has to do with an old, old story." This was all he felt he should tell her tonight. It would not have been easy for Ben Adhem to tell his dream that night to anyone but God.

A little later he heard Lela sleeping and felt the peace in his heart a husband feels when he knows that all is well with his wife, that he has done nothing to cause her heartache, and that she can sleep the sleep of a little child who has been lovingly tucked into bed with a kiss.

* * *

They were in the orchard when he began to tell her. They'd strolled all the way down to the dock and back, and he had been feasting his hungry thoughts on memories, stopping now and then to inspect locations he had loved long since and lost awhile. He was, at the moment, studying critically the now-healing scar on the Jonathan apple tree. "Give that tree a little more time—and a little loving care, of course—and the wound will be only a memory. And what's one little memory, if the tree itself keeps on bearing fruit? Scars are not for display. If possible, they should be hidden by fruit—right?"

Her eyes were studying the tree. One of the lower branches was loaded and hanging low with apples. He heard her humming a familiar melody, one he had loved since boyhood, a part of Americana for many years: "In the Shade of the Old Apple Tree." Then she spoke. "I think I will always love that little ditty. It makes me feel like a young lover again."

"Only *again?* Has there been an interruption of some kind?"

"True love doesn't have interruptions or vacations or funerals. It lives always. But sometimes it gets a new burst of life, as if it may have had a little nap and has wakened refreshed. It's always there, even though it may not at the moment desire to express itself."

He rested his cane against his knee. Now, he was sure, was the time to tell her of his own reawakened realization of God.

He began by quoting a line he had discovered in Chaplain Conrad's library in London: "British novelist Charles Kingsley, one-time professor of modern history at Cambridge, wrote almost a hundred years ago, 'Never lose an opportunity to see anything beautiful. Beauty is God's handwriting.' "

He turned to her, lifted her chin, and studied her eyes. "At the risk of seeming overly sentimental, I *have* to say, I know a certain person who herself is the handwriting of God."

She sighed, "Thank you, but you don't always see the real me. Oh, Joe, I'm so happy. God has been so good to bring you back."

He had not meant to sound pessimistic or to ask for sympathy. He only wanted to introduce the theme that was like a new sunrise in his heart: "He didn't bring back all of me; somewhere in an unmarked grave is that part of me which is missing in action." He tapped his ankle with the cane.

Then, after an interval, he moved into his story—of the cross that rose above "the mists that round the mountain curled," and of the words of the Apostle John, which he had seemed to understand for the first time: "These are written, that ye may believe that Jesus is the Christ." This was the new and beautiful realization he had of the presence of Christ.

130

The rustling of the leaves of the apple tree, the drone of bees in the adjacent apiary—these were also the handwriting of God, as if to confirm the words of the Book, "That believing ye might have life through his name."

"Why," he now said, "should I have to go all the way to London to find what was within the reach of simple faith? Why Normandy and the boy and—"

He stopped. What had he almost told her? He must be careful. Quickly he lifted his right foot, tapped it with the point of his cane, and continued. "A little loss, a little time, in exchange for a bigger slice of eternity." He reached up, picked an apple, handed it to her, and quoted from the Song of Solomon: "Comfort me with apples."

Again there was silence as she turned the apple in her hands. She was first to speak, "Remember what Elizabeth said about her losses? 'God bless all our losses.' "

He remembered.

"I've been waiting to tell you that your wife has accepted what God in His providence has allowed to happen to us. And when we face life together, for better or for worse, even the worse can be better, don't you think? It's like something I read in one of *The Silver Lining's* new columns the other day—Daddy has decided we need one on the problems of young marrieds. Here's what it says, 'In the world's broad field of battle, in the homemakers' bivouac of life, it must always be *us* against the world; never you against me, nor me against you, but only *us,* and forever.' "

He felt her warm tears against his cheek and said gently, "When your tears flow down *my* cheek, that's true togetherness."

"And now that you've let me have my way—made you see our baby first—and waited all night, we can drive around to see what the builders have done to our home."

There was a brief delay while she ran into the house to see if Mother Blanchard had Junior under control—or vice versa—and then they were driving out onto the highway. "He's perfect in the daytime," she said gaily. "Never causes any trouble, naps on time, calls for his meals on time, gurgles and coos almost every waking minute—and only the first night his daddy is home does he decide to show who's boss around the place."

They came to the Y in the road and took the lane that led to the new dock built especially for the future residents of Cardinal Hill.

Jestingly, he said, "I wonder if there are any bigger fish in the lake than the beautiful one I landed a few years ago."

"I've been wondering that myself. I landed a fish, too, you know, that same night."

Contentment rode beside them as they drove through their happy past into a happier future. Familiar places along the lane caught his eye—goldenrod tossing haughty plums, tall mullein stalks, spangled with yellow flowers, standing like miniature saguaros, and at the end of the lane, near the horseshoe-shaped dock where the Blanchard dinghy was often moored, the wide-spreading beech on whose bark someone had carved a heart with a cupid's arrow piercing it.

The beautiful beech, so solemn and so gay, had made no protest against the wounds made by the knife of love, he thought.

Lela spoke now, as the car nosed up to the tree and stopped: "This tree always reminds me of Kilmer's poem." She quoted the first two lines:

> I think that I shall never see
> A poem lovely as a tree.

"How sad that Joyce Kilmer had to die so young," he commented, remembering a column he had written in his pre-Normandy days. With the help of Janice who had done the research and with this very tree in mind, he had begun:

"In deserving pride, the beech tree said, 'I am different from other trees. Frost does not take my leaves, as it does those of the flamboyant maples. Mine cling to me to keep me warm all through the winter. I make lonely hearts glad when they see me silhouetted against a snowbound hill, especially when the sky is blue and the sunshine bright. The sun gets its brightness from me, you know.' "

Janice, in her research, had learned that Joyce Kilmer was Joyce *Albert* Kilmer—"Joyce" was sometimes used as a masculine name—and almost with a sob she had said when she handed him her data, "He was only thirty-two when he died. He was killed in World War I."

"I loved your column," Lela now said. "It almost broke my heart when I thought of a mind like that being snuffed out when he was still so alert and so filled with dreams."

132

Joe remembered the epitaph on little Jimmie Granada's tombstone and thought, Kilmer had sacrificed much more than his strong, young body. He had given his mind also, with all its potential, with never a chance to sing again nor to create a song for others.

She led him past the tree toward the boat house, planned before he had been inducted. With a key from her ring she unlocked the door, opened it, stepped back—and it was like the raising of the curtain on a spotlighted stage.

Riding the waves which lapped gently at its stern was a white powerboat with a flaming red cardinal painted on its prow.

He swallowed, his eyes moist. Almost everything he had seen since coming home was an expression of her love.

"Let me count the ways *you* love *me*," he said and thought how very much he would like to take the helm now and go flying out across the lake. Even on a stormy day, the *Cardinal* would be the master of wind and wave.

"See?" Lela's gay exclamation brought him back. She pressed a switch on the shelter's facade and an overhead garage door lifted. She pressed it again and it lowered.

"Ready now for your next little surprise?" she asked. "You have to be blindfolded first. You aren't allowed to look until we get all the way there."

She led him up the slope. "OK now! Off with your blindfold!"

He waited briefly, his eyes still closed, remembering the architect's plans drawn up and OK'd before he had been inducted and wondering now what he would see—the area still very much as he had left it or a house in the process of being built?

It was unbelievable, the panorama which now crowned the once-devastated shrine of the great god Ra: A beautiful home, strikingly landscaped, with flagstone walks losing themselves in the woods and a paved drive leading to a double garage. The entrance was shaded by a spreading ponderosa; pink panelling and trim set off the cedar siding; the foundation was veneered with red rock, matching the stone fireplace chimney; grass was growing on the landscaped lawn; and a rose trellis boasted a climber in its initial stages of growth.

For a moment he indulged an alien thought: What had they done to his own private domain on the overhang?

When he looked, he saw nothing to indicate any building had been

133

done there, only the winding juniper-bordered footpath leading to the mesa-like area above. It was still crowned with maples and aspen and he hoped—and would soon know for sure—still carpeted with wild flowers. He could see the splintered spire of the ponderosa pointing toward the sky like a finger of faith.

Beneath that steeple he would build first his replica of Thoreau's cabin of a hundred years ago. There, in the solitude that would be his most enjoyable companion, he would write as he had when he was only fifteen in the lake country of the north. From this rustic throne he would broadcast the ideas and ideals with which the locker of his mind was filled to overflowing.

"The Call of the Cardinal" would still be heard. As before, the column would be a call to peace, only now there would be new and different modifications, a metamorphosis of the original theme, with overtones of the music of the Creator of all music.

Lela broke into his reverie to exuberate, "When Daddy learned what had happened to you in Normandy and thought how we might like to walk into the finished home, just as we had planned it, we all decided to go ahead. Isn't it beautiful? Don't you love it! And just wait until you see the inside. Janice designed Junior's room, and set it up for us."

"Janice?"

Her answer seemed evasive—or was it apologetic? "Oh, that was another surprise. Dr. Halford Raymond is the new doctor I wrote you about, who had recently set up his practice in Wilkerson. And his part-time nurse is Janice Granada. I'll be eternally grateful for all she did for us when Joe Junior was born. Your former secretary has also been helping Daddy with *The Silver Lining*—proofreading and taking care of some of the fan mail for the feature columns. There was just too much to do, what with the new column for young marrieds. That column is drawing an avalanche of mail. Janice thinks it ought to be syndicated and go all over the world."

"Janice!" he repeated. She had moved to Wilkerson. She was taking over Dad Blanchard's office, taking over Lela, helping with the interior decorating of the home of the Joe Cardinals, and designing their son's room!

Lela seemed to have sensed that he was displeased, for she said, "She's been wonderful, so helpful, always being sure we approved

134

before making any major decisions or editorial changes. And it was just as if she felt *The Silver Lining* and the various features were her own special responsibilities."

Joe postponed his desire to climb to Hawthorne's Haunt and moved with his radiant wife toward the front stoop. At the door she handed him the keys, saying, "Your house, sir."

He unlocked the door, held it open to her, and with a gesture of gallantry, stooped, lifted her, and with faltering stride, carried her inside. He was all the way in before she remembered, quickly released herself, and said, "Oh, my darling husband! You shouldn't have!"

"Physically, no. Mentally, *yes*," he answered, and entered into her dream.

He followed her as one in a labyrinth of wonder, while his greater desire was to climb to the overhang.

The new house, just as they had planned it before he had been inducted, was—or should have been—a delight to his heart: the cabineted kitchen, the living room, the fireplace with bookshelves on either side, and, down the wide hall, rooms on either side—for their future children, each to have a room of his own.

In the alcove of an ell, planned originally for a small nature center, was a large office-type desk, an executive chair, file cabinet, and, shelved on a windowless wall, an artistic arrangement of knickknacks and reference books. The titles of some of the books caught his eye: *Mothercraft, Bible Mothers, Bible Babies, Birds of the Midwest, Roget's Thesaurus, Your Baby's Name, Old English Furniture, Dictionary of First Aid, A Parent's Guide to Better Babysitting, Husband Care, Cat Culture, One Thousand Beautiful Things,* and a dictionary. One book among them all captured his attention. Its title, *Just Enough Shadow,* startled him. The author's name below the title was simply "Cardinal."

Calmly he said, "I see your husband has finished his new book. I thought it was still in manuscript—and only half done."

She seemed to feign indifference, "Oh?" Then she reached for it and handed it to him. "I had an artist do us a colorful jacket, and I've wrapped it around another book just to see how it would look on a shelf."

"I like the art work," he said.

135

"The idea of a night scene, with a three-quarter moon nesting in the top of the evergreen—does that remind you of anything?" she asked.

His answer was: "I have never needed to be reminded. I never forget it."

When he had released her, he complimented her with: "Why *shouldn't* you have a working library? You're a writer, too—as well as mother, chief cook, babysitter, homemaker, husband-pacifier and inspirer. Oh—oh! I see your husband has written another book."

He slipped out of its place another "dummy" book with a strikingly colorful dust jacket,—another night scene, a boat tossing violently in the midst of a storm, a jagged lightning flash streaking through wildly rolling clouds—and beyond the shadows, streamers of light fanning out from the horizon, focalized in the red fire of a rising sun.

Hanging in an arc just above the horizon, in letters of gold, was the book's title: *East of the Shadows*. Superimposed on the crest of a wave was the figure of a man in white, with outstretched arms, moving toward the terrified crew of two in the floundering little bark.

In the lower right hand corner of the jacket was: "A novel by Joe Cardinal."

Joe stood immobile, his hands clasping the book.

She smiled brightly. "You like it?"

"Very much, but usually I don't decide on a title before I've written the book."

"You *have* written it, almost all of it. All you have to do is bring Vern and Judy out of their shadows and set the sail of their beautiful little boat so the storm itself will drive them toward a sunrise made especially for them. You see—"

"Before I decide whether I like it—how much, I mean—I need to know whose idea it was, yours or—"

Her answer was with a smile and a little gesture of humility: "I borrowed a phrase from Henley's 'Thick Is the Darkness.' Remember? 'Dawn harbors surely, East of the shadows.' "

Their eyes met and clung. Then he said, "That day in classroom B was the day our own little boat set sail for our own very special sunrise."

After an interval of tenderness he suggested, "And now the tour

136

may continue. Lead on, my dear Queen Midas. What else have you turned to gold?"

From the master bedroom they stepped across the hall. "This, Your Majesty, is Junior's den. Isn't it adorable?"

It was astonishing, artistic, and just right. All in pink, sailing ships on one wall, toys, and a giant panda sitting upright in a canopy crib whose hardwood frame, including the panels, was finished in ivory enamel with pink and gold shading.

"See?" she demonstrated. "The canopy is high enough for a mother to take care of a baby without having to stoop—or for that matter, high enough for a *father* to do it, while the mother gets her beauty sleep."

He was not sure he *ought* to like it. It reminded him of a portable throne. On it a crowned Joe Junior could be carried down the street, his followers crying "Long live the King" or "God save the King" or "Heil Hitler" or something. It introduced the thought of the great god Ra whose shrine once covered acres.

The illusion faded, and on the throne was Queen Janice.

"You *don't* like it!"

His answer was: "Should I? Wouldn't she expect me to?"

There was an arena in his heart. Everywhere he went and in every conversation and situation, it was Janice. Janice did this, Janice thought of that, Janice came up with a positively brilliant idea.

When they were in the hall again, he asked, "How *much* of the interior decorating was planned by Queen Janice?"

She must have sensed how he felt, for she asked: "Do you really mind? She's been such a dear, and so helpful, so completely self-effacing. She's been like a second mother—a sort of fairy godmother. I don't know what I would have done without her at times."

He turned to her and spoke in a tone he afterward felt was too stern, "It's this way, Lela: I married just one woman—not two—and I think I should warn you of something you may not wish to hear—if you give Janice enough rope, she won't hang herself with it, she'll tie *you* hand and foot. She'll do your thinking for you. She'll make all your plans and then convince you that you thought of them first."

She drew back. "I'm sorry," she said, "but you don't understand. Her friendship has been wonderful. I've never told anyone, but if it hadn't been for her, our Junior might not have been born, and you might not have had a wife at all. The doctor was in emergency surgery at the time, and only Janice seemed to know how to help me. We owe a lot to her, and yet she never acts as if she expects any kind of reward. She only wants to help. She actually cried for joy when Joey gave his first cry announcing his arrival."

"OK! OK!" he said, and wrestled against the giant of resentment in his mind. He decided now it simply would not do to tell her that once upon a time Janice Granada had been in love with him—and very probably still was.

"And now," she announced, as if determined to erase the friction between them, "the most important of all."

They climbed the hill together and found the mesa just as he had left it—the flower fields, the silver maples, the evergreens, the fallen ponderosa bole, and one thing more. Her eyes were alight with anticipation as she watched, waiting for his reaction. Beside the log was a neat standard on which was lettered in old English: HAW-THOREAU HOUSE

He turned to her. "You're a genius! The name is perfect. How'd you ever think of it!"

"Well, women have an intuition."

"Women? Plural?"

"I," she answered, "thought of it myself. I *do* have a mind of my own—as you may be finding out, and for which I am sorry if I shouldn't have."

The atmosphere of rule 6 was fast fading.

In his mind Joe visualized the completed Hawthoreau House. He became enthusiastic, "It will be just ten-by-fifteen, with only one window—on the north facing the lake. Just a little, one-room cottage like the one I used to work in when I was fifteen, only it'll be a little more weatherproof."

He did not welcome her suggestion when she said, "But that will be too small—a little bit—I mean—or maybe it won't. *I'm* sorry!"

He moved out of his dream to realize he must have indicated his displeasure at her trying to help him build his dream house or she would not have apologized.

"I'm sorry, too," he said, and sought her hand.

After a brief interval of adjustment in which neither of them spoke, she asked, "Are you going to build your house of wood, of straw, or of brick?"

He shrugged, "Will it make any difference?"

"Of course! When your wife gets lonely to hear your voice or see your face, and comes huffing and puffing up the hill, she wants the kind of house she can blow in."

Seeing the love-hunger in her eyes, he said, "You, little pig; me, big, bad wolf." And he began to eat her up.

A vagrant breeze stirred the maples and set the needles of the pines to sighing, but the two seemed not to notice—not until there was a sound behind them—like Riley's "husky, rusty russel of the tossels of the corn."

Lela, hearing first, said, "Look! We have company. Another spy— not a cute little kitten but a wood rat."

Joe looked where she indicated, caught a glimpse of the intruder— a long-haired, yellowish-brown and black, prominently whiskered rodent, working its way along the trunk of the fallen ponderosa. It was visible for only a few seconds. Then, either from fear or from surprise because his domain had been invaded by the human species, it scooted across the open space to the ponderosa stump, darted around it, and disappeared.

"You must have frightened him," Lela said. "He's not used to seeing a man around the place. He and his wife have a nest in an outcropping over there. I've been feeding him—and maybe shouldn't have, but it was so much fun—and every time I came back up, he had brought me some little tidbit in exchange. Once I lost a hair curler, and he actually had found it and deposited it right here."

"I thought they were nocturnal—worked secretly, and only at night."

"That's what I thought, too. But Daddy says no, that sometimes, whenever it suits their fancy, they let themselves be seen. Says it's their curiosity."

Joe sighed, "The storybook didn't say anything about a bushy-tailed wood rat interrupting the big, bad wolf while he was eating up his favorite little pig."

"Sorry, I forgot. Besides, I don't remember which one of us *was* the old wolf anyway."

It didn't seem to matter. After such a long and anguished separation they had regained their paradise, and it was going to be better than before.

Startlingly now, there was the sound of a motor in the area below, a car door opening and a man's voice calling, "Lela! Joe! Come quickly! Something's wrong with Junior, and Mother doesn't know what to do!"

Chapter 17

Lela found Joe Junior on the wide bed in the downstairs living room. The baby's eyes were rolled up, his body was twitching, and his breath was coming in heavy gasps. He was frothing at the lips and tossing about convulsively. She heard Eloise Blanchard at the telephone calling desperately for Dr. Raymond: "But we *have* to have help! He's going wild."

One fear swept into Lela's mind when she saw *how* wild he was acting. One fear, one hope, and one quick instinctive action. She jerked off the blanket Mother had put over him in which he was entangling himself. The prenatal clinic she had attended the month before his arrival had been very specific about how to give first aid for convulsions.

"Don't take time, as the popular notion once was, to put the child into a bathtub of water. That is dangerous, as the child may hurt himself on the sides of the tub—or get out of control and drown. Sponge him instead. Keep on sponging him, first one arm, then the other, the legs, the chest, and the back. He may be having a high fever, and this will reduce the fever. Don't cover him with blankets! Not while you are trying to get his temperature down."

Why doesn't he respond! she thought. *Why does he keep on twitching? They said convulsions didn't usually last long unless something is seriously wrong. What is wrong! If he keeps on thrashing about, he'll hurt himself. He'll bit his tongue!*

When his first two lower incisors had come through at only four months, Dad Blanchard had expanded his chest and said, "It's a sign of intelligence, when a baby teethes early!" which of course it wasn't. Mother, hearing the jesting claim, had deflated him with, "George Blanchard, if I remember correctly what your mother told me, you sprouted *your* first lower incisor when you were *eight* months old."

And dear old Dad, wise in the ways of pricking dangerous balloons, remarked, "Oh, well, the *exceptionally* intelligent humans *teethe* later."

Joe Junior, writhing now and still frothing at the mouth, had recently pushed through his first *upper* incisor, and of late he had been drooling and biting and fretting. He *could* bite his tongue.

"Mother!" called Lela. "Get me a clothes pin—one of the wooden ones."

"Clothes pin?"

"Please!"

Lela inserted the soft wooden clothespin between the jaws to keep them separated and to save the precious tongue from possible injury. She held it in place with one hand, and with her free hand she kept on sponging her child. "My child," she prayed. "Joe's and mine—and *Yours!* There's a future out there for him, somewhere, and You've given us the job of taking care of him, preparing him for it—*saving* him for it."

It had been a wild ride—leaving the lake and following the narrow lane out to the graveled road, with Joe's command in her mind: "You go, Lela! I can't get down the hill fast enough! Take the car and *go!* Dad and I will come in *his* car!"

Never had such a short ride seemed so long, and never had her heart pounded with more fear. As always, she sought for strength from the truths stored in her memory. Somewhere in her subconscious was the needed medication for her aching heart—to control her panic and to keep her steering carefully.

> God is never so far off
> As even to be near;
> He is within; our spirit is
> The home He holds most dear.

During Joe's absence, in her moments of meditation alone with the Book, watching the orchard birds busy with homemaking and thinking of Joe in Europe, eager for some word from him to say that he was all right—some word that God had protected him and that he still loved her—she had felt the strength that came from companionship with God.

But now, as on the lonely night of Junior's birth, she was on her own battlefield, and Joe Junior was in desperate need of a mother in control of herself. Mother Eloise did not know what was wrong, and she had sent Dad for help. Joe Junior was on a battlefield also, and there was no guarantee that he would come out unscathed—if he came out at all.

She swung into the drive at the Blanchard ranch, drove down the lane, skidded to a stop near the side porch, and was out of the car and into the house in time to hear Mother say into the phone, "But we have to have help! He is going wild!"

And then Lela had taken over.

She kept on stroking the trembling little body with her wet hand, holding the clothespin in place, keeping little Joe on his side so that if he should vomit, he would not choke—another reason for keeping his jaws apart.

She remembered now, also, and this helped a little: "If you cannot reach the doctor immediately, don't worry. The convulsion is usually over before the doctor can get there."

Don't worry! Don't worry! Don't worry!

Am I worrying?

What *is* worry! If it is intelligent concern that does something about the *cause* of worry, then a little worry might be good.

Please!

There was the sound of a car in the drive now—and voices. Dad Blanchard and Joe Junior's father.

Calm now, Lela.

"Just a normal little-child convulsion," she said, when Joe was at her side. "It should be over any minute now. At the clinic I learned it's usually over before the doctor can get there. In times like these, when most doctors are in surgery in the mornings—"

"He's vomiting!" Dad Blanchard exclaimed. "Get him over on his face so he won't swallow anything!"

"The bed's too soft," Joe put in. "The way he's tossing around, it's better to keep him on his side or he might smother."

By the time the doctor's car had swung into the drive and stopped, a relaxed Joe Junior was asleep in his mother's arms, and the tornado of fear was past.

It was not the doctor, however, who had come, but his nurse, Janice Granada.

Joe saw her push open the car door and come hurrying to the

house, a doctor's bag in her hand and her nurse's uniform crackling. There was efficiency even in her walk—determination and an air that said, "I'll know exactly what to do."

"Everything's just fine," Lela announced. "It was just a little convulsion—nothing too serious. Have you met my husband? Joe, your former secretary, Miss Janice Granada, and now research secretary for *The Silver Lining,* also Dr. Raymond's part-time nurse."

Lela startled him for the moment by adding, "You two run on out to the lawn and reminisce awhile, till I get this little trouble-maker taken care of. I'll be out in a few minutes."

The few minutes stretched to fifteen before Junior was fully cared for.

In Joe's mind, the storm was past, but its remains were like Shakespeare's description of a woman's temper: "Yet working after storm."

He offered Janice a chair near the barbecue pit and seated himself across from her, studying her serious blue eyes and thinking, *Anybody oughtn't to hate anybody.*

"You're very fortunate, Joe—Mr. Cardinal—to have married a girl with such good judgment and such presence of mind in an emergency like that. I'm afraid that even with my nurse's training, if it had been my baby, I wouldn't have done as well."

He looked across the lake to Bluebell Island. "You'd have done all right, I am sure," he returned. "You're like Lela—the type of person who can rise to any occasion. I found in the past whenever you undertook anything, you carried it through."

"Except, in one important matter," she said, and bit her lip. "I think I never appreciated Ella Wheeler Wilcox's poem 'Keep Out of the Past' so much as I have since being released from the most wonderful position I ever had. I felt, as you maybe know, that at last I had found my true lifework."

"I don't seem to remember the poem."

"It was the second stanza that spoke to me," she explained.

> Keep out of the past. It's haunted;
> He who in its avenues gropes,
> Shall find there a ghost of joy prized most,
> And a skeleton throng of dead hopes.

The expression on her face was as if she herself were fleeing a skele-

144

ton throng of dead hopes, as she went on: "There's a maturity in your look, Joe, and something I can't quite place. It almost frightens me. I think I might be afraid to be your secretary now. There are so many things separating us—your year away, and your marriage.

"I do enjoy doing research for Mrs. Cardinal and proofreading for *The Silver Lining,* as you know, and now that we've started the runaway column, 'Magnetizing Your Marriage,' I feel I'm a little nearer my purpose for having been born."

"You're also helping in Dr. Raymond's office, I believe."

"Only part time, and mostly as a receptionist. He lets me make out statements and go early to get his mail—things like that." She stopped, biting her lip.

"Keep out of the past," he said lightly.

He never liked to see tears in a woman's eyes—for how could a man know their cause? A woman's tears had a way of saying to a man, "You are to blame for something or other."

"I was just now thinking," she interrupted her tears to say, "there can't actually be anything wrong in carrying a little of the past in a person's heart, can there? By the way, I've seen your beautiful new home. As you know, Mrs. Cardinal let me share in some of the interior decorating—or did she tell you? That was another thing I tried some years ago—but it didn't satisfy."

"She told me." He stood now, looked toward the house to see if Lela might be ready to come out, and for a moment, having forgotten his artificial limb, he staggered to keep his balance. He looked down at her apologetically, and she in a motherly tone commiserated, "You do remarkably well, Joe. I was just thinking how completely unnoticeable your artificial limb is. With your shoe and slacks, it looks almost more like a real foot than a real foot does." The way she said it took him back to the office in The Towers when he had told her, "When you sign my name, it's more like my signature than my own is."

She added now, "I suppose you sometimes have phantom pain?" And it was like a mother crooning over the hurt of a little child who had fallen and skinned a knee or run a sliver into his finger.

"I try to keep out of the past," he answered her question. "I left my foot over in England, remember?"

"I remember. I think about it sometimes—buried over there, and no marker. But they didn't bury *you*, Joe. The *real* you came back—stronger and better and more mature, and I'm proud to have been your friend—and secretary, of course—and I hope you'll let me keep on being secretary to your wife. I'll try not to take over," she added.

She was standing now, because Lela was coming down the steps with the baby.

"Mind if I hold him a minute?" Janice asked. "He's such a husky little fellow—and so handsome. Have you ever noticed how much he looks like his father—such strong fists, the same firm chin, the dimple in the same place and in the same cheek."

In Janice's arms their child slept on, unaware that he was the subject of conversation. Or *was* he? Joe thought. For it seemed to him that when Janice was looking down into the face of Joe Junior, she was seeing also the features and personality of the boy's father.

When Janice had gone, Lela said, "Want to hold our boy awhile? He needs a father's consolation after winning such a hard battle. He did have a *very* hard time. But he's such a sturdy little guy. He can take anything, just like his father. And he *is* handsome."

"You can tell by looking at him that he's the kind that will rise to any occasion, just like his mother." Studying the features of the sleeping child in his arms, Joe felt the proud emotion he supposed a young father ought to feel and was thankful for so many things—*so* many things.

He was startled now by his wife's question: "Are you sorry you didn't marry Janice?"

His answer was as if he had anticipated her query: "I think Elizabeth has expressed it better than I can. If I remember correctly, she put it something like this: 'God bless all our losses.' "

Their eyes met, and she moved toward him, adding in a very wifely sort of way, "And all our gains? I *am* one of your gains, aren't I?"

Playing upon an often overworked expression, he philosophized, "I didn't just lose a research secretary; I gained the best little mother in the world."

When, an interval later, Dad Blanchard came upon them on his way down to the dock, he stopped, looked appraisingly at the three of them, and especially at Lela, and remarked, "You never know what a woman is crying about. Young man, have you been hurting my daughter?"

Lela's answer was, "I've been hurting *him,* maybe. That's why I'm crying—I think."

"You never know why a woman is smiling, either. Oh, I almost forgot—Pastor Wellman wants you to phone him. They're having a baby dedication service this Sunday at the church. He thought maybe you'd like to bring Joseph George Wilcox Blanchard Cardinal. There'll be three others, he said. You're to call him back after a while. I told him yes, but that I'd check with you for a final decision."

Chapter 18

The final decision was to bring baby Joe to the morning worship service of Faith Memorial Church where, after the sermon, there was to be a dedication of infants.

In the meantime, there were five days in which Joe Senior suffered through the confusing process of adjusting to civilian life. There were the minor disillusionments that came with the realization that his wife, so flawless when he had been overseas, was now not an angel but a woman with a woman's intuitions and imperfections—and so very human.

There were times when he needed her in the way a little child needs his mother, and there were other times when Chaplain Conrad's rule 3 was painfully prophetic: "When your man gets home, he will probably enter into a period of lethargy and apathy. He may appear depressed and lazy. This will be a perfectly normal phenomenon. Do not goad him."

He climbed to the Hawthoreau House area, dreamed of the day when Thoreau's replica would be finished, strolled as Wordsworth once strolled—lonely as a cloud that floats on high over vale and hill, lay pensively as had Wordsworth on his couch, studied the deep blue sky, and quoted to himself Thoreau's descriptive line: "The bluebird carries the sky on his back."

These poetic phrasings had been his inspiration in former days, and through them he had been consoled with the comfort that beauty brings. They were the motherings his spirit had needed, and in their arms he had rested.

Once, on a quiet afternoon, when the lake was a wide blue mirror with never a roll on its surface, he strolled to the dock, only absently aware of Lela's kitten playing erratically alongside, behind, and ahead of him.

The *Cardinal* lay at anchor at the end of the pier, and in an interval

148

of history relived, it became an LST with wounded soldiers aboard, buffeted by a wild and boisterous wind.

His thoughts moved to Ned Boynton, still, as far as Joe knew, on his hospital cot, writing, thinking, praying, and being chaplain to a dozen other men in ward 7.

What had happened to the poem Ned had given him? Its beginning lines came easing into Joe's mind now, and in them he searched for meaning for himself:

> I need the shadows,
> The storm-tossed sea to cause my heart to fear;
> I need the shadows,
> That I His blessed Peace, be still! may hear;
> As birds at twilight seek their nest,
> so shadows call my heart to rest,
> I need the shadows.

"Thanks, Ned. Thank you very much. But your poem doesn't say how *much* shadow. There has to be just enough—not too much."

He strolled out onto the dock, felt a sudden breeze fanning his cheek, and stooped to pick up and hold in his arms the kitten which had followed him. "I wonder, little vagrant, which generation you are. We know who your mother and grandmother were, but as for your father—you are an orphan, do you know that? A very cute, very friendly little orphan, and you are not to blame for having been born. *Look!* See what happened out there in the water? Do you know what Henry David Thoreau said about a movement on the water like that? Listen:

" 'When a playful breeze drops in the pool, it springs to right and left, quick as a kitten playing with dead leaves.' How about that, little friend! How about that!"

Lela had not goaded him to work, to laugh, to play, to write, nor to be more attentive.

"You're *my husband,*" she told him, "and my husband, I want you to know, is not going to be controlled by his wife. I may try it at times—when I forget—but if you'll always remember that I don't *want* the black feathers you see in my wings, you'll be patient with me —a little, anyway."

"I like black feathers," he said. "They offer variety. I need the shadows."

"You're a darling," she told him, "and as far as I'm concerned, you're on vacation. You don't have to write so much as one line until you find your muse. Do you know what? Janice was saying just yesterday—I mean—" She stopped and tousled his hair with her free hand—the other hand was busy holding Junior. "The little pig said maybe if we'd hurry and get Hawthoreau House finished—"

Rule 6 caught fire in his mind. It was with desperate will power he answered, "She may be right. I think it would be a good thing if we ordered the lumber and got started. But please, *please,* let *me* do the interior decorating?" And the question mark in his tone seemed to cut through her heart like a serrated knife.

When she did not reply, and he saw her tears, he realized she was not at fault but her husband. He had allowed self-commiseration to twist the original Joe into a disagreeable caricature of what she had believed him to be.

He would have to take himself in hand, he would *have* to go to work.

He had tried writing at a folding table near the fallen ponderosa, but his thoughts were like a rainy day in spring—cold and gray and overhung with clouds.

Perhaps when Hawthoreau House was finished and they had settled down to homemaking—when he could lose himself in the solitude of his spirit—the river would flow again.

On a lonely night he walked among the trees of the orchard, following the weaving path of his flashlight. And every moment he was aware of the unintentional pressure upon him from without. The world was expecting him to produce, to write brilliantly, to strike out with flaming swords against the injustices in the world, and to lead weary, straggling sheep beside still waters. What, they were probably thinking, would his first Cardinal columns be like? How long after his return would the wearer of the Purple Heart continue to wait and wait and wait before his song would be heard?

He stopped at Lela's favorite rendezvous, where she sometimes prepared her talks for the College Brain Trust.

That was another thing. She had invited him to sit in next Sunday morning and, if he desired, say a few words to her class on some such theme as "What the War Is Really All About," or, as she had expressed it, "Tell them about Ned Boynton—and the secret of his triumph over handicap." And then she had stopped, embarrassed, and he had felt: She is trying to get me to triumph over my own—and I cannot! I simply cannot. Why does she keep goading me—in such sweet, unassuming ways?

Charles Boynton had called self-pity "the great crippler." But how can a man keep from pitying himself when his whole self is such a pitiful cripple!

He directed a beam from his flashlight toward the trunk of the apple tree, focused it on the once-ragged but now-healing scar, and remembered Normandy and *Ein' feste Burg ist unser Gott!*

He recalled now a scene from the New Testament: A lonely Man was on His face under an old olive tree in Gethsemane, sweating "as it were great drops of blood" and saying, "Not my will, but thine, be done."

So now, Joe buried his face in his hands, crying with convulsive and desperate words: "War! War! I hate it! *Hate it!* There has to be a better way for the world than to take the sword and perish with it!"

And there Lela found him. He heard her calling, "Joe? Where are you?"

He stood to welcome her.

There was no complaint in her voice, only sympathy. "Are you all right? I missed you!"

"I missed myself," he said, "so I came out to see if I could find me."

They walked like young lovers back to the guest house, where they had been staying until the final touches could be made on their new home. At the door they stopped, and there, with her hand on his arm, she asked, "Have you ever read the little poem 'Tomorrow' by Myrtle Burger?"

"I've never read it, but Charles Boynton quoted it to me once. One of his pupils wrote it on the blackboard in the school he was teaching. You remember him, don't you? He lost both legs in World War I."

It was she who seemed to want to change the subject. "On a night like this it's almost a shame to waste it in sleep. Hear the locusts? I love their songs, even though they're always a monotone. And they *don't* sing all the year round—only in the heat of summer."

From his store of textbook knowledge he answered, "The drumming

151

of the harvest fly is made only by the male. But you were going to tell me about the Burger poem."

"I've been one of your best pupils this past year," she said. "I've memorized a lot of beautiful things, and 'Tomorrow,' I thought, was one of the finest. Would you like to hear it?"

And while she quoted the brief stanza, he stood in a little one-room school and watched a dark-haired, blue-eyed little girl writing it on the blackboard.

For an interval there was silence between them, and only the sustained whirring of the cicadas reminded him that this was not tomorrow but tonight, and they were a man and a woman, a husband and a wife, a father and a mother, whose son, in the years ahead, would be among the little children marching.

"Joe," she said gently, "Where have you gone? Your wife is in your arms and you don't even seem to know it."

His answer was as from a deep cavern of anxiety, "I saw tomorrow marching, and Junior watching. The crowd was in the street, and he was their leader, and was trying to find out where they were going so he could lead them. I wonder where the future *is* going. Does anybody know?"

The next day he tried to write again, but the power of will could not ignite the sleeping fire in his mind.

Then came Saturday, before tomorrow's dedication of their child and of themselves to God. Standing under the wisteria, Lela suggested, "Let's go for a spin on the lake, take the camp stove, cook our dinner in the open, and just play. There's nothing I'd like better than to laze around over there, wading, swimming."

He shook his head, "I haven't tried swimming since—" He shrugged and lifted his new foot. "You know, I'm not exactly a bathing beauty."

He did decide to drive over to the island—but alone, and to this she agreed.

She walked with him to the dock, helped him into his life jacket, and saw that his portable typewriter was on board, along with his attaché case and his little box of reference books. In a few minutes he was out on the lake, the *Cardinal* gliding smoothly through the water and its motor purring without strain, even at top speed.

He drove first toward the overhang, cut a wide circle, turned back, looking for the Great Stone Face, and thought once he had seen it.

But it had disappeared as swiftly as Longfellow's arrow and could not be found again—not even in the heart of his friend, the Muse.

You did let me see *Your* face, he prayed, and I thank You— I thank You for Your Son and my Saviour. But I've lost the sense of His presence. My story is dead, and I cannot revive it. World War II still rages on, and the Cardinal's call is being smothered out in the fury of it. I cannot even hear it myself.

He steered toward the island, circled it, came back to the new pier Dad Blanchard had had built there, and drove the *Cardinal* in behind the breakwater, just in case the wind should rise and try to toss the beautiful new boat against the rocky shore.

He looked toward the vacant throne of the little god Joe and noticed that from here one could see the artist's cap at the top of the fireplace chimney of their new home.

He lifted his typewriter from its case and set it on the folding table Lela had suggested he might wish to bring along. "Only a suggestion," she had said and smiled, and he had understood her to be saying, "I am not trying to control you nor to supervise you. I am only being a wife."

To which he had answered, "I sometimes wish I didn't have so much ESP. Especially when it comes to reading my wife's thoughts."

"You couldn't possibly read nicer thoughts of a nicer wife, sir. Now, be gone! 'And a murrain seize thee!' "

He hadn't thought of that expression in a long time. It had been used in literature somewhere as a mild imprecation. He answered with a chuckle, "A plague o' both your houses!"—and couldn't remember who had said that, either.

He laid his reference books in a little semicircle on the deck and rolled a sheet of paper into the typewriter.

The boat was rocking gently in the quiet water, with only now and then an interruptive lurch when a larger wave came moving in.

Searching in his thesaurus for a substitute word for "fear," he ran down the list: "apprehension, anxiety, care, alarm, dismay, despair." He felt he was in a boat on a Galilee night:

> The tempest was raging,
> The billows were tossing high,
> The sky was o'ershadowed with blackness,
> No shelter or help was nigh.

153

In the past, he had been able to begin his writing day simply by beginning—by writing just anything, even irrelevant matter, until the river of creation began to flow of itself.

A folded sheet of paper, probably used as a marker at some former time, slipped out of the book and was whisked by a vagrant breeze to the deck. In another second it would have been gone. He lurched to retrieve it and felt a stab of pain somewhere in England.

"That, sir," he addressed the offending phantom, "is not fair! You are no longer a part of me! Please remember, I am trying to stay out of the past!"

He unfolded the sheet of paper and scanned the written message. It was not in his own handwriting nor in Lela's. It was the smooth, confident script of a former secretary, to whom he had once said, "When you sign my name, it's more like my signature than my own is."

It was, he noted, a letter.

"Dearest Lela:

"Thinking of Dr. Wellman's latest column this morning, I was browsing in an old commentary for something new and fresh for you to give him, and I ran across this. It's something I never had seen or heard before. I hope you will like it:

" 'We who believe in the second coming of Christ and expect to see Him face to face at some future time in the history of the universe must remember that the Bible speaks also of a *spiritual* presence; that He, the Son of God, is here *now*.'

"I especially liked the writer's comment on John 14:23: 'The promise of the Saviour is very clear: "If a man love me, he will keep my words (obey my teaching): and my Father will love him, and we will come to him, and make our abode (home) with him.' "

"I think I never saw it before. *Love* is the whole thing, Lela—love and obedience. Because we love the Saviour, we obey Him; when we obey Him we place our hearts at the disposal of the Father, and both He and the Son come to make their home within us.

"And so we do not have an absentee Christ, far off somewhere among the galaxies of the universe—though because He is deity and omnipresent, He is there also—but we have His presence here and now. He is a *now* Saviour. He is here now; we talk to Him now; He strengthens us now, in this time of trial, in this moment of heartache and disappointment. He will not allow us to be tested beyond what we are able, but will NOW make a way of escape that we may be able to bear it NOW.

"Do you think maybe Dr. Wellman would like to use this? To me it is living water from the well.

"Love,
"Janice."

Joe could not define his reaction to the letter. There was no date for its writing. But it must be recent, for only a few days ago, when he had used the book, the sheet had not been there.

A deerfly swept in from the shore, buzzed noisily about his typewriter, and powerdived at his ankle. He brushed at it, saw on the boat deck another slip of paper, and picked it up. It was only a leaf from a notebook, in Lela's hand, as if written slowly and very carefully. It was a line from Goethe:

"Every man has within himself a continent of undiscovered character. Happy is he who proves the Columbus of his soul."

Joe was torn between resentment and appreciation. Had Lela purposely inserted the quote in his treasure house of words, knowing he would eventually find it? Was she using this indirect way to tell him there were vast areas within himself, undiscovered, waiting exploration and exploitation, and that until now he had discovered only a small island, narrow and circumscribed with self-pity?

Was this her way of "goading" him?

Or had she written it for her own inspiration?

In any event, it seemed now he had exactly what Vern Gregg needed. Gregg needed to realize that his life until now was only insular, that if he would he could become the Columbus of his own soul—and that beyond the little circle of his thoughts there was a vast continent of truth awaiting exploration and appropriation. There was a *now* Saviour, a *now* power, a very present *presence*.

Joe began to write as if addressing Vern himself, "What you need, sir, is an awareness of God. He is not only with you in your valley but your valley is past. You have come all the way through. You have done more than discover the continent of yourself, you have discovered God."

155

And as he wrote, Vern Gregg became Ned Boynton lying on a hospital cot in ward 7, bed 19, learning to help others; his notes of encouragement were shade trees to shelter his buddies from the heat of their desert—oases from which they could drink living water from *the* well.

The words continued to come—many words, expressive words, phrases, plot ideas, nuances, action and more action. Vern Gregg was learning to speak with his pen, to speak also in a guttural whisper, and he was going to come back to America and to his Judy who, also needing the shadows, was finding the strength generated by a realization of God's presence.

Joe's fingers flew over the keys as page after page rolled through the typewriter and were tucked safely away into his attaché case.

Across the lake the dinner bell rang, and though he heard it, it was as if it had no right to ring, no authority to interrupt the river of his creativity.

Resting his eyes a moment he looked toward Cardinal Hill and then to the right. Suddenly he saw—and also heard—the dinghy coming at high speed, a woman at the helm.

He wouldn't mind the interruption now. It was at just the right time. He had found his muse, and rule 3 was going to be forever history.

Would she, perhaps, bring with her the camp stove, and would they still climb to their nook where they had first heard the call of the cardinal?

She was waving her arm, a gesture he had learned to love because of the way she did it. A great gladness welled up within, and in a moment of ecstasy, he cupped his hands to his lips and called to her: "Hurry up! I've been waiting for you!"

He busied himself closing books, standing them in his box, fitting the typewriter into its case, and folding the writing table.

When he looked again, he was caught up in a bewildering emotion, for the lady pilot of the dinghy was not his Lela but dark-haired Janice Granada!

Janice, part-time nurse in Dr. Raymond's office, research secretary for Mrs. Cardinal, and former little pig, was coming toward him—and perhaps secretly still huffing and puffing at his door!

Chapter 19

When the dinghy was within half a dozen rods of the pier, the pilot shut off the motor and lifted an oar to steer the boat in to the beach. Joe, in an inadvertent gesture of a man trying to help a woman who probably wouldn't need any help, rose from his seat, and forgetting his right leg was still in England, he staggered, turned, and sat down, saying, "Sorry—I forgot—I keep forgetting!"

She laughed, and it was the old familiar laugh of room 1214 in The Towers.

"I hope I haven't interrupted anything," she apologized, "or done anything that will keep Vern and Judy apart any longer than the plot calls for, but I lost a very important letter, and I thought I might possibly have left it in the *Cardinal* somewhere. I was cruising around in it yesterday."

She was out of the dinghy now, beaching it, and talking, explaining why she had come. "I've found the *Cardinal* a wonderful place to think. I've been bringing my research books and just cruising around until I find a good place to anchor, and in almost no time I'm walking beside the still waters."

"This look like anything you lost?" He indicated her letter to Lela, explaining almost apologetically, "We always read each other's mail —with permission, of course."

"Of course. I believe it's only secretaries who are not supposed to read personal mail."

"Keep out of the past—unquote."

He felt her watching him, and when he looked up to where she now was, standing on the pier, their eyes met, and he thought he saw in hers something new, something he had never seen there before. It was puzzling, confusing, and embarrassing, reminding him of a crappie just caught, lying on the beach, gasping for life.

"It wasn't *just* the letter to Lela. There was another, one marked

157

personal, and it was to Halford—Dr. Raymond, I mean. Perhaps I should have left it in the mailbox, but he was out of town and won't be back until late tonight."

"It still might be here somewhere—you know how absentminded I am at times. I may have seen it on the floor and slipped it into some other book." He leafed though his Webster, an Audubon book, and *The Psychology of Dealing With People* and searched in his attaché case.

She sighed. "I shouldn't have bothered you, but you didn't come when we rang the bell—and the binoculars indicated you were about to wind up your day's stint—you know, like you used to at The Towers—stop, look away, yawn."

She frowned and bit her lip. "I was up on Cardinal Hill yesterday, dreaming a little, and planning just how I'd like Hawthoreau House if I were an author, and I might have dropped it there.

"Well, here goes. Lela will want to see the water I've pumped for Dr. Wellman's column!"

Janice turned back to the dinghy, lifted the anchor, set it inside, and with the skill of one proficient in boat launching, had the prow off the sand and the boat out into the water without getting her feet wet. She rowed out beyond the breakwater, started the motor, and was off.

He watched until she was perhaps a hundred yards from shore, when her motor coughed, sputtered, coughed again, stopped, and she was adrift.

"Motor trouble?" he called.

She was looking into the gas tank. "I'm out of gas, looks like! I *would* have to have been born a woman! A *man* would never have started without looking first to see if the tank was full."

And so it came to pass that Joe offered to give her a tow, and because she had no choice other than to row, he came alongside, helped her put the dinghy's anchor into the *Cardinal,* and guided her over the gunwhale and into the boat beside him.

And it came to pass also that Lela, who had been watching through the binoculars, saw the *Cardinal,* with the dinghy in tow, swing to the left and steer for Cardinal Hill—and in it was her husband and his former secretary.

She saw Janice point toward the overhang and thought, "She sees the Great Stone Face. She's telling him."

A storm of jealousy swept into the mind of Mrs. Joseph Cardinal. The old big bad wolf may have gone up in flames in the guesthouse fireplace, but now it had risen from the ashes like the mythical phoenix that was the embodiment of the great god Ra—cremated, yet rising to life from its own ashes.

Jealousy, that once before had been like a "most vehement flame," leaped into furious life.

In her mind the *Cardinal,* with the empty dinghy in tow, became a lovers rendezvous; the passengers were Evangeline and Gabriel fleeing the British in the *same boat!*

And now from the house there came an interruption, a baby's fretting wail, calling for a mother's attention in the only way he knew.

* * *

Lela found nothing seriously wrong with her son, and in only a little while he was on his customary good behaviour.

"How little you know about the major problems of adults," she crooned to him, "but someday you will begin to find out. So tomorrow we are dedicating you to the only One who can lead you all the way through life. You be a good little guy, now, and get plenty of sleep today and tonight so that tomorrow, when you are being looked over and cooed by several hundred people, you will be in a good humor—and *that's an order!"*

Baby Joe, who did not know it was a command, nor that at the moment his mother was not in a gentle humor, drifted into sleep.

"I have to run up to the house," Lela explained to her mother. "Since we're moving in Monday, I'd like to—well, just sort of look around a little to see what else we may have to have—for the first few days, anyway!"

Mother Eloise, having just come in from the orchard to take over the baby-sitting chores, searched her daughter's eyes and said, "You have a heartache?"

Lela's answer was, "I have a *head*ache—and I hope that's all."

"Are you sure you ought to go? Won't they suspect your motive? A man does like to be trusted, and as far as I'm concerned, your husband is more deserving of absolute trust than any man I know—unless it's my George. After all, she was his secretary for a long time, and it's normal for them to have things in common."

"I know—but it depends on *what* things—and just how common!"

Fighting tears, and controlling them, Lela drove onto the highway.

"Jealousy is as cruel as the grave," she was quoting to herself, "its fire a most vehement flame." And she felt the fury and passion of it in her heart.

But was all jealousy evil? Did not a wife have a right to exclusive devotion?

* * *

She parked near the recently built shelter which was to house the *Cardinal* in winter and protect it from storms in other seasons and noted that the dinghy's anchor was lying on the *Cardinal's* floor. The sturdy little boat itself was riding without complaint on the waves outside the shelter, an unaware satellite of its new and beautiful successor.

"Second place for you, dear little dinghy," she said as she hurried past on her way up the slope.

What possibly could be going on in the minds of the two who now were alone yonder among the maples, aspen and evergreens at the site of Hawthoreau House? *My* secretary—*his* secretary.

At the top of the incline she heard talking and laughter, and one voice whose laugh was so cheerful, whose colorful personality helped make the office of *The Silver Lining* a place of enjoyment.

Joe, with his wry humor, had probably said something to make her laugh. Joe could do that, even in serious moments. His sense of humor had helped her fall in love with him in the first place—and it had helped their love to grow. It had probably gone with him as he had walked with God through the valley of the shadow that was the theater of war.

What she was about to do now did not make sense to herself, but she knew she was going to wind her way up the slope to the overhang, where the laughter had its source. I do live here—or will, beginning Monday. I will be climbing this hill often in the years ahead.

She stopped and listened. She was almost there now. Janice was saying, "I can't imagine where I lost it—unless it could have been over on the island. I was there yesterday looking for columbine. Halford—Dr. Raymond, I mean—wants a wild flower garden in his backyard, and I promised him I'd help. He especially likes columbine —and he's started a butterfly collection. That *man!* Look! There's a bed of mariposa lilies! Hal wants a valance of them bordering the

160

porch railing. Would you mind if I come up someday and help my-self?"

"I'll ask Lela. She happens to have a special love for what she calls her 'lavendar butterflies.' I think she might be willing to let you have a few."

In the silence that followed, the vehement flame sputtered and was about to go out; then Janice spoke again, and what she said was especially flammable: "Of course. I guess I keep forgetting you're married—and I must try not to do that."

The voices were nearer now, and Lela hid herself behind a cluster of junipers.

In only a little while she saw Joe and Janice below her, moving toward the front stoop of the house. She also noticed that Joe was not limping at all, and she knew him well enough to be pretty sure he was making a special effort not to.

And now he was taking the key from his pocket. She saw him un-lock the door, saw Janice go in ahead of her husband—and smothered a desire to cry out, "Wait!—It's me—Lela! Joe Cardinal's wife! You can't go in together when I'm not there!"

Chapter 20

But they *could* go in together, and they did.

Her heart pounding, her mind aflame with jealousy, Lela flew down the hill, circled the house and let herself in through the back door. She rationalized her actions with the thought, "I have a deadline to meet on next week's column. I can make it to the typewriter without being seen."

She tried to compose herself with Mother's counsel: "After all, she had been his secretary for a long time, and it is normal for them to have things in common."

Normal, yes, but dangerous, she thought, and remembered an old epigram often quoted by her father: "One cannot depend on woman's friendship, for she gives everything to love."

Suddenly the house was full of music. Janice was at the piano, her fingers storming their way through a Liszt rhapsody.

"I," Lela pitied herself, "am only an ordinary housewife. I do not play the piano with such finesse."

From Liszt to a Mozart overture and finally to the saccharine notes of "Clair de Lune." Then there was silence.

Janice was talking now. "Sorry. I didn't mean to stop so abruptly. I remembered how you loved the moonlight, and that took me to Debussy, but did I hear a typewriter? Is Lela here, do you suppose? She did have a finishing touch to put on her column. That's why I broke loose on Liszt just now—he was her feature last week. This week it's Chopin, and next it'll be one of the Reformation composers —Martin Luther, I think."

And now again the house was filled with music. Janice was playing Luther's majestic, "A Mighty Fortress Is Our God," striking the chords with strong and determined rhythm, as if she were declaring to the world her own sure faith.

Lela was startled to hear her husband call out: *"Stop! Don't play that!"*

The interruption was so abrupt and so impassioned that Lela felt both resentment against her husband and pity for the girl who, unawares, had displeased him.

The silence that followed was tense, its pain reaching down the hall to Joe Cardinal's wife, seated at her typewriter.

"What did I do?" Janice asked.

"It's all right," Joe apologized. "I was just reminded of something that happened over in Normandy."

That moment seemed to be the right one for letting her "guests" know that the lady of the house was at home. Lela rolled a sheet of paper into her typewriter and began to type vehemently: "Now is the time for all good men to come to the aid of their party."

Even as the words staccatoed onto the page, Lela knew that this was, for her, one of the tensest moments of her life. In a crisis like this, when emotions were seething and there was little self-control, women had been known to give way to unladylike temper explosions. Her husband and his former secretary seemed to have just too much in common.

It was Joe who, quite by accident, came to her rescue. Afterward, she told him, "I had my jealousy grave almost finished and was about ready to leap into it when you called down the hall, 'Lela! You here?'"

She had answered with still more vehement speed at the typewriter: "Now is the time. Now is the time."

What to do—what to say—whether to do anything except type—and what to say when she said anything—if she did.

She decided now to call back facetiously, "Joe? I didn't know you could play like that!"

And he, in a completely unaffected tone, answered, "Want to hear me play again?"

And now, as before, there was music. This time it was a thunderous Mozart composition.

Coming down the hall and into the room, Lela said to Joe, who was standing near the fireplace, "I should have guessed it. Only Janice could play like that."

Was there a sudden flush on the pianist's face as her fingers raced through the Mozart?

When she had finished her number, Janice stood, bowed to a crowded concert hall, and said, "There are many who prefer Mozart

163

to Beethoven. One well-known music lover has expressed his preference in words like these: 'Whenever I hear a Beethoven number, I get the feeling he worked long and hard to perfect it— that he created it himself; but when Mozart music is played, it is as if I am listening to a *discovery*. That his music, in a sense, *always was,* and he just happened onto it and wrote it down for the world to hear.' "

Janice bowed again, to the right and to the left. "We who compose the music for our own little sphere of influence create so laboriously. Our personal world, so beautiful at times, is often distorted under our creative hand, and in our frustration we become discouraged, disillusioned and at first unable to keep on creating. And then, suddenly, we hear music in our own soul, and we cannot wait to write it. How thankful we should be that we do not die with all our music in us."

Janice gave a final bow, sighed, and said in a completely different tone of voice, "I have lost what may be a very important personal letter. It was to Dr. Raymond. He will be coming home tonight from the medical convention in Chicago, and if I don't find it, it will be very embarrassing!"

The three looked through the house, climbed to the overhang, combed the whole area, and searched again in the *Cardinal,* the boat house, and the wastebaskets in Lela's den. Yesterday Janice had been doing research there. They leafed through every book—even the cookbook.

They found the letter on Hawthoreau Hill. Searching the area near where a beheaded violet had once caught on a mullein stalk, clung a moment, then had fallen over the edge, Lela saw near a rocky outcropping a little pile of sticks, leaves, stones and bones and—covered with dust—an envelope addressed to Dr. Halford Raymond. The address was handwritten and marked "Personal"—and in the lower left-hand corner were the initials "B.B.W."

Janice breathed a heavy sigh of relief and said, "I never lost a personal letter before—did I, Joe—Mr. Cardinal?"

Joe, studying the red-penciled initials signifying "Big Bad Wolf," knew that between Dr. Raymond and his secretary there was a camaraderie that made for a satisfactory secretary-employer relationship.

"Those darling little pack rats!" Lela exclaimed. "They'll borrow anything you leave around unclaimed! But they're very thoughtful;

they nearly always leave something in exchange—that's why they're sometimes called trade rats. If we can find what they've left, and where, we'll know exactly where you were when you lost the letter."

Beside the trunk of the fallen ponderosa, they came upon a little pile of cones, a small white stone, and an old cocoon.

Joe studied the empty chrysalis and remarked, "When the monarch crawled out of this little dungeon, it was forever. Want to take a memo, Janice?"

"Sorry," his former secretary returned, "but I forgot my notebook."

"There's blank space on the back of the letter; I'm sure Hal wouldn't mind."

Once again Lela felt herself on the periphery of an exclusive little circle as she listened to Joe dictating as to a recorder and saw Janice taking shorthand notes on the back of Dr. Raymond's letter:

"In all the literature on the metamorphosis of the butterfly there is nothing to indicate that, once the insect has attained the imago, or the perfect state, it ever returns to the larva or pupa stages. It stays forever out of the past. Like Holmes' 'chambered nautilus,' it leaves its outgrown shell by life's unresting sea.

"We of the human species may learn from the insect—there is a past that must remain forever history. Though we are forever a part of our past, because our past is forever part of us, yet we cannot go back. In the providence of God, we, through faith in the ever-present Christ, have become new creations: old things are passed away, and all things are become new. This is a new birth, and it is of God. Happy is the man who has experienced it. Happy—"

Janice interrupted to say, "I'm sorry, but I'm out of space."

Joe looked toward Bluebell Island and said as if his thoughts were far away, "That's all right, that's all I wanted to get down before I lost it. I'll weave it into my first column since coming home. You sure you got it all?"

"Every word. Would you like me to see what else I can find on the monarch? I have a book on insects, and it has a special section on moths and butterflies, with pictures in full color. The caterpillar is even more beautiful than the butterfly itself. Could you make any comment on that—such as, even though it is beautiful in its larval stage, it is destructive; but as a butterfly it is a thing of beauty and a joy forever?"

Lela heard her husband sigh, and when he did not answer but continued looking toward the island, she said to Janice, "If you can find a little more space, maybe on the other side of the envelope—if you think Dr. Raymond wouldn't mind, can you take a note for his marriage column?"

Echoing her husband's style of giving dictation, Lela began: "The brushy-tailed pack rat is chiefly nocturnal in its habits. It works secretly and in the dark. Its thieving tendencies are not limited to its needs, nor does it consider the original owner. It takes what it likes, and often gives only rubbish in exchange. It has not learned 'Thou shalt not steal.' Nor has it—"

Janice had stopped writing and was only listening, and Lela thought she saw both pain and misery in her expressive blue eyes.

"Mind if I add a line or two of my own?" Janice asked. "Something like this? 'And even though the trade rat may sometimes give much in exchange for what she has only borrowed, she is still a rat.' "

Inadvertently, Joe eased the tension when he proposed, "Let's tie up the dinghy and take a spin around the island."

At the boat shelter Janice said, "An electric device for opening and closing the door was your wife's idea." And it seemed to Joe she was trying to say, as she had said once before on the Blanchard lawn, "You are very fortunate to have married a girl with such good judgment."

They filled the dinghy's motor with gas, left her tied up at the dock until someone could come back for her, and took off for Bluebell Island. Joe, at the helm, was aware of a feeling of pride, an emotion born of ownership, of conquering resistance—but of worry also. There was an atmosphere of war which ought not to be—and must be dissolved.

Lela was first to speak, "Wagner is next—after Mozart and Chopin. I have the research completed, and I'll turn it over to Dad tomorrow!"

"But you shouldn't have," Janice protested. "You were going to let your little pack rat bring you all the material."

The bayonets were still busy, Joe thought, and he felt himself being jabbed with every thrust.

"I've been doing a bit of research myself," he interjected. "That is, *my* little pack rat, Judy Frost, did it for me. She's musical, too, you know, working toward her degree. She ran across something every

166

pastor and layman in the world ought to know. As most every music student already knows, Richard Wagner was a violent personality, made enemies wherever he went, and was a defier of convention, as were Liszt and Nietzsche, with whom he associated.

"Judy, trying to find something commendable other than his striking compositions, stumbled onto an illustration of the gospel—one of the finest I've ever seen. When she tells it to Vern, who is the skeptic in the story, as you know, it opens his eyes. I was writing it yesterday here in the *Cardinal*. Anybody want to hear what Judy wrote in her thesis?"

It seemed that "anybody" did, so, while the *Cardinal* cruised around the island, and while the atmosphere was still strained, Joe quoted from Judy's manuscript:

"When Wagner died in February, 1883, his second wife, Cosima, daughter of Liszt, cut off her long beautiful hair and laid it in the coffin on her husband's breast, as if to say to the world, 'When my husband died, I died with him. From now on, I live only to perpetuate his name and fame.' "

The *Cardinal* was making its third trip around Bluebell Island when Joe finished. "Judy applied the story this way: 'So, we who trust in Christ are to believe that when our Savior died, we also died with him. Upon our acceptance of Him, His death becomes a reality for us. Our own biographies as unbelievers and sinners end when we trust in Him.

" 'I, Judy Frost, no longer live, but Christ lives within me. I now use my time and talent to keep alive His wonderful name. Unlike Wagner, who died and remained dead, Christ lives for and within me. If any man be in union with Christ, he is a new creation.' "

Inadvertently Joe opened the throttle, and the *Cardinal* shot forward. "This," he thought, "is the way it ought to be. Every Christian ought to believe that his biography as a sinner forever ended when he yielded himself to the living Saviour." He breathed a sigh of relief and said, intending Janice and Lela to hear, "Thanks, Judy. Thanks very much."

They were back on the lee side of the island when Janice exclaimed, "*Look!* There's Hawthorne's Great Stone Face!"

Joe cut the motor, circled, and looked back toward Cardinal Hill, but saw only the rugged outcroppings, the tree-spangled overhang,

167

and the somber, splintered stump of the once-mighty ponderosa.

The sun and the clouds had had their moment and lost it. The image was no more.

"I'm sure I saw it," Janice defended herself. "I wasn't just seeing things."

Joe unleashed the motor and they drove again toward the island. Twice they circled it and came back to the area from which the Face had, on other occasions, been visible. But as before, there was now only the ragged features of the overhang, and below it the boathouse, its door closed, and, near the parking area, the beech tree, its leaves trembling in the green fire of the afternoon sun.

When Joe had throttled down the motor and they began the long smooth glide to the Blanchard dock, Lela's hand reached out to his in a little gesture of oneness—and Janice in the prow saw the diamond on her finger and the wedding band, smiled, sighed and looked again toward the place of the Face.

Seeing the smile and hearing the sigh, Joe felt an ache in his heart and breathed a prayer that someday, hopefully soon, the queen of The Towers would find her quest. Having lost her kingdom in Madison, she had come to Wilkerson in search of another. He thought, *We seek and when we find, we lose again—we are set to sail in different ships.*

Dad Blanchard saw them coming and hurried down to meet them. He announced, "Doctor Raymond just phoned from Chicago and asked if he could have the *Cardinal* tomorrow. Wants to go over to Bluebell Island for a few wild flowers—mariposa lilies, I think he said, and some columbine.

"Anybody want to volunteer to go with him to show him where to look?"

Joe, aware still of a certain atmosphere in which three had been, and still was, a crowd, decided to toss in what he hoped would be interpreted as a facetious remark: "Would he like a man, woman or beast?"

Janice, as if to accept the veiled accusation—or whatever it was—volunteered, "I think he is looking for a beast—described by Funk and Wagnalls as 'a sentient creature inferior to man,'—a rodent of some kind, perhaps."

And with the self-incriminating confession, the three became a very large crowd.

Grandmother Eloise came inadvertently to the rescue when, from the wisteria-shaded porch, she called to say, "Somebody's r.other is needed in the nursery!"

"Let me," Janice volunteered. "I need to do something for somebody—OK?" She accepted Dad Blanchard's help and was quickly out of the boat and onto the pier.

"Thanks, Dad. You're the nicest adopted father I've had in a long time," and the nurse—stenographer—interior-decorator, wistful-hearted Janice Granada, hurried up the slope to the house.

Following her with his eyes and suffering for her, Joe thought: *She's still searching for purpose in life, and she doesn't know she has already found it and has been living in its splendor ever since she was a little girl writing on the blackboard in Charles Boynton's school, "I saw tomorrow marching on little children's feet."*

Janice herself was tomorrow, as was every man and woman in the world, beginning at birth.

Dad Blanchard also was watching. To Lela and Joe, still in the boat, he commented, "She needs a father."

To which Joe added, "And a brother—and maybe a sister." He looked toward his wife, who bit her lip, turned away, and busied herself with getting out of the boat.

"And of course *you* need a father too," the editor of *The Silver Lining* remarked as he steered his daughter onto the dock.

"Thank you," she said and added, "I already have the best father a girl could ever have."

With that confession, Lela took off up the slope—not to help Janice look after Junior nor to supervise the work, but to salvage a bit of herself from the turbulence that was still seething within.

As she hurried along, she said in soliloquy, "I don't like myself for feeling the way I do. Am I jealous because she seems to have taken over not only my husband and my father but now, perhaps, my baby also? How *can* such a wonderful person be so unaware of what she is doing to me!"

To Dad Blanchard, Joe commented, "There, by the grace of God, goes the best wife a man could ever find—the *very* best. Not only does she rise to every difficult situation, sometimes she washes it away with her own tears."

169

"You haven't found any of her flaws—any imperfections inherited from her parents?"

"A very few, but I have a small cemetery for burying them."

A little later, when the two were in the *Cardinal* enroute to deliver it to its new garage and to bring back the dinghy, Dad Blanchard explained, "I told the doctor the redbird would be ready and waiting and where to find the key—just in case he wants her while we are still in church. He *might* decide to come to church, though. I told him about Junior's dedication, and he feels a sort of godfather interest in him. Also, for some reason, he has been dropping in more or less regularly. I think it is Pastor Wellman's sermons—or else it's the world situation that sets men searching for answers. Dr. Wellman is making a lot of our professional men aware of the inadequacies of the philosophy of materialism. They're reading his column first and then coming to church to hear him preach."

"More power to *The Silver Lining,*" Joe answered.

"And to Dr. Wellman's research secretary. Thanks for letting us have her while you were away."

The *Cardinal*'s powerful motor purred softly as if to say that, although the whole world was caught in the holocaust of war, there was an eye in the hurricane where all was peace.

As they neared the place where the replica of Hawthorne's Great Stone Face was sometimes seen, they circled the area twice, but though the rocks of the cliff stood out in detailed outline, no face was discernible.

"When you get Hawthoreau House finished," Blanchard said, "I'll want to put up a lightning rod on that old ponderosa stump. It's one of the highest points up there, and it's right near where you're going to build. I was planning to have it cut down and sawed into fireplace wood, but Lela said no. She said you wanted the place to look rugged—something about the great god Ra, I think she said."

"My little cemetery is up there," Joe commented, "and that old stump makes a fair-sized headstone."

"Big day tomorrow, eh?" Dad Blanchard commented presently, as he throttled the motor preparatory to gliding to the dock where the dinghy lay at peace, waiting to take them back.

"Very big," Joe answered, and was caught up into what he felt must be a high and holy emotion. It was very good to be a father.

170

Chapter 21

Pastor Wellman's sermon topic was "Hiding Among the Trees." After a brief introduction, in which he retold the historic event of the world's first homemakers in the Garden of Eden, he began his exposition and application by saying: "There are many *religious* trees in today's gardens, where the descendants of Adam try to hide themselves to keep their sins from being detected—and in some instances to keep their own hearts from admitting any guilt at all. They seem determined not to come to the Light, lest their deeds be reproved, not realizing that the God who searches is also the God who saves."

Religious trees offering only transparent shelter were listed as: *Psychological Religion,* which seeks a hypnotic adjustment for tension and frustration; *Emotional Religion,* which offers the seeker psychic thrills and mystical exaltations but does not give life; *Sacramental Religion,* which depends upon certain rites and/or ceremonies for salvation but in reality may be only a form of godliness, like cream puffs without the cream; and *Theological Religion,* which may be nothing less than a coldly scientific acceptance of the abstract truth of the Scriptures.

Among these trees men hid in vain, alternating between feelings of security and secret fears of the future—fears of what will happen when the soul stands alone before God in the white light of His holy nature.

"There *is* a place to hide. It has been expressed in the words of the hymn: 'Rock of Ages, cleft for me, Let me hide myself in Thee' and in the words of yet another hymn, 'Thou blest Rock of Ages, I'm hiding in Thee.' You cannot hide *from* God; you can only hide *in* Him.

"When the Holy Spirit in his gentle and loving way has reminded you that you have sinned, and your heart is aching for shame—fly to Him on the wings of faith and hide your face and your whole self

171

against his loving breast. There humbly confess, and there, because of Calvary, you will be forgiven.

"Are you satisfied to be only a spectator? Or are you a participant? A professor or a possessor? Many *applaud* Christ but do not *appropriate* Him.

"There is forgiveness and there is peace for those who by experience enter into union with Christ."

Seated now beside his wife, Junior asleep in her arms, Joe struggled to keep out of the past and could not. Much more of him was in Europe than a discarded leg: a German lad was buried over there somewhere who, like himself, had not wanted to fight—had not wanted to kill or be killed.

Pastor Wellman was saying, "The secret of complete release from self-condemnation because of our remembered sins is to remember Calvary and to stand in our thoughts at the foot of the cross which still towers over the wrecks of time—and the wrecks we may have made of our own lives.

"Hear the Saviour say, 'Why, my child, do you make a lash of your remembered sins, and with it scourge yourself—striking again and again and again with cruel and merciless blows? Why, when you may claim my forgiveness? My blood, shed here, has washed them all away, and My Father, who has forgotten them, holds them against you no more.'

"Should you remember sins which God has forgotten?

"If He has forgiven and forgotten, then should you not also forgive yourself?"

And in that moment, Joe knelt at the foot of the cross and gazed in wonder at the nail-scarred wounds still dripping with blood. He raised his eyes to the eyes of love beneath the diadem of thorns.

The voice of Pastor Wellman was saying now in tenderness—pleading, almost—"Throw them away—all those lashes you have made. Do not make a purgatory of your memories. Only in the cross is there forgiveness—through the One who suffered there, and it was in your stead."

But he was such a young boy, and he didn't want to die!

Into Joe's mind now came another thought: *The Man of Calvary was young, clean, fine, strong, and filled with love. He took the lash of sin for me. With his stripes I am healed.*

172

And in that moment, in a new way, Joe Cardinal, the sinner, flew swiftly on the wings of his own faith and hid his face against the breast of God, saying as with the poet of long ago, "Jesus, Lover of my soul, let me to Thy bosom fly."

The sermon finished, there was the announcement of a hymn. Lela, beside him, Junior in her arms, touched her husband gently with her elbow, indicating the hymnbook in the rack. He came to attention and with her help, because she had heard the page number and he had not, turned to the section of the hymnal designated as "Favorite Hymns of the Church."

The organ marched into the exulting strains of "A Mighty Fortress Is Our God." The hymnal in Joe's hand became a bayonet and the song that of a German teenager sobbing, *Ein' feste Burg ist unser Gott!*

First a bayonet, then a lash—but as the words of Luther marched on, they became a mighty fortress. Another young Man, gentle and strong, the Son of God, the great I AM, was calling from a cross on Calvary's hill, "It is finished!"

A door opened in a far corner of the auditorium, and as the organist began to play the martial hymn, "Onward Christian Soldiers," a parade of children entered and moved down an aisle—dozens of them, scores of them. They filled the reserved seats in an alcove, overflowed into the sanctuary, and still they came—in colorful dress, some serious, others smiling, still others searching the audience with their eyes to locate a parent or friend or other person they knew.

The children's church had been dismissed early so these young people might share in the service of the dedication of infants.

The children seated, Pastor Wellman spoke briefly, saying:

"What we have just witnessed is one of the finest sights ever a man can see—as Myrtle Burger has expressed it:

> I saw tomorrow marching by
> On little children's feet;
> Within their forms and faces read
> Her prophecy complete.
> I saw tomorrow look at me
> From little children's eyes,
> And thought how carefully we'd teach,
> If we were really wise."

Joe's thoughts winged swiftly into a long-ago past, saw Charles Boynton at his desk in a little stucco school, saw a little girl who hated war, writing on a blackboard, and heard her asking, "Do you believe in God, Mister Boynton?"

That little girl was now doing research, it was apparent, for Pastor Wellman. Her kingdom had moved into Faith Memorial Church, and from there she was reaching out to the whole community. And behind that little girl and her faith was a teacher who was really wise, a man whose wheelchair and gravestone were pulpits proclaiming the grace of God.

If a man with two missing legs can walk with God, why not a man with only one?

The pastor was speaking: "Tomorrow *is* marching. Our hymn has said, 'Marching as to war,' meaning the Christian warfare. Such warfare is in harmony with the will of God. But there is a march in which we may all become participants—true sharers, not just spectators.

"Every day, every moment, there is born a prospective recruit—and we have, this morning, for dedication, four little tomorrows. They will come forward now for induction:

Joe Cardinal, veteran of World War II and winner of the Purple Heart, led the way, with Lela following. Soon four couples stood in a semicircle in front of the dais, where Pastor Wellman was waiting.

*　　*　　*

"And do you, Mr. and Mrs. Cardinal, promise that you will train this child in body, mind, and soul for service and fellowship with God —that you will so live yourself, and so teach, that he will, of his own free will, desire to receive Christ as his own Saviour as soon as he is old enough to understand?"

"We do."

As was the custom, the parents turned to let the audience see the faces of the newly dedicated infants. Joe, standing with his son in his arms, searched the auditorium and noted the pride-filled expressions on the faces of the George Wilcox Blanchards. And in the back row, with little Jimmie in her heart, was Janice Granada. As on other occasions in The Towers office, there was a look of apology that seemed to say, "I'm not sure what I have done wrong, but whatever it is, I'm sorry—and I won't let it happen again."

174

And there was more—as if she had not wanted to fight in the war of life but had had no choice, and someone—who also did not want to fight—had plunged a bayonet into her heart.

Joe rejected another scene that intruded itself, and it seemed he was answering her apology with: "I did not want to hurt you, Janice, but this is the way life is, and you will just have to rise to the occasion."

It was as if he were making a promise to her to bring up the son of Joe and Lela Cardinal to be strong, self-reliant, governed by high principles, a lover of all things beautiful, and a hater of war and all things evil. And he would never hate any human being—never.

Following Dr. Wellman's closing prayer, Joe, receiving the benediction, thought how wise was the Heavenly Father, whose many children the world around were watched over and loved by Him. How protective He was of His own to set over His church such a thoughtful and loving pastor, whose sermon on the cross was not a pageantry of emotions but was heaven come down with comfort and hope and peace.

"O storm-driven world, O terror-filled hearts! Do you not know there is still a God in heaven, and a Saviour still on earth, and that those who love and obey Him will know His indwelling presence!"

After the benediction, while the worshipers were funneling their way through the main exit, there were many congratulations, handshakes, and words that said to Joe, "We love you; we're glad you're back; you'll want to join our Disabled American Veterans group; we need men like you."

It was grandfather Blanchard who carried Joseph George Wilcox Blanchard Cardinal down the stone steps, with Eloise beside him, accepting with grandparental pride the many compliments, congratulations, and ego-inflating words of praise.

* * *

In the afternoon Joe and Lela drove to Cardinal Hill.

Before they left, Dad Blanchard called after them, "The weather report has a storm warning for this area. You might be on the lookout and not get too far from shelter, just in case. The humidity is climbing fast."

They were delayed a little longer when Mother Eloise came running out with their raincoats, saying in playful derision: "Children! Always have to be looked after! *When* will you ever grow up!"

175

"Never, I hope," Joe answered, and added, "if I can always have such wonderful parents-in-law."

He was remembering Wordsworth when they came into view of the lake: "Beside the lake, beneath the trees, fluttering and dancing in the breeze."

The commonplace was dressed in beauty and there was heavenly pageantry in everyday things, because God Himself was the Architect of beauty.

Always he would love this place: the beech tree with the cupid's arrow through the heart, the arrow and the heart in the process of being healed, the waves of the lake laving lazily at the dock posts and at the new boathouse.

Far out near Bluebell Island, the *Cardinal* moved slowly, a man and a woman silhouetted against the dark green of the trees.

Beyond the island there was a buildup of cumulonimbus clouds—sky-deep wool packs, tier on tier, the kind of horizon familiar to those who recognize the gathering of a storm.

They parked beside Dr. Raymond's car. Taking a peek inside, Joe noted the doctor's bag and a woman's reversible raincoat with a matching umbrella. He looked again toward the sky and wondered how soon the rain would come. The ever-efficient Janice had overlooked the little matter of being prepared.

"I'd like you to have a neat reversible like that sometime," Joe said.

"Not *exactly* like that," Lela reminded him. "No woman can stand having another woman wearing a coat, suit, or dress just like hers."

He studied her face, saw she meant it, and fumbled in his jacket pocket for his notebook. "Judy," he said, "is going to run into a similar problem at a parent-teacher meeting. She'll be slightly unhappy all evening, and when her husband asks why she is giving him the silent treatment, she will leave a tear or two on his shoulder, and the family fight will be on—or over, whichever the author decides it should be. What do you think of that for a filler in a chapter that otherwise might be rather dull?"

"The filler," Lela answered as she took his arm for the climb to the mesa above, "could grow into a shrine that covered acres—if neither of them knew how to dethrone the great god Pride."

In a little while they reached the crest and were in their new home.

Standing for an interval, looking into the fireplace, already laid and awaiting a match, he remarked, "That would make a good chimney for an old wolf to come bounding down."

"If I remember the original story," she said, "the Old Wolf landed in a kettle of hot water—or was it a kettle of matrimony?—and has been in hot water ever since."

Joe moved into the future, saw lazy flames lapping at crisscrossing logs, and remembered a line from Lela's beloved Elizabeth: "The little cares that fretted me, I lost them yesterday."

He was catapulted into the present when he heard an unfamiliar sound behind him and turned to see his practical wife wielding a dustcloth. She was moving from one piece of furniture to another. Each movement of the cloth was like a caress. This particular housewife with a dustcloth was, to him, like an angel writing in a book of gold.

They moved into the kitchen and stopped to make a cup of tea. Sitting across the table from each other, they talked and ate the cookies which, along with the raincoats, Mother Eloise had thrust upon them before they left.

She filled his cup, handed him another cookie, and mused, "When today's tomorrow has become tomorrow's yesterday, we will stand on Cardinal Hill and look toward the Bluebell. And from somewhere high in the trees we will hear the call of the cardinal and be glad we found each other. Then we'll go down the slope, press the switch that opens the boathouse door, and Evangeline and her Gabriel will go sailing away together—and the cruel British will never be able to catch them—never."

"Quoth the raven, 'Nevermore.' "

Time marched on—too much of it, too fast—so that it was an hour later when he remembered something special he wanted to tell her.

Outside, he noted the heavier humidity, studied the sky, and remarked, "Looks as if our beautiful cumulonimbus clouds have been joined by what storm-watchers call 'mammatocumulous.' There just might be a lot of wind as well as rain."

At the site of Hawthoreau House they measured distances, using a tape he had brought for the purpose. "You," he said, "are a very necessary person. Your suggestion that ten by fifteen was too small set my subconscious to work—and this morning it came up with a bright idea. A subconscious is almost as necessary to a man as his wife."

Their eyes met, and when he saw what he interpreted as a mischievous gleam, he said, "I mean, his wife is almost as necessary as his subconscious. Anyway, here is what I saw with my mind's eye this morning: Build a replica of Thoreau's cabin, and let it be my sanctum sanctorum. Let the rough weatherboarding of the facade be the back wall of the main room, or so-called reception room, where guests, if any, will be welcomed, where my wife can sit and wait until I am available for conference, and where an occasional secretary will work. But the sanctum sanctorum is only for the king himself."

"Not even for your wife? Somebody'll *have* to come in at least once a year to help you hoe out and to sweep up the brain dust."

The present moved into the future, and Joe saw Hawthoreau House completed and himself ensconced in the solitude of his dreams. His valley of the shadow had been long and lonely, but he had emerged into a great awakening light. A shadow was proof of the light, a valley was likely to be more fruitful than a mountain top, and a walk *through* the valley was better than to be hurtled into it, never to emerge.

Here he would lose himself in creative solitudes and find them more companionable than any human companionship. Visitors might come to see his domain, and their exchange of words, ideas and dreams would be like sparks from the anvil of the soul.

The future was ushered startlingly back into the present by a long and rather violent rumble of thunder. The cumulonimbus were capped now with a gray green canopy of cirrus.

From the buildup a fiery leader of lightning streaked downward. Its simultaneous thunder declared to the world that it was charged with violence, that it sought an opposite charge somewhere on the earth, and that when the two should meet, there would be an explosion of the kind that destroyed, that drove through walls and trees, and that killed whatever lay in its path.

Joe pressed the automatic return button on his tapeline, and watched the tape snap back in the housing. He looked again toward the sky. "Might as well be good little children and obey your mother," he said. "Here, get into your storm coat, even if it isn't as beautiful as the reversible down in Dr. Raymond's car."

178

Lela, looking through the binoculars, exclaimed, "The *Cardinal* is coming back—and they'd better hurry. Somebody's secretary is going to wish she had taken her coat along."

There was no reason why he should have wanted to defend his former secretary against a possible oversight, but he did hear himself saying, "She probably thought that *if* it rained, the canvas top would keep them dry—unless, of course, there's a high wind."

"There is a wind now—hear it?"

The wind was already driving hard, whistling through the trees and turning the lake into a churning caldron.

To Lela, who had always loved to watch a storm driving across the lake, there came, as often before, the lines of a favorite hymn:

> Though the angry surges roll
> On my tempest-driven soul,
> I am peaceful for I know—

But this time there was no joy in the lilting phrases—for suddenly her husband was gone, calling over his shoulder as he broke into a run down the slope, "I'll go down and get the door open. Maybe they can make it before the rain!"

He was only half way down when the storm struck. There was rain and a wild wind that was like the sound of a freight train thundering across a trestle.

The beech tree far below was fighting back with flailing strokes, her branches tossing wildly in protest at the interruption of her tranquillity and this violent attack against her shrine.

A hundred yards out, the *Cardinal* was being driven and tossed, and there was no Man on board to rise and say to the wind, "Peace, be still!"

The boat top tore loose from its fasteners, lifted, and was hurled into the water. The boat itself was a plaything controlled by the waves.

Lela saw and was afraid—for Janice and Hal, as well as for her husband leaping and running and staggering down the slope.

It seemed she must follow him and help him in some way. My husband! My darling husband! It was not like him to be rash in his decisions.

A flock of birds was driven helter-skelter like autumn leaves across the sky. A lone gull near the shore, zigzagging in a desperate struggle to stay in flight, was hurled against the trunk of the pine to which, in her own flight to the boathouse, Lela had been forced to cling or be thrown to the ground. The gull fell with a cry of pain and weeping of wings at her feet—and then she saw that it was not a gull but a dove, and her pity for it stabbed deep into her heart. A dove was such a dainty thing, so gentle in its manners. Even in moments of happiness she mourned plaintively, as if there were no peace anywhere.

Far out above the lake and above the shadowy outline of the island, a funnel cloud rolled, driving fiercely toward them, wielding serrated swords of fire.

Lela saw her husband now, clinging to the gray bole of the beech, pressing hard against it.

Again there was lightning—and it was as if a streamer of fire leaped from the land to answer the mating cry of a leader from the sky; the simultaneous thunder was like the detonation of tons of TNT. Lela saw Joe stagger and reel. His cane flew from his hand, and he slumped to the ground.

"Joe! Oh, Joe!" she cried, and ran through the rain and the wind and the terror of her thoughts to her fallen husband.

* * *

In his headlong drive down the hill, Joe felt a stab of pain with every step, and the pain was in the foot which, somewhere in England, was disintegrating into dust.

If only he could get to the boathouse in time to press the switch that would lift the overhead door, Hal and Janice might be spared the worst of the storm.

Joe now saw the boat top torn from the *Cardinal,* and the craft became like a redbird shorn of its crest.

He saw the funnel cloud, a sky-high spinning goblet capped with mountains of gray green foam, spewing wind and fire and terror of thunder.

The crestless *Cardinal* became a fishing boat on Galilee, the tempest was raging, and a little crew of men were crying out for fear. Now was the time for a voice to call, "Peace, be still!"

But the wind and the waves on Bluebell Lake could not be silenced, and to the bewildered Joe, they became the noise of battle. The ponderosa stump piercing the sky and the dim outline of Cardinal Hill were the cliffs above the Normandy beach. The rain and the wind

180

were bullets and bombs and shrapnel. He stumbled over a root, and it was the body of a fallen comrade.

He was crawling and running and sobbing in his spirit. He was in a hand-to-hand battle for survival—dodging, parrying, and jabbing with his bayonet. He had not counted on this. He had only wanted a setting and an atmosphere for the hero of his novel—and now a German lad lay dying, sobbing with terror and faith and unbelief: *"Ein' feste Burg ist unser Gott!"*

Joe was clinging now to the trunk of the beech tree, his fingers digging into the scars made by the knife of a young lover long ago.

"When the bombs are crashing all around you, and you have no foxhole, there is only one wise thing to do—and don't wait to find out whether or not it is wise—*drop flat!*" The command came barking into his memory from a day in training.

The bombs were falling faster now, and the noise of battle was more terrifying. He could not stand it if he should have to use his bayonet again, for how could he come before the judgment of God with blood on his hands! He must get rid of the evidence. He dropped now to the ground, hurling his bayoneted gun as far as he could, and lay with his face buried against his arm, waiting for the battle and the judgment day to pass.

And as he lay and the storm roared over him, he seized the lash of his own remembered sin in the Normandy orchard, and with it he beat and beat upon himself, forgetting that between two thieves another person had taken the lashes for him in vicarious suffering, and there is therefore now no condemnation to them that are in Christ Jesus. He would never come into the sinners' judgment, because he had already passed from death to life.

He heard now the terrible explosion of the ball of lightning, and it seemed he felt the savage hissing of its fire in his drenched clothing.

And there was a woman's voice, like the screaming wail of a loon from across the lake, crying, *"Joe! Joe!"*

Chapter 22

Before the storm that drove them on their wild ride across the lake toward the boat shelter, it had been a gala afternoon for Nurse Granada and young Doctor Raymond. For a long time their hearts had been reaching out to each other like the coming of timid spring, when sunshine touches the pulse of the dying winter and withdraws again and yet again until the time of spring is come.

The time of spring seemed to have fully come this afternoon. They strolled hand in hand through little brown paths winding in and out of the shrubbery and along the beach, stopped now to examine the nest of a protesting wood thrush, saddled upon a forked branch of dwarf oak. "If one didn't know otherwise, he could decide it was a robin's nest," he commented. "It has the mud lining and the interwoven sticks and twigs."

"Dad Blanchard calls it the 'Wood Robin,'" Janice said. "He has pet names for all the birds in the area. He even calls Eloise—Mrs. Blanchard, I mean 'Bonnie,' after the old love song, 'How sweeter dear, yes dearer far than these, Is blue-eyed, bonny, bonny Eloise.'"

"Every woman," Hal returned, "should have her name changed." To this she did not reply, but as if to change the subject, she suggested, "Columbine grows just over the ridge, down among the aspen. It's low there, and the soil is moist."

"And," he continued, "every man should take a lesson from the birds. A certain man I know loves his freedom, his eyes are on far hills and green pastures—but, as every bird that catches the worm knows, or ought to know, he must eventually settle down to nest-building. When he lays his surgical instruments aside for the day—or the night—he likes to go home to a cozy little nest—"

"As I was saying," she interrupted as if she were not hearing, "The aspen—I mean the columbine—is just over the ridge. Come on! Let's get them dug before it rains!"

"Rain?" he looked toward the sky and saw the buildup of tall white clouds, like a giant cauliflower topped with liver-colored cirrus. Even shaped like a liver, too, he thought, conforming to the contour of the diaphram.

"You should be thankful Lela's father is generous," she told him. "For in some states the columbine is protected by law from vandals."

While he carefully dug about the roots of a cluster of the deep blue aquilegia and talked defensively about vandals who stole the hearts of women and had such a difficult time because the roots clung so tenaciously and would not let go, she, in turn, defended the columbine by saying, "Maybe they prefer the independent life to becoming merely ornamental in a man's garden."

Between his counter remarks, she told him, "I was doing research last week for Joe's column and ran across some very interesting data on the columbine. Its name is from the Latin *columbinus,* meaning 'dovelike.' Its inverted flower, as you can see, and as one dictionary suggests, has a fancied resemblance to a group of pigeons. The word 'columbia' has also an ecclesiastical meaning: the columbia is a dove-shaped vessel for the sacrament. In astronomy, Columba is a southern constellation located near Canis Major. It is also called 'The Dove,' or 'Noah's Dove.' "

"Quite interesting," he commented as he gave an affectionate pat to the ball of burlaped columbine roots. "I was just thinking that *canis,* in the world of mammals, includes the dog, the fox, the jackal and the wolf. Has it ever occurred to you that a certain old wolf might eventually tire of sparring with his elusive little pig and some day come right straight out and demand an answer?"

"In the Bible," she went on, "in the Song of Solomon, the dove is a term of endearment. A person may be regarded as being as pure and gentle as a dove. Song of Solomon 2:14 puts it this way: 'O my dove, . . . let me hear thy voice.' "

Dr. Halford Raymond straightened up, the burlap ball in his hands, and said to her sternly, "For the past half hour I've been trying to tell you something. I've suggested that every woman ought to have her name changed, that every man ought to settle down to nest-building, and that a certain old wolf gets lonely sometimes. And you have answered that the columbine might not like to surrender her independence to become a mere ornament in a man's garden. Don't you know

183

the only true independence in the world is in discovering your destiny and surrendering yourself to it? You are giving me a hard time, Janice, my dove. Let me hear your voice!"

"It *is* going to rain—hear the thunder? Besides, you promised you'd tell me what was so important in the personal letter I lost and Lela found for you."

"Just as soon as you promise to help me build my nest and agree to let me change your name and transplant you into my garden—You're not listening!"

"Sorry," she apologized. "I was just thinking of Joe and his problems."

"When you were Queen of The Towers and his secretary, I understood, but Joe is married now, very happily so, and—"

Her interruption was gentle, "Joe is the kindest, most thoughtful person I have ever known. Without his friendship I might never have found myself. I think I *was* infatuated with him, and *maybe* in love, but there was a barrier.

"Sometimes the wall was not between us at all, but we were together sitting high upon it, looking out upon life and discussing it, looking down upon a world that struggled and fought and killed, and built nests, and tore itself to pieces with words as well as weapons.

"No, I'm sure I was never in love with Joe in the way a woman should be if she were going to be his wife. I'm not sure I've ever had that particular emotion—or conviction, or whatever it is that makes a woman want to start helping a man build a nest—"

Again there was thunder, a loud and threatening roll. It sent them scurrying back over the ridge, and down to the dock. They were in the *Cardinal,* ready to take off, when he introduced the letter. "You sure you don't need your shorthand notes?"

"I transcribed them last night before I turned the letter over to you. Joe will need them tomorrow for his column."

"And you," he said, "will need what is on the inside. I was going to keep it from you until after you decided to accept my roundabout proposal. But now that I seem to be getting a no, I think I'll just withdraw my suggestion about the old wolf and the little pig going into partnership."

"You haven't gotten a no," she answered. "Only a postponement of a yes."

"For what reason?"

"Does a woman have to have a reason?"

"Maybe not, but a man does."

"The right-now reason," she explained, "is the fact that there is a very bad storm coming up. It's about to strike any minute, and a boat in an electrical storm is not the kind of setting I had planned on."

"You *had* planned the setting, then?"

"Nothing so definite as a plan. Only a career woman *does* have to think about what will happen to her years of training and experience in the business world and whether or not she is willing to surrender all her rather wonderful past for a hazy future."

He set the motor adjustment for Start, pressed the switch, and the *Cardinal* took off for the mainland. His answer to her evasive but common-sense statement was philosophical: "If you had said yes in too big a hurry, I would have been disappointed. Any doctor knows that it takes a heap of living and loving and self-denial to make a home. This doctor has seen beautiful relationships shattered, or, as they say, shipwrecked on the shoals of disillusionment and selfishness. In every marriage there are times of bitterness, blindness, grudges, financial crises, tears, and the things that cause them. A woman has to believe that love will conquer all and that it will survive after the aura of sweet romance has blown away. Thanks, Janice, thank you very much for asking me to wait."

The storm broke with a crash of violent thunder and a rush of wind and rain, and the usually tranquil Bluebell Lake became a sea of violence.

Under the canopy of the *Cardinal's* top, Janice sat watching the strong, muscled man at the helm and noting the set of his jaw and the steady control of his emotions. Here was a man who could not be dominated yet would be gentle and always thoughtful. He might be tactful enough to let her *think* she was guiding his own thinking—and she would love him with all her heart and mind and soul.

They would move down a church aisle, stand before Pastor Wellman, listen to the routine questions, which, in her mind she had already answered—and on another day there would be a scene like the one this morning, and her heart would burst with pride and gladness because she would have a child of her own to love.

At the wedding itself, there would be the first question: "Who giveth this woman in marriage?"

"Joe," she decided. "I will want Joe to give me away." She did not know she had spoken aloud until Hal asked, "Still thinking about Joe?"

Her answer was: "I was just thinking that if I ever do accept your proposal, and if we have a formal wedding in the church, I'd want Joe to take the place of my father and give me away."

To which dream he countered, "Sorry, but I've planned *him* for the best man. You might be willing to settle for Dad Blanchard. There's a man whose ego enjoys inflation more than any man I ever knew— the higher type of inflation, of course."

The *Cardinal* gave a lurch and was swung about sharply, caught by a crosswind. She felt sudden fear, clung to his arm, and whispered to herself, I think I need to be afraid, because I need a man to tell me to be calm. I need somebody to adopt *me!*

The *Cardinal* was wallowing now, fighting the wind, which, for the moment, was blowing from the direction of the overhang. "Don't you worry one little bit—if you're capable of worrying. Just consider yourself under sedation, and this little old boat the operating table; and when you come out from under the anesthetic, you'll be in the recovery room of Cardinal House. And your fiancé will be holding your hand."

Only once before had she seen such a storm, and that had been in the home community at Cranston. The wind had toppled the steeple from the church and the belfry from the school across the road, as well as felling two of the great old maples in the churchyard and tossing them like matchsticks into the cemetery. Little Jimmie's marker, and mother's and Charles Boynton's all had been crushed into the ground.

"We just might blow our top!" she heard herself yelling to him above the screaming of the wind. "We'd better put on the storm coats! Dad Blanchard keeps a pair in the hatch for emergencies!"

With the efficiency of a nurse handing instruments to a doctor during an operation—or a secretary knowing exactly where to look in the file cabinet for a certain document—Janice had the hatch open and the slip-on, all-purpose coats out and unfolded. In another minute the two were ready for the emergency which was already upon them.

She had just said, "I was a bright girl to leave my coat in the car. Otherwise I might never have found out how to use one of these," when the wind caught the boat top, tore it from its fasteners and hurled it like a fly-away kite up and out. It landed twisted and crumpled in the water a hundred feet away.

"*Look!*" she cried. "There's Joe! He ought not to be out in the rain! His metal leg could draw lightning!"

Then came the fireball and the terrifying simultaneous explosion of its blast. The tall, splintered stump of the old ponderosa leaped into flame, the resin still in it making it especially flammable.

And now Janice saw Joe under the beech tree, saw him fall, saw Lela running toward him and change her course and fight her way toward the boat shelter, saw her reach for the switch that would open the overhead door, and remembered from past research on lightning: during a storm, keep away from trees, remain in the open, don't use a steel umbrella in an electrical storm, and never touch an electric switch with wet hands.

Chapter 23

There were four in the recovery room of Cardinal House, but it was only Joe who was the patient. His first words sounded strange to him as he struggled to sit up. The window drapes were drawn, there was a fire in the fireplace, and on the stone mantle a kerosene lamp burned, casting eerie shadows about the room.

Was it night? How could so many hours have passed since he fell in battle—and how did he get here all the way from Normandy?

"What happened?" he now asked.

It was Dr. Raymond who answered. "A fireball struck the old ponderosa stump. When we found you in a daze under the beech tree, we thought lightning had struck it, too. But you'd probably have been spared even if it had, because current always flows through the best conducting path—in your case, your wet clothes.

"As it was, you did get a mild shock—the kind a man sometimes gets under severe mental or emotional strain."

Joe took a deep breath. It felt good to breathe, to be aware of life and of being alive, to be here rather than in Normandy in hand-to-hand battle for survival—dodging, parrying, jabbing with his bayonet, hearing the wailing sob of a teenage boy quoting the first line of Luther's old hymn.

"You go down and get the body," he said, "and we'll bury him on Hawthoreau Hill."

He lifted his hand to his forehead, felt the throbbing of pain, and heard his breath coming short and fast.

"Lela!" he called out. "Are you all right? There was a tornado! I saw one over the island!"

And then he felt his wife's hand stroking his forehead and heard her crooning, "Everything's all right. I'm all right, the folks are all right, Janice and Dr. Raymond are all right. Our baby is all right—he slept right through the whole storm. The tornado never came down. And you're all right, too, Joe!"

The kerosene lamp on the mantle swayed dizzily for a moment, and he struggled to come all the way back from his journey into the past. "I vowed to myself I would return, and I did."

He closed his eyes and sank back onto the pillow. And with the increased flow of blood to his brain, he relaxed, sighed deeply, searched among what seemed like a clutter of things in the storeroom of his mind, and then said, "Janice, want to take a memo?"

And now Lela knew her husband *was* all right. Whatever had been wrong—mild shock, temporary amnesia, a wild excursion into some secret battlefield of the soul—God had given him back to her.

Lela looked toward Dr. Raymond to see if he, too, realized that Joe had fully regained consciousness, as she believed. She saw him gesture to Janice, search in his jacket pocket for something on which to write, come out with a weathered envelope, and handed it to her, saying, "There's a little space on the back."

"Ready for dictation," Janice announced to her former employer.

Joe sighed, and with eyes still closed, he began:

"It was the hand of God, the great I Am, who sees all things from the beginning. He knew the fireball would strike the old ponderosa stump, and He could not let it happen while two of his children were standing beneath it. He filled the heart of one of them with fear and used that fear to drive him down the hill to the boat house. He sent that man's wife hurrying after him, and in this way He removed them both from the place of death, because He was not yet ready for them to leave this world. He had planned for them a new and wonderful tomorrow in which there would be just enough shadow to remind them constantly of the overshadowing of His love."

Joe's voice trailed off, he began to breathe rhythmically, and it seemed he had drifted into sleep.

But a moment later he opened his eyes and saw everything in the room in true perspective.

He sat up and was not dizzy—and his wife, beside the couch on which he had been lying, breathed a sigh of happiness. He let her cry against his shoulder, and remembered something her father had once said: "You never know for sure why a woman is crying."

189

He also remembered a little word game they sometimes played and said, "A nicer wife couldn't cry on a nicer husband's shoulder."

As if for the moment she was unaware of others in the room, Lela answered, "If I were a little pig, and you were the big, bad wolf—"

"I *am* hungry," he began, but was interrupted when Hal said, "If I were a writer doing a novel about four young people I know, I think I'd title the book *Two Little Pigs and the Two Big Bad Wolves Who Ate Them.*"

Hal's voice took on an authoritative tone: "Now is the time for a certain good man to come to the aid of an *un*certain party. I take pleasure in announcing the engagement of Miss Janice Granada to Dr. Halford Raymond. The wedding will probably be within the next few weeks, just as soon as—"

Janice interrupted, "But I haven't said yes. I was waiting for a more appropriate setting. There ought to be a moon—"

Dr. Halford Raymond, physician and surgeon—and now a determined suitor—took his nurse by the shoulders, shook her gently, and said determinedly, "This, young lady, is all the setting you are going to get!" And a very positive big, bad wolf led an elusive little pig toward the hall.

At the door Hal stopped, looked back, focused his eyes on Joe, and announced: "I have prescribed for your former secretary a new wonder drug named 'Complement,' but she doesn't know the meaning of the word. So, if you two will excuse us, I'll try to interpret it for her."

Alone in the room, while pine logs crackled in the fireplace and love and thankfulness burned warm in their hearts, Lela said to her husband, "I liked very much what you dictated about the fireball and the old ponderosa. The tree is still there— the rain put out the fire."

"I'm glad. Because up there is where I have the cemetery where I have buried all my perfect wife's very insignificant faults, and that old stump could never be replaced. In addition to its being a landmark, it is the headstone to remind me that they are actually and forever gone—but you wouldn't know about that. When your father was talking with me one day, he said every husband ought to have a fair-sized cemetery in which to bury all his wife's little faults."

She released herself, looked steadily into his eyes, and informed him, "My father told *me* I should have a fair-sized cemetery for my *husband's* faults."

There was a moment of silence. Then she asked, "Remember the decapitated violet that once fell over the edge?"

"How can I forget?"

"It's buried up there, too. I had it cremated first in a most vehement flame."

Down the hall, Dr. Raymond glanced over his fiancée's shoulder and saw in Joe Junior's room the sailing ships on the wall, the canopy crib, and the giant panda. "Joe Cardinal's wife is a very artistic person," he said. "Do you suppose that maybe in some far distant future she would be willing to visit the home of the Dr. Halford Raymonds and design a room like that for us?"

To which Nurse Granada replied, "She just might. I'll go ask her in a minute, but first I'd like to know what was so important in that personal letter. You know, of course, that it was not only addressed to you but it was in your own handwriting."

"I know. I wrote a letter to myself, commanding me to stop letting a certain little pig live alone in her lonely little apartment. I gave myself an ultimatum—I identified it as a personal letter, but I hoped my secretary would open it. When she didn't, I had to try something a little less roundabout, something like this—"

"Do you know what?" she interrupted.

"What?"

"That letter is going to be framed and hung on the wall of our den. Then, if there is ever any doubt about who proposed to whom, I'll have the proof."

Janice released herself from her fiancé's arms and said, "There's something very important I have to do right this minute." And she hurried back down the hall to the living room.

Suddenly the house was filled with music; a skilled pianist was playing the majestic refrain of "Master, the Tempest Is Raging":

> Whether the wrath of the storm-tossed sea,
> Or demons, or men, or whatever it be,
> No water can swallow the ship where lies
> The Master of ocean and earth and skies;
> They all shall sweetly obey My will;
> Peace, be still! Peace, be still!

The music rose to a thunderous crescendo that was worthy of the words, then moved swiftly into a rippling cadence like laughing water flowing down a canyon—and as Joe listened, it was like the sound of tomorrow marching into a new day where the love of Christ would reign at last and the great god War should eventually become only a filler for crossword-puzzle makers.

With the eye of the mind he saw a little boat tossing violently in the midst of a storm. The tempest was doing battle with the power of the Creator Himself, and east of the shadows, a Man was standing with outstretched arms, waiting.

About the Author

PAUL HUTCHENS' name is well known
in the field of Christian fiction. He au-
thors the best-selling *Sugar Creek Gang*
series. Since Moody Press began publish-
ing these pre-teen adventures, more than
700,000 copies have been sold in American editions alone.

Presently there are 35 books in the
Sugar Creek line.

East of the Shadows is not the author's
first venture in the field of adult fiction,
for he has written 18 other full-length
novels. This is his first since 1954, when
he began concentrating on youth books.

Hutchens and his wife, Jane, live in
Colorado Springs, Colorado.